Dedication

To the many wonderful friends I've made playing *The Secret World* and *Secret World Legends* over the years. And to P.J., my sweet fluffy Chihuahua, who passed away in October 2018. You were a good boy, and we miss you every day.

D1738294

Acknowledgments

When I was writing the first book in the Unofficial Legends of The Secret World series, *To Sir, with Love*, it was vital for me to "see" the book as a real thing, so I took great pleasure at writing the acknowledgments at the beginning of that process.

This time I got all the way to the end of writing the second before I attempted them. There are quite a few folks who deserve acknowledgment for their participation in the process of the development of this book.

First of all, Michael Payne, who was a tremendously good sport about letting me take outrageous liberties with his Secret World alter ego, Sevenoir. Not only did he give me carte blanche to write the story, but he filled out a character sheet questionnaire to help me paint the Sevenoir on the pages into a rounded mentor/sidekick for Wedd and read it while it was still in rough draft form to help me get things right. Thank you so much for your encouragement and assistance, Sev, and above all, your enthusiasm!

And while I'm on the topic, Mark Innes (aka HolloPoint) is as enthusiastic a partner in crime as I could hope for. His artwork is fantastic, and his talent takes my breath away. When he mocked up an early cover draft for *London Underground* about 15 minutes after he'd finished up the final version for *To Sir, with Love*, he inspired me to get the next book started. I'm not sure when you sleep, Mark, but I'm thrilled to have you illustrating the covers for this series. Your recent forays into 3D animation bode well for all of us who enjoy your work.

Also, to other *Secret World Legends* players and friends Gypcie, Drenneth, SnowDrifter, Lurdtz, and Kinii for allowing me to use their character names and/or likenesses for this bit of fiction, I hope you enjoy seeing them on these pages.

Thanks to readers and advisors who came back to help me again with the second book: Trista Emmer, for her excellent feedback and editing; Kelly Dewnsup, for her encouragement and advice on fencing and blade work—readers, if there are errors, please note that alone I am the cause. Other advance readers and old friends deserving a shout out for their feedback and support include Jenn Gibbs, Regina Napolitano, Courtney Righter, and Brian S. Williams.

And of course, once again, I owe a profound thanks to my husband, Mark Reviea (aka Hadad) for his encouragement. He discussed aspects of the plot with me at random times of the night and day, gave me feedback and ideas when I was stuck, and held me tight when we lost our pup P.J about a week before *To Sir, with Love* launched. I love you great big bunches.

Last, but certainly not least, I want to thank Terri P. and Andy B. at Funcom. Without your help, this story and *To Sir, with Love* would not have seen the light of day.

LONDON UNDERGROUND

An Unofficial Legend
of *The Secret World*

Blodwedd Mallory

What's Happened So Far

So, we trapped the murderous wraith in a photo slide and got the thumbs up on graduation from Innsmouth Academy. Gypcie and I have our respective invitations to join Secret Societies.

What do you do after the world ends? After you've trapped a wraith from Hell and gotten the invitation to join the Templars? As the old saying goes, you chop wood and carry water.

Lately, I've been trying to rent a flat in London. I'm headed there soon to take my initiation. I've been in contact with a landlady named Miss Plimmswood, who seems nice, although the rent in London is *ermahgerd* expensive.

I can't wait to go there, see the sights, and start my training. And of course, meet Richard Sonnac, the head of the new Templars. I am also hoping that being at Temple Hall will give me the opportunity to get more news about my mom. She's a Templar too, and on assignment somewhere that keeps us from being in regular touch. That worries me a lot. There's scary stuff happening in the world right now, and Solomon Island is no exception.

Here at the academy, things have settled down to a new normal. Yeah, we still have creepy, dangerous familiars and murderous specters. Not to mention the whole host of zombies—some of them my former classmates—running around outside the academy yard walls. Ms. Usher and Headmaster Montag pretty much keep us close to base, also known as the Administration Office, although Carter, Gypcie, and I have moved back into the dorms. We've set up a system of wards and traps that keep us safe enough to sleep at night. Our days are filled with doing what we can to help keep the island as sane and safe as it can be, but that's a far different picture than was laid out in the school prospectus.

The Sheriff's Office in Kingsmouth and the Council of Venice help with that. The soldiers are still holed up in the Faculty Lounge, although recently they've traded out some of the traditional soldiers for Gaia's bees, who, like Carter, Gypcie, and me, are more suited to combat the supernatural threat we're all facing.

I'm going to leave for London soon, but I'm torn about leaving my friends and old school behind. I know what we're facing here.

It's ugly. It chatters. It glides through walls and lurks in the corners of the yard. But, it's the known evil.

What awaits me in London remains to be seen.

A Flashback to Tokyo

"It's all shut down, Kaidan-cho, everything, from the park to Orochi Tower..."

The voice was urgent, young, and feminine, with an English accent. I opened my eyes to find myself lying on the floor of what appeared to be a subway station, artificial light flickering, the cold tiles pressed against my cheek.

In front of me, I could see three people arguing, two women and a man, standing in front of a gray metal gate blocking the entrance to the platform areas beyond.

My heart beat loudly, and my eyes blurred as I tried to focus. I could see a dirty hand stretched out in front of my body—I was laying on my left side—but it didn't look like my hand. Above it was the sleeve of a white leather jacket with blue leather trim cut to look like a flame. That confused me further. I didn't have a jacket like that.

"SDF quarantine. Good news for Tokyo, bad news for us." The other woman spoke, her voice softer, although still young and feminine.

I pressed up on one elbow. The floor in front of me was littered in the grime and trash typical to subways, but there was something new. A strange shiny black substance covered it, spreading out in thin offshoots like the roots of a tree. In places, the substance was pooled into thicker pods and had started to climb up the nearby wall.

"I thought the Dragon thrived on Chaos?" the man spoke now.

The second woman retorted, dryly, "Someone once told me the Illuminati had all the answers."

Dragon? Illuminati? My head spun as I continued to try to focus my eyes, my breathing shallow. My body had a dull ache as if I'd been knocked down. My left hip was sore. This was a strange nightmare and very vivid. I couldn't ever remember being aware of pain while sleeping before.

My heart thumped loudly. What was I feeling? Was I afraid or merely curious? The detail in this dream was unbelievable. I could smell the mechanical, oily tang of the subway trains and the faint institutional funk familiar to places where people traversed in large numbers. My eyes blurred again. I shook my head and focused on the three speakers in front of me.

A young platinum-haired woman dressed in a ribbed, white V-neck sweater, jeans, sturdy boots, and a puffy red winter vest stood nearest on my right. She was wearing an off-white knit toque, which pressed her short shag cut hair down over her face, covering her left eye. There was a shotgun on her back, held in place with a thin leather strap, which wrapped around the vest.

"They're saying a bomb. It's never just a bomb."

The other woman with the softer voice, who was standing nearest the gate, responded. "Something worse. Something that brought the Filth with it." She looked vaguely Asian and was wearing headphones, a rust-colored cropped off-the-shoulder T-shirt, and low-slung yoga pants, with a katana-case strapped to her hip. Ornate dragon tattoos embroidered her shoulders, and her black hair was gathered back into a ponytail.

I noticed she said "filth" like it had a capital "F." I looked again at the black substance covering the floor. Was this some biological outbreak? Where was I? The first woman had said something about "Kaidan-cho." Was that in Japan?

"So we fight," the first woman spoke again. "That's what us Templars do."

Templars! Understanding flooded me. Now this dream made more sense. I was fantasizing about my future with the Templars. But, the dream was so real, so vivid. It was unnerving.

"I enjoy a good fight. It's just that these bloody trousers are velvet," said the man, who stood off to the right, gesturing at his pants. He was wearing a long, dark-brown duster and had short, spiked brown hair. He appeared to be in his mid-30s, while the two women seemed younger, early-20s-ish. Were they agents of some sort?

The Asian woman looked over at me as I struggled to my feet. "Sarah! Thank Gaia! Are you okay? How are you feeling?"

I staggered as I stood up and swallowed hard as my stomach lurched with the movement. Who was Sarah?

I looked down at my body but didn't recognize my clothes, or, truth be told, the warm brown color of the skin of my hands. I held up my arm to see the blue-flame details that ran down both sleeves of the white leather jacket I was wearing. I had on a pair of gray jeans and old high-tops. I reached up to touch the wide cloth headband on my head. Maybe it was a scarf. My hair felt different, smoother, finer, and shorter. I turned slightly and could see the black ends of it touching my shoulders. That wasn't right. I had long, auburn hair that I typically wore in a bun.

This was some dream. Who was Sarah? I'd never been someone else in a dream before, but I was too fascinated to let the strangeness bother me. I didn't know what was going on here, but there was only one way to find out. I nodded my head at the second woman to let her know I was okay.

She nodded back, then turned to the first. "If Zuberi was here, he'd tell us this is the worst time to argue."

"Well, he's not. He's down there somewhere," the blonde responded, gesturing through the locked gate. "Sarah, get your gun."

I jerked with a start. She meant me. I spied a shotgun on the floor near my feet with an anxious thrill in my stomach. I'd never used a shotgun before.

How hard could it be? I picked it up, holding it gingerly with both hands, muzzle pointed toward the floor in what I hoped was proper safety etiquette. I prayed silently that there were shells in it because I sure didn't know how to load them.

I looked around the room and spotted the subway exit behind us, a back-lit sign identifying it in English and what looked like Japanese kana. It gleamed in the dimly lit room. A small, deserted news kiosk sat along the wall to the right of the stairs, with newspapers and magazines lining its display shelves. I could see more tendrils of the stuff—the Filth?—reaching across the floors like blood vessels in a circulatory system amid the trash and old newspapers. A brightly lit vending machine offering candy and cigarettes stood at the right of the kiosk, providing a strange contrast of normality to the otherwise grim scene.

A large thump echoed from the stairwell beyond the gate in front of me, and I turned back quickly at the sound of footsteps running toward us. From the stairs emerged a frightened woman.

5

Spying us, she grabbed the gate and began shaking it frantically. "Let me out!"

"Open the gate!" the blonde woman in our group yelled. The Asian woman crouched down and struggled with the latch at the bottom, trying to pry it up.

"I'm trying, Rose! It's inside the electrics somehow, the Filth..."

"Let me out!" The woman trapped behind the gate screamed more urgently now, the gate ringing as she shook it.

A man sprinted up from the stairs behind her. My mind boggled for a moment as I took him in. He was wearing a buttoned-down white shirt and gray trousers like a businessman, but his face and head were covered in black, shiny tar, with two tentacles waving wildly from it. Was he infected with something? Was he contaminated with this Filth they kept talking about?

Before I could contemplate it any further, he jumped on the woman behind the gate and knocked her down, tearing at her face and arms with his teeth. She shrieked pitifully as she attempted to push him away.

"No!" the Asian woman cried out as she stepped away from the latch, covering her eyes, as the monster ripped the trapped woman apart in front of us.

"Fuck me!" the guy in our group yelled.

"Oh. My. God!" Rose echoed.

My eyes were wide, and I shook at the sight. "We have to help her!"

I aimed the shotgun at the gate and attempted to fire, but nothing happened. Looking down I realized the safety was still on. I flipped it off and raised the gun to try again, but I was too late. The woman had stopped struggling. The infected man jumped off his victim and ran off the landing down the stairs to the left beyond my line of sight.

Acid poured into my stomach as horror flooded me. This might have only been a dream, but seeing the woman torn to pieces in front of me was very real and upsetting. Her body lay on the landing beyond the locked gate, blood pouring from a wound on her throat, her sightless eyes clouded in death.

I swallowed hard and turned my gaze away. With my left hand, I pumped a shell into the chamber. Next time, I thought with anger as I bit back tears, I would be prepared to fire.

A low knocking sound came from my left. What was that? My heart rate jumped again, and my eyes widened. I turned quickly but kept the muzzle of the shotgun low.

To the right of the kiosk and vending machine, the wall of the subway station had three large vents midway up to provide air circulation underground. They were large enough for a human to stand in. My adrenaline spiked as I realized the covers on two of them had been torn off, revealing the blackness beyond the reach of the artificial light of the area in which we were standing. The others also turned and faced the noise, dropping back into postures to prepare to fight.

"Watch out!" the short-haired man called out as a Filth-infected creature appeared in the rightmost ventilation duct. It jumped down and threw itself at us.

The Asian woman drew her katana and brandished it at the creature, but I was ready this time, and, holding the shotgun up to my cheek, I fired past my companions at the infected man. The blast caught him in the stomach, and he fell back against the wall, dead or incapacitated.

Ha! My shoulder stung from the recoil of the shotgun, but I felt a deep satisfaction in having hit and downed my target.

"Nice shooting!" The blonde woman, Rose, yelled at me from over her shoulder.

She was interrupted by a raw hissing scream. It echoed from deep within the tunnels, warning us that more infected specimens were on their way.

"How many have they got in there?" the short-haired man asked.

"It's gone viral so fast... If this gets out into Tokyo..." Rose responded.

"It doesn't. We stop it here. Whatever it takes." The Asian woman glared at us as she swiped down with the katana to make her point.

"Shouldn't we consult the Council of Venice first?"

"Shut up, Alex," Rose responded sharply. "Mei is right."

The short-haired guy, Alex, had said that in such a dry, sarcastic voice that I knew this was an old argument between them.

I also knew what the Council of Venice was. I had worked with them firsthand at the Innsmouth Academy on Solomon Island when they arrived last fall to assist with the familiars that were over-running us. Why did Alex make consulting the Council of Venice sound like a bad thing?

Before I could finish my thought, six more infected breached the vents and jumped down to attack us. Rose raised her shotgun and took the opening shot, blasting away from the left side. Mei swept her blade before her on the right, holding them at bay, while Alex threw fireballs from a little further back. I positioned myself sufficiently that I wouldn't shoot any of my group, pumped the shotgun again, and aimed at the infected with both barrels as they swarmed towards us.

Rose gave them the full salvo, her shotgun making a *bang, bang, bang* sound as she laid waste to the infected lurching toward her with fast, repeated blasts. Mei decapitated the filth man nearest her, her blade moving like a tsunami, barely visible with the speed of her strikes. Alex continued to bombard the infected with fireballs, his arms flowing forward as the flaming energy erupted from his palms. I did what I could, one shot at a time, trying to hit my targets with the new weapon.

Because this was a dream, I didn't have my chaos or blood foci. I was effectively as dangerous as a newborn, my earlier lucky shot notwithstanding. Thank goodness my companions were capable fighters.

Before long, the infected were dead and covered the floor in front of us. I took in a shuddering breath. Screeches and hissing in the distance indicated there were more on the way. Who knew how many would breach the ventilation ducts this time?

"We have to get the gate open and move deeper into the subway. Here, we're sitting ducks," Mei said as she crouched down again in front of the gate's locking mechanism, grunting as she fiddled with the latch. I heard a click as it finally gave and she raised the gate up, jumping to push it up into its casing.

The opening yawned like the entrance to a netherworld. Alex must have felt the same, as he quipped, "Abandon all hope, ye who enter here."

"Thanks for the encouragement, Alex," Rose said with a scowl.

Mei cut her off with a gesture. "Let's do this. Take it like all the other occult disasters, right?"

"We really have to stop meeting like this." Alex pulled a lighter from his pocket and toyed with it. Rose grabbed it from his hand and stuffed it in her vest pocket as he sputtered in protest.

We started down the stairs to the next landing. I turned away as we moved past the torn-up victim of the first infected man. Shame and sorrow burned in my chest at her death. The Filth had to be stopped, and I was ready to fight it.

Below I could see another gate between us and the actual train platform. I couldn't read the signs posted on the walls, which probably described where the trains traveled, because they were all in Japanese kana. But it didn't matter. The infection was right here, covering the floors, the walls…everything.

As we moved out onto the landing to the next set of stairs, the wall to our left began to bulge, as more of the infected ran up the stairs toward us. With a squeal and a crash, the tiles lining the wall split open, and a cloud of black filth exploded outward. A piece of flying shrapnel from the wall hit me in the chest, and I was knocked back, the air leaving my lungs in a whoosh. I hit my head hard against something behind me, and the scene faded to black.

CHAPTER ONE

Ordinary World

June 13, 2012

THE SMALL CLOCK on my nightstand buzzed as the alarm went off, flipping on the radio. The BBC announcer's voice filled my tiny dorm room with the 8 o'clock morning news briefing.

"…A new development in Tokyo, where the military is maintaining a heavily guarded perimeter around the site of last month's terrorist attack. The Japanese government has stated that an unidentified radical political group released a biological agent in the Tokyo subway less than one kilometer from Orochi Tower."

Weird. I lay there on my bed listening to the news and contemplating what I could remember about my dream. Maybe I had tuned into the radio waves while I was sleeping. The news coming out of Tokyo was terrible. There had been some bomb released there on the subway a month ago, which must have set the stage for my dream. No wonder. The world had been a crazy place recently.

On Solomon Island, a dense fog had rolled in after the return of a lost fishing boat. With that fog came a siren's call that pulled many of the inhabitants of Kingsmouth town out into the sea to drown. Only those who had been somehow unable to answer the call had survived. The wards on the campus walls had protected Innsmouth Academy at first, but many students had died in the aftermath as the residents of the island came back to shore—dead, but animated by whatever dark magic had pulled them into the sea in the first place. On Halloween, we were attacked *en masse* by the zombies, and the wards had failed, leaving the students and teachers at Innsmouth Academy vulnerable.

Those of us who survived that night had spent the past few months trying to pick up the pieces, secure what was left of the island from more trouble, and protect the survivors that remained, including ourselves.

"Although the area has been evacuated, there have been eyewitness reports of activity inside the perimeter, including ongoing fighting between Orochi security personnel and armed civilians," the voice on the radio continued. *"Authorities are denying these reports and the military has barred anyone from approaching within one hundred meters of the temporary perimeter."*

Last autumn seemed like a distant memory now. Things had been relatively quiet and stable for months on the island. I had graduated from Innsmouth Academy on schedule and was now planning to take the next step forward in my life by initiating with the Templars. The recent events in Tokyo were disturbing, but Japan was a long way away from Solomon Island, Maine, with plenty of ocean in the middle.

I stretched on my small dorm cot, about the size of a twin bed. The sun crept in through the windows on the south wall, beneath the coverage of the roll-up shades. As I rubbed the sleep out of my eyes, I thought some more about the dream. Who was Sarah anyway? She was a young woman for certain, but I wondered what her role was and why she'd been in the dream. I also wondered what had happened to Alex, Mei, and Rose in that subway. It had felt more like an intense and horrible movie than a nightmare, and I felt a little bereft that I did not get to find out how the story ended. Silly, but I hoped they'd made it out all right.

Probably too much orange drink, I thought. Nah, most likely it was the cup of coffee I'd bummed off the Council of Venice soldiers before I headed off to the dorms to bed.

The Council of Venice. Alex had said something about them. What was it?

The dream continued to linger in my head as I propped myself up on my elbows and contemplated the day. I looked at the open suitcase sitting on the chair next to the closet. A thrill went through me anew. I needed to finish packing. I was headed to London to join the Templars!

I climbed out of bed and reached for my leggings and a clean T-shirt. I quickly got dressed and threw my hair up into my trademark bun. My best friend, Zandria McCullough, known as "Gypcie," was also leaving this week, but for New York City. She was planning to initiate with the Illuminati. I couldn't wait to tell her about my dream, mainly since the Illuminati were in it too. I think that had been Alex. Mei must have been a Dragon, like Renee, this guy I'd occasionally been dating when he visited Solomon Island in his travels. Rose, the one in the red vest, must have been a Templar.

I thought about how Rose was dressed in my dream as I opened my closet door to see how much I still had to pack. I was taking just a few of my best outfits with me to London. I had no idea what a Templar agent wore, and most of my clothes weren't suited to a big city or an opportunity like this one. Whatever didn't fit in the suitcase was going to be given away or thrown out.

I'd spoken to a recruiter last week to finalize the details. I recalled the conversation clearly although it was very one-sided. I hadn't gotten the chance to get a word in edgewise while the woman had rattled off the details in a crisp English accent.

"I represent an organization headquartered in London," she had said. "A very large organization with branches across the globe and connections in every government. Although we see ourselves as a, hmm, a silent partner. We pull strings. Big strings: prime ministers, presidents, kings. Dark days are coming. The world is in turmoil, and we're recruiting. Soldiers, agents, adventurers...Crusaders.

"And we offer good terms. A fresh start. A network unlike any other. Unlimited resources, a fantastic medical plan, and a way to harness and use your incredible powers. It may be a big transition, but look at it this way: This is a unique opportunity. You have been chosen. You have been granted powers beyond what most can imagine. So you can either be an outcast in a world that will never understand or accept what you've become...or you can join others like you. Take a stand against the rising darkness and embark on a journey into the unknown, into the hidden places. Into the secret world.

"The choice, as we're so fond of saying, is entirely yours, but know this: Your emerging powers will attract plenty of attention. And not everyone is as, hmm, as accommodating as we are. On your own, you'll be easy prey. You might not last the week. Choose or don't choose, it's your prerogative. Either way, you won't hear from me again. I trust you'll make the right decision," the recruiter had concluded, then hung up the call.

I sat in stunned amazement for at least a minute after it ended.

What the recruiter didn't realize, of course, was that I needed very little encouragement. My mother was a Templar agent and was currently deployed on a mission somewhere in the world. I was excited to sign up. I'd been waiting for it for years. It was why I had talked her into letting me go to Innsmouth Academy after I swallowed Gaia's bee.

I didn't know yet when I would be heading to London other than it would be "soon," according to Ms. Usher.

There was a quick rap on my dorm room door, and I put down the shirt I was folding to open it.

"Ready to go collect some anima charges?" Gypcie stood in the doorway, looking fresh and chipper in a T-shirt and shorts with some lace-up work boots, her brown hair laying in soft layers around her face. "Time to renew the library wards again."

"Is it Wednesday already?" I stuck my tongue out. "I'm not going to miss this chore when I head off to London."

"Oh, come on. It's simple enough. We'll get it done and get back to packing before noon," she coaxed me.

"When do you leave for New York? Have you heard yet?"

"Two days," she said. "Ms. Geary said they were going to send someone to get me on Friday."

"Wow, that's exciting!"

My enthusiasm for her was not feigned, but I felt sorrow well up in my throat. Gypcie and I had been friends the entire time I had been enrolled in Innsmouth Academy, but our friendship had deepened as a result of our adventures together in the last few months.

Through a series of mishaps and "learning experiences" last fall, Gypcie and I had captured a vengeful wraith who was bent on destroying the Innsmouth Academy Headmaster, H.J. Montag. The confrontation had been challenging and at times painful, but it had given us some hands-on experience with magical combat. I expected I'd be getting a lot more shortly with the Templars.

Other than that, our daily chores consisted of helping hold down the fort, so to speak, which mostly meant containing the familiars loping around the campus and renewing the wards on the yard walls and buildings every couple of days. That was to keep the other monsters roaming around the islands—the sea draugr and the former residents—at bay, and away from the mighty magical tomes inside the Innsmouth Academy library. The wards fed on anima and needed to be renewed regularly to control the chaos and protect the island.

Headmaster Montag and Ms. Usher helped coordinate the overall security of Solomon Island as well, so Gypcie and I were well used to taking on the responsibility for the wards. I wasn't quite sure what would happen once we were gone. Carter, our friend and the only other student left at the Academy, was a couple of years younger than we were and she was still working on her control over her powers, which tended toward thermonuclear.

A trickle of unease filled me. What would Ms. Usher and Headmaster Montag do when Gypcie and I were gone? Sending Carter off to renew the wards alone was a potential disaster in the making. The Council of Venice soldiers who were stationed at Innsmouth Academy now were mostly just that, soldiers, without the magical skill to collect the charges and convert them to shards to power the wards. But recently, Venice had started sending some Bees of their own to back up our meager defenses.

I also knew there was a fairly steady trickle of agents—Illuminati, Templar, and Dragon—who stopped by the Academy on assignment willing to help out. That was how I'd met Renee Laveau, my erstwhile boyfriend. Well, okay, we'd gone out on a couple of dates when he was in town. He was a few years older than me, so things had been very casual, but I liked him. He was Creole, handsome and dark-haired, and had an absurd sense of humor that cracked me up. I was always glad when he was in town, and I could sneak out to spend some time with him. I didn't know where the relationship was headed, but I was enjoying it while it lasted. Plus, sneaking out was fun, provided Montag didn't catch me at it.

Ugh. Once again the prospect of all the changes ahead stopped feeling exciting and started feeling worrisome and sad. Would I see Renee any more after I went to London? And what about Gypcie? Indeed, I could write to her and send her emails to stay in touch, but New York was a long way away from London.

"What are you frowning about?" Gypcie prompted me, drawing my attention back to the present.

"Oh, I'm just thinking," I said glumly. I shook my head to clear it and dug deep for some enthusiasm. "Let's go get those charges so we can get back to packing. I'm sure you're anxious to have it done, so you're ready for Friday."

CHAPTER TWO

Call to Adventure

WE STARTED COLLECTING CHARGES in the yard, where there were a host of familiars running around. By running them into the existing wards, or hitting them with a fireball or blood curse, we were able to disintegrate their bodies and collect the anima charges that animated them.

Once we had five charges, we could use the W.A.N.D. Anima manipulator to create an anima shard, which was then used to renew a ward. There were at least ten wards inside of the Main Hall as well as at least that many on the Academy yard walls, so we had our work cut out for us. Our adventures last fall had given us a full appreciation for the need to renew them. Luckily, Innsmouth Academy seemed to have an unending number of familiars that could be harvested for this purpose.

"Gotcha!" Gypcie yelled as she incinerated a Sparring Partner that had been running circles around a lamp post on the right side of the main stairs with a fireball. "That makes five. Shall we renew the front gate ward or keep collecting shards until we have enough to do all the yard wards at once?"

"One sec, busy," I grunted as I drew the intricate blood glyphs necessary to cast two Dread Sigils in short succession at a pair of Sparring Partners hiding in the bushes near the front path to the stairs. They sizzled and dropped to ashes, and I ran over to grab the glowing gold charges left where their bodies disintegrated. Familiars were not alive *per se*. They were animated by the charges, which had been donated by the students who created them originally as part of their Innsmouth Academy magical education. Unfortunately, or fortunately, depending on your view, their animation did not require their original maker to still be at the school or even still alive. That left us with plenty to harvest even all these months after the fog rolled into Solomon Island.

"OK, got two more. I say we do the front ward while we're here. We can finish the yard and then move inside to do the wards in the Main Hall. We'll leave the library for last, once we've had a chance to thin out the population a little today."

Gypcie nodded her agreement and pulled out the W.A.N.D. to create a shard.

"Girls!"

I turned to look over my shoulder at the call. Ms. Usher was standing on the steps at the entrance in her neat, dark-red suit jacket and plaid wool skirt, her curly auburn hair pulled back into her usual messy ponytail. She had fabulous hair. Mine shared its color somewhat, but I didn't have her natural curl, which Ms. Usher came by honestly as a Scotswoman. She was the Academy's Witch Doctor and had been a friend and mentor to both Gypcie and me since we'd arrived here.

"Hi, Ms. Usher," Gypcie called in return, looking up from the W.A.N.D. "What's up? We're just working on the wards."

"I need to talk to Wedd for a moment. Can you finish up, Gypcie? I can send Carter out to help if you like."

I looked over at Gypcie with wide eyes. Her lips quirked up in a smile. She was guaranteed an exciting morning if Carter came to help.

"Sure thing. Send her out," Gypcie responded, laughing at my comical expression of doubt. Gypcie was far more capable and patient than I was at helping Carter. After all, she'd had lots of practice dealing with the unpredictable running around for the last few months with me.

I nodded my agreement and ran over to give my collected charges to Gypcie before heading up the stairs to join Ms. Usher.

"Let's find somewhere private to chat, Wedd," she said as I joined her in the foyer. That seemed slightly mysterious, but I was excited to learn more about what was planned for me.

She called through the gap in the Administration office window for Carter to help Gypcie. We walked across the foyer and then turned right to step into the Faculty Lounge. Ms. Usher asked the two Council of Venice soldiers stationed there, dressed in their typical white uniforms with light blue berets, to give us the room for a moment. They nodded and stepped into the back portion of lounge, leaving Ms. Usher and me alone in the front.

"I wanted to talk to you for a moment about your initiation into the Templars," she began. "As you know, Innsmouth Academy is largely funded by the Illuminati in keeping with the faction's history on this island. What you may not know is that I am not Illuminati."

My eyes widened a bit at the information, although it wasn't an incredible surprise. Even though the Illuminati funded the school, it served students with many different backgrounds, which was part of the reason I had been able to convince my mother to send me here. It made sense to me that some of the instructors came from different factions as well. I said as much to Ms. Usher.

"It also helped that your mother and I were acquainted."

"Well, yes," I said, not understanding. "You met her when she dropped me off at Innsmouth Academy four years ago."

Ms. Usher smiled gently. "That is not when we first met, Wedd. We met at Temple Hall about 15 years ago, when I began my faction training to become an agent."

My jaw dropped. Ms. Usher was a Templar?

"My family are Templars, proper old Templars. The house of Usher, aye, that's hilarious," she noted, with a dry smile. "Once I finished up with the basics, I decided I didn't want to be an agent, and I was tired of the bustle of London besides, so I took this position to trade an overcrowded island for a quiet one, for a peaceful life."

She pursed her lips. "Before life went and said bollocks to that."

I nodded firmly in agreement. It may have been a sleepy place once upon a time, but there was nothing quiet about Solomon Island these days.

"There was something pure ironic about the move too, you know. My kind weren't popular in these parts three hundred years ago," Ms. Usher gestured vaguely in the direction of Kingsmouth Town. "Witches, not Scotswomen."

She gave me a sly wink. "It's occult suffrage in action."

"But what did your family say when you moved here?" I asked.

"They didn't disown me when I said I wanted nothing to do with anyone's army or the posturing and scheming. The 'my cabal is bigger than your cabal,'" Ms. Usher said. "That's worked out right well for us so far, hasn't it? I didn't come here for the Templars or the Illuminati. I came here for the kids. And that's why I'm staying. I came here for kids like you and Gypcie. For the ones who come back, for the ones who won't. For Carter, who's brushing up to be one of the most powerful mages on the Atlantic seaboard, but just wants to be a girl. One out of two's fraught enough."

She paused, lost in thought.

My head spun as I considered the implications. Ms. Usher, a Templar here, in an Illuminati school, teaching magical children. Who else knew this about her? Her next words jolted me back to attention.

"Are ye sure about this, Wedd?"

I cocked my head at her in confusion. "Sure about what?

"Are ye sure ye want tae join th' Templars?"

She held up a hand as I opened my mouth to assure her I was.

"Jest hear me out," Ms. Usher continued. Her brogue was starting to surface, so I knew that she was serious about what she was telling me and perhaps just a little upset. "Ah ken ye're excited tae put on th' red uniform and gang tae London tae join th' barmie to sae th' warld, but there's a lot ye don't quite kin yit abit the…complications bein' an agent brings. Th' varoous factions, despite whit yoo've seen haur at Innsmouth Academy, hae troubled relationships. Things will be required ay ye that may…change how ye feel."

She took a deep breath to calm herself as she worked to get her brogue under control, looking at me gravely. "The Templars are all abit tradition an' loyalty, but 'at can be a burden in and ay itself. Havin' th' reit bluid." Ms. Usher paused as if waiting for me to understand what she meant. I was a little confused. Brogue or not, I followed her words, but it sounded like there were broader implications.

"I ken ye want to follow in yer mother's footsteps, and that ye ha' a fine Templar family name, but ye have been chosen by Gaia as weel. That alone means the implications of joining any faction for ye are vera long-lasting. Ye ha' choices. I want ta make sure ye ken what ye're getting into. Ha' ye done any research on yer other options?

Of course, I knew about the Illuminati, having come to Innsmouth Academy to school, and meeting Renee had given me a little insight into the chaos-focused perspective of the Dragon. I told her what I knew.

"There are other factions as well," Ms. Usher said, her brogue pushed back into hiding, "which we don't hear as much about because they're not as large. Druids, Ourobori, Freemasons, even the Phoenicians. The Council of Venice keeps them all in line and away from each other's throats, most o' the time."

I looked at her in surprise. I hadn't realized there were so many different factions. Still, I didn't want to be in any other faction. I wanted to be a Templar, like my mother. Even if she wasn't a Bee.

Ms. Usher cleared her throat. "Here's the point, Wedd. Once ye're in, ye're in. It can be difficult to…change course or leave. Ah was only able ta come here tae Innsmouth Academy because the Templar leadership felt Ah was in a position tae influence up-and-coming agents, loch ye."

Why would anyone ever want to leave the Templars? I wondered. I'd been waiting my whole life for the chance to join! Still, her words had given me pause.

Ms. Usher looked at my face and bit her lip, unhappiness crinkling her brow. "Ah've said tae mooch already. And Ah certainly don't want to dampen yer enthusiasm. It's yer life. I suppose I've jist become attached tae ye girls an' I'm nae ready tae lit ye gang."

She put an arm around me and gave me a hug.

"But, of course, my history puts me in the position to be of a little more assistance to you, Wedd," Ms. Usher continued, speaking slowly and clearly. "I still have contacts at Temple Hall, which is how I've been able to get word to you about your mother. I spent three years there before I moved to Solomon Island to take this teaching position."

Ms. Usher put both hands on my shoulders and looked at me squarely.

"During that time, I met many of the people you'll be meeting soon. Dame Julia. Brigadier Lethe. Richard Sonnac—he was still just an agent then," she said, smiling as my eyes lit up. I suspected she knew about my little crush on Richard Sonnac. It was a poorly kept secret on campus. Probably because I talked about him all the time.

"I knew your father somewhat better than your mother. Now he was a dab hand with a sword. Your mother only stopped in for brief visits here and there, since she was busy raising you at the time. Before she went active again as an agent when you came to us."

Now she had my full attention. My father?! And he was a swordsman? Was he also a Templar? It sure sounded like it. Of course, I was clear that I had a father somewhere in the world, but my mother had raised me by herself and was decidedly closed-lipped about providing details about him. I wanted to ask more, but Ms. Usher was still reminiscing.

"I give them a lot of grief, but the Templars were ahead of the curve among the factions in pushing for a proper magical education. Oxford, Uttar Pradesh, Cairo, et cetera. Of course, their reasoning was a bag of shite. It's got bugger all to do with entitlement and everything about sorting out your place in the world. But, you'll run into them that still hold those opinions when you get to Temple Hall."

She shook her head. "Och, I don't want to influence your views any more than I already have. You'll find out soon enough what's in store and make your choices as you do."

Ms. Usher nodded her chin firmly to punctuate the comment, then changed the topic. "I'm sorry tae say it, but your mother isn't able to come get you right now to take you to London herself."

That wasn't really news. I nodded. I wasn't happy, but neither was I surprised. I'd hoped I'd get a chance to see her and have her help getting settled in London, but she stayed really busy out in the field on assignment. It wasn't unusual for me not to see her for months at a time.

"So, I've contacted Temple Hall and made arrangements to have an agent come to pick up you. They should be here tomorrow."

A thrill went through me. Tomorrow! I had to finish packing. I'd leave before Gypcie even. I'd be traveling to London and meeting a real Templar agent!

She smiled at my obvious excitement, then added. "It's no secret, really, these things that I've shared with you. But, it's also not something that I broadcast, if you get my meaning. So, in your excitement, there's no need for you to share the parts of our conversation that don't pertain to you in particular, eh?"

I nodded my agreement. I was headed for London tomorrow!

"Ms. Usher!"

We both turned at Gypcie's urgent call. She rushed up to the threshold of the Faculty Lounge but slowed to a stop as she stepped through into the door. We had both had to learn not to startle the Council of Venice soldiers who normally stood armed with assault rifles at the inner doorway.

"Ms. Usher, come quick!"

"Whit is it?"

"Carter has…has accidentally lit the dorm building on fire trying to kill a pair of arcane cadavers. We could use some help," Gypcie panted out, bending over as she struggled to catch her breath.

"Och! Let's gang swatch. That lassie will be th' death ay me," Ms. Usher headed out the door Gypcie had just rushed in and ran across the foyer and down the front steps to the yard with Gypcie and me hot on her heels. "Carter! Carter! Ur ye aw reit?"

CHAPTER THREE

Refusal of the Call

66 "I've CHANGED MY MIND. I don't want to go."
I started taking the shirts I'd folded out of my suitcase and reached behind me to grab a hanger from my small dorm room closet.

I couldn't get the picture of Carter out of my head, her face covered with soot, standing helplessly in front of the dorms, as Ms. Usher ran over to put the fires out. She was working so hard on gaining control of her powers, but in the stress of combat, they were unpredictable. By the look on her face when we ran up to her, I could tell she felt terrible about it. Ms. Usher had things set to right in no time, and the bricks were only slightly scorched, but I felt awful about it, too. Innsmouth Academy needed more help, not less, to deal with everything these days.

"What? Don't be ridiculous, Wedd. You've been planning for this for years," Gypcie said to me incredulously. She was sitting cross-legged on my bed hanging out with me while I finished packing. "What is going on in that head of yours?"

I set the pile of shirts down on the bed next to her, then bowed my head and scratched my forehead, the obnoxiously short chunk of my bangs that never seemed to grow out swinging forward as I did. I sighed in irritation and sorrow. "I can't bear the idea of leaving Ms. Usher and Headmaster Montag with no help. How will they keep the wards refreshed? Who will be here for Carter? To make sure she has someone to talk to and someone to hang out with?"

"Uh, you mean like Danny?" Gypcie said dryly and stuck her tongue out at me. "She probably would prefer hanging out with him anyway. That is if she can talk Montag and Ms. Usher into letting her go to Kingsmouth."

"I still don't think she and Danny are dating." Danny Dufresne was a local Kingsmouth boy who holed up from the zombies in the Kingsmouth skate park. Carter had gotten into a pile of trouble a few months ago sneaking out to meet him and had been on house arrest more or less ever since, after giving the headmaster a near case of apoplexy.

"Whatever. If it walks like a duck and quacks like a duck." Gypcie grabbed the pile of shirts from the bed and stood to put them back in my suitcase. "You've got some martyr complex, you know. Who says it's your responsibility to fix this? The Illuminati will send some agents or something to help out."

"I don't want to leave you either," I wailed.

"Well, too bad," she said intently. "I'm going whether you go or not."

She put a hand on my shoulder to take the sting out of her words. "Wedd, this is just change. We'll get through it, and we'll stay friends, regardless of where we are in the world. I'll write to you every week and let you know what's happening and you can do the same for me. Ugh. I can't wait until you get a cell phone. It would be so much easier to just text or tweet to you!"

It was true. We could stay in touch despite my lack of technology and exchange addresses once we both arrived at our new locations. I know Gypcie thought it was weird I didn't have a phone, but I didn't have anyone besides my mother to call, and with her being out on assignment most of the time, I couldn't call her anyway. Being a single mom, she'd decided that particular expense could wait until I was older. Maybe I'd be able to get one once I was in London.

I nodded to Gypcie in acknowledgment, but I was still glum about one thing in particular. I decided to share my pain with her.

"I don't know how to get in touch with Renee," I said quietly. "I don't know if I'll ever see him again."

"Oh, Wedd," Gypcie said, her face filling with understanding. She gave me a quick hug. "I'm sorry about that. Do you have a phone number for him? I could try to get in touch with him."

I shook my head sadly. "We only went out when he was in town. I never got it from him because…no phone. I don't know how to get in touch to let him know where I'm going."

"Maybe Ms. Usher would be willing to give him a message?"

"Ugh." I pulled a face at the thought. "That's presuming he actually asks her about me. Remember, I've been trying to keep it on the down low. He knows I didn't want her or Montag to know I was seeing him."

Gypcie tipped her head to the side as she listened, crooking an eyebrow at me.

"What? All we ever did was have coffee in the Faculty Lounge. I didn't need them to—I don't know—forbid it or something."

She nodded at that. "When did you see Renee last?"

"It was in March," I admitted. "I was supposed to see him again in May, but then the Tokyo thing happened, and he didn't come back here. I'm a little afraid he got sent to Japan to deal with the aftermath."

"He's a Bee, right?" Gypcie asked. I nodded my head in confirmation. "Well, then, we know better than anyone how hard we Bees are to kill. He'll be okay, Wedd. You'll just have to trust that if he wants to see you again, he'll find you."

With that, Gypcie reached down to the floor of my closet and grabbed my old blue and white Innsmouth Academy gym bag and started shoving pairs of shoes into it.

"Wait! Don't pack all of them," I said. "I'm thinking of getting rid of some."

25

She held up my favorite purple ankle boots with the cute straps and three-inch heels. "Like these?" she said mischievously. "I'll take them! You will need red ones where you're going anyway."

"Nice try, but no. I was thinking more about the shabby track shoes or these old flip-flops."

Gypcie held the flip-flops up and turned her nose up in the air with a dramatic flourish. "Yup, those can definitely go. You've had them since you got here, I think. At least they smell that way."

She grinned at my look of disgust. She knew she'd distracted me from my reservations.

"Now," she said, smugly. "What are you going to wear tomorrow?"

Gypcie and I spent the rest of the day finishing up my packing, throwing the clothes I planned to take into my suitcase, and my other meager possessions into my backpack. With that on my back, the duffel bag on my arm, and the suitcase in hand, I could manage to carry my stuff pretty well. I'd be fine as long as I didn't have to walk too far. I had a box of other things that Ms. Usher agreed to hang onto until I knew what my new space in London would hold, but it didn't contain anything critical, just a few posters, a small microwave, and a couple of pictures. My framed photo of and the letter from Richard Sonnac were securely packed in the backpack along with my chaos and blood foci, my address book, and a couple of my favorite novels.

Before I knew it, everything was packed and ready to go, and all that was left was to wait until morning.

CHAPTER FOUR

Meeting with a Mentor

I GOT WORD my escort had arrived shortly before noon the next morning. I shuffled into the Administration Office, my face shiny and red from hauling my bags down the stairs in the dormitory and schlepping them across the Academy yard, and then up the stairs of the Main Hall. I got hung up on the door frame as I tried to wedge all my bags into the back room of the office. I muscled my way through and dropped them with a grunt in front of a table along the wall.

I was already regretting my choice of clothing—I had on a short, red leather jacket, a white button-down shirt, and a black bandage skirt with black low-heeled pumps. My feet were not going to last long at this rate, and my shirt was already wrinkled beyond repair.

"I hope you're not expecting that I'll carry any of that," a dry, male English voice said. "Let's hope you're one of those liberated young American women, shall we?"

I looked up from the pile on the floor to see a tall man with white-blond hair scowling at me from the threshold of the inner office. He was wearing a superbly tailored red, black, and white

Templar uniform and, incongruously, a pair of ridiculous looking bunny ears on his head.

"Oh, Wedd, there you are," called Ms. Usher as she moved past him through the doorway over to me. "I'd like you to meet Agent Michael DePayen. He's come to assist you in traveling to London." She put a hand on my shoulder and gestured toward him. "Michael, this is Blodwedd Mallory."

"Nice to meet you, Michael." I held out my hand to shake his, but he captured my palm and held the back of my hand up as if to kiss it, but smacked the air above it instead.

"I prefer 'Sevenoir,'" he said. "Charmed, I'm sure."

I smiled uncomfortably at him. Okay. So, was his agent name Sevenoir or something? And what was with the bunny ears? I knew the English were eccentric at times, but this was random.

"Now Annabel, we need to get on our way. I have important things to get back to," he said stuffily.

"I prefer 'Ms. Usher,'" she said with a sly wink at me as she pressed a £20 note into my hand. "And I believe Wedd is ready to depart when you are."

"Very good. Come along then."

Sevenoir moved past me toward the exit to the Administrative Office. I gave Ms. Usher a quick hug and thanked her, then I leaned into the inner office to blow a kiss to Carter and gave Headmaster Montag a grave bow. He nodded briefly and then turned back to the window.

I picked up my duffel bag and suitcase and twisted slightly to get my backpack straight before following him out into the foyer and down the stairs. At the bottom of the stairs sat a motorcycle, with a black tank and fender detailed with red and yellow flames. I looked at him in astonishment as he reached into a saddlebag and pulled out a World War II helmet and handed it to me. I put down my bags and attempted to strap it to my head.

Sevenoir rolled his eyes and reached under my chin to fasten it, tossing the handle of my duffel bag over the safety bar and strapping my suitcase to the top of the right saddlebag. Then he climbed on the bike, his bunny ears flopping precariously.

"Hurry up then," he barked. "Hop on."

I looked down at my bandage skirt doubtfully. Well, at least it was somewhat stretchy. I threw my right leg over the seat and scooted myself back behind Sevenoir, resting my feet on the passenger foot pedals. I reached around his body with my left hand, while holding my suitcase with my right, trying not to let my bare legs touch the metal engine parts. They were pretty cool now, but they wouldn't be once we got going, I knew from experience riding on the back of a motorcycle as a kid. I didn't know how far we had to ride on the bike before we got to a boat to take us to the mainland. Or, maybe we were going to a charter plane at the Kingsmouth Airport.

The engine of the powerful machine rumbled as he pulled slowly out of the Innsmouth Academy yard and onto the dirt road that constituted the front drive. I twisted my head around to look back at the Main Hall as we moved away, causing the bike to wobble with my motion. Ms. Usher and Carter were standing on the top steps, waving, as Gypcie ran up from the side yard where she'd been renewing the wards, waving to me with both arms over her head. Tears filled my eyes, and I waved back to my friends, sniffling, as I rode away from my home of the past four years.

"Hold still!" Sevenoir scolded, and I reluctantly turned back to front. The trees that lined the Academy drive were full and green in the warm early summer day, and there was just a nip of salt in the air from the ocean.

On my right, a still-animate member of the Kingsmouth Track and Field team loped along the wooden fence on the berm separating the drive from the fields surrounding the academy, drawn by the noise of the engine. We were traveling fast enough on the bike that encountering the zombie wouldn't be an issue, but it gave me a stark reminder of how much chaos still ruled on Solomon Island and how much was yet to be done. I would no longer be around to help.

At the entrance, I could see the tall Ferris wheel from the Atlantic Island amusement park looming over the trees across the road. Sevenoir turned left onto Illuminati Way, which was a paved two-lane road and picked up speed. We passed a car still parked in the street, abandoned by its owner when the dead began to rise. We drove by stone fences and fields leading to the more populated areas of Savage Coast, the houses getting bigger and more elaborate as we drew up to the main highway that encircled the island, Solomon Road.

Sevenoir stopped carefully at the red stop sign, before turning left onto the highway heading west. Apparently, we weren't going to Kingsmouth Airport. We must be headed to catch a boat to the mainland.

I pondered the full stop Sevenoir made at the sign as we drove up the road. There was no traffic to speak of, but he stopped nonetheless. He believed in rules, apparently, and followed them even when no one was watching.

We rode past more houses, a playground, and a construction project that was a time capsule into the past. A backhoe, shovel poised over the hole it had been digging, stood unmoving where its driver had left it. Feral groups of zombies clustered on either side of the road, scratching for sustenance on whatever ragged bits of sinew and bones that remained of the bodies that lay where they had fallen last October.

On our left, we drove by the mostly abandoned Sycoil Oil gas station. "Mostly abandoned" because there were still groups of zombies straining at a chain link fence at the back of the property. We followed the highway until we came to the covered bridge over the Miskatonic River when he slowed and took another left turn onto a small dirt path. That startled me. There were no boats for rent down this path. Just a few small dinghies at the Academy boathouse. Where were we going?

We rode a few yards down the path before he slowed to a stop and put down the kickstand on the bike and told me to get off.

"Where are we?" I asked, taking off the helmet.

"This is it," Sevenoir said.

"This is what?"

"The entrance to Agartha."

I looked around me with confusion. To my right was a steep path down to the bed of the river. In front of me the dirt trail continued along the river, and I could see the shadow of a wendigo, a flesh-eating monster, hiding behind a tree, ready to jump out at unsuspecting passers-by.

Sevenoir unstrapped my suitcase and handed it to me. I gave him back the helmet, then pulled the duffel bag off the safety bar, balancing my load as I tottered on my pumps on the dirt path.

"Head down the embankment to the river, toward the crevice in the rock wall beyond," he instructed.

I gave him a baleful look as I took in the rock-strewn path down to the stream.

He rolled his eyes again. "Oh for pity's sake. Why didn't you wear some more reasonable shoes?"

"Because I thought I was going to an airport or a dock," I snapped at him.

"Why, in Gaia's name, would you do that? Porting through Agartha is far easier, and there's no fare required." He grabbed the suitcase and duffel bag from me and started down the steep path.

I followed him best as I could, muttering at him under my breath. "Wait, for me you... Mean. Stupid. Englishman."

"You know I can hear you," he called dryly up from the bottom. "And I was born on Berwick-on-Tweed, so I consider myself Scottish, by the way."

Being no expert on British Isles geopolitics, I grunted noncommittally. I grabbed the bigger rocks on each side of the path to use as a makeshift handrail as I climbed down into the sandy bottom of the stream, effectively soaking my good black pumps. I scowled at him, blowing the obnoxious piece of my bangs out of my face. This was an adventure of my least favorite variety.

"All right then. Just in through that crevice and out to Agartha with you," Sevenoir said, handing me back my suitcase and duffel, then pointing to an opening in the rock. I stared at the crevice beyond the clumps of grass growing up on the far side of the stream bed. Faint golden light was visible behind it, but only if you were looking for it. I might have walked by the opening a hundred times previously without ever noticing it.

I moved toward the opening. As I neared, the golden light grew brighter, illuminating what appeared to be a natural cave—natural that is, except for the multitude of tree roots lining the walls and ceiling. I could smell dark soil and loam and could hear a loud buzzing of bees coming from deeper within the cave.

I turned back to Sevenoir. "What is Agartha?"

"What is Agartha? You *are* wet behind the ears. Agartha is the hollow earth where the world tree abides. You're standing before the entrance to it in this part of Solomon Island," he said, not unkindly. "There are other entrances here as well, but they are not generally advertised to the uninitiated."

We both spotted a piece of paper fastened to the cave wall with a small knife. Sevenoir flipped the corner of the paper with a chuckle. "I suspect that some of the local boys may be familiar with this one. The League of Monster Slayers, eh?"

He turned around to head back up to his motorcycle.

"Wait?!" I cried. "Aren't you coming with me? I thought you were supposed to take me all the way to London?"

"Yes, well about that." Sevenoir stopped and turned back to me with his arms crossed. "I've had something come up. I need to scoot down the road to wrap up a problem in the Blue Mountain area before I head back to London. Something far too dangerous to bring you along. Why do you need me to come with you?"

"I've never done this before," I said with a bit of a whine in my voice. "Can't you come with me now and come back later to wrap up your...thing?"

"You'll be fine." Sevenoir rolled his eyes. "You'll face far scarier things as a Templar than Agartha. Just move deeper into the cave. You can't miss the entrance. Look for the bees and walk through to the light. It's as easy as walking through a door."

He climbed up the rocky path near the stream bed and got back on his motorcycle, starting it.

"I'll see you later in London," he yelled to me as he rode off.

CHAPTER FIVE

Crossing the Threshold

PULLING MY BAGS to my body with a huff, I tromped forward into the cave. I wasn't going to be bullied by a rabbit-eared jerk. I could do this.

The smell of ozone and dirt was intense from the entrance, as was the glow coming from within it. Waist-high grass covered the cave floor, and the walls looked naturally carved with massive tree roots breaking through the seams between the rocks. It was a reasonably wide passage to start, six feet across at least, but it narrowed as I walked deeper. I rounded a slight curve, and at last, I could see the portal of which Sevenoir spoke. Big fat bumblebees, some the size of small birds, buzzed back and forth around the entrance, filling the space with a loud hum.

A round structure of tree roots, like a picture frame, stood before me, and through it, haloed by the golden light, was a strange scene. I could see an area comprised of more tree parts and foliage, but arranged to look like a sort of grand room with small alcoves, and what I could swear looked like a sign or mailbox.

Taking a deep breath to calm my nerves, I stepped through the portal, which enveloped me with a sizzling tingle, into the golden light. The hum of buzzing became a deeper throb of noise, like jets flying overhead, making a kind of eerie music. I could hear the sound of gears churning and something squeaking faintly every few minutes. A deep chime resonated, adding another note to the sound, like the start of a symphony. Faint voices in a chorus surfaced from time to time, as I stared with wonder at the scene before me.

Hundreds of giant trees, larger than the largest redwood, lined the horizon as far as the eye could see. From these trees grew a variety of branches, dozens of them, maybe even hundreds. The branches, which were the size of roads, had weird knobby growths that looked like alcoves. Golden lights shimmered from within them. I could see floating wooden platforms with more knobby nooks. The air was dense but pure. It smelled sweet, like honey but with an undertone of machine oil. I had a vague sense of being underground, and yet when I looked up, I couldn't see any ceiling, just tree trunks extending endlessly upward. The area was filled with a golden glow, like a sunlit day, but there was no sun in the sky. And it was stultifyingly warm, like the inside of a greenhouse.

I was standing on a wooden platform suspended in midair, it appeared, although it felt perfectly sturdy. I dropped my bags and turned around immediately to look at the portal through which I'd come. A knobby circular alcove—similar to those I'd seen on the branches and platforms—stood behind me. It had been grown, not constructed, the wood grain of the platform curving to form the shape.

Through the window of the alcove or portal, I could see a faint image—not of the cave I'd come from—but of the Innsmouth Academy, the picture shimmering and rippling as I stared. The same golden light I'd seen in the cave leaked from around the edges of the image. I moved to the side of the platform and looked down, feeling vertigo as I realized that although I could see more platforms and branches below, as far as I could tell, there was no bottom.

Nearby, a small robotic automaton made of copper and gears marched along the platform, startling me, and I stepped away from the edge of the platform to avoid falling. The device was no larger than a cat or a little dog and seemed to have no interest in me, as it wandered by on its task.

There were two more circular alcoves on the platform. Through the one to my left, as I faced the Innsmouth Academy portal, I could see a faint image of the Kingsmouth Sheriff's Office. My mouth dropped open of its own accord. This must be one of the other portals Sevenoir had mentioned. On the right, the alcove showed an image of a dark, mysterious looking mansion. I was unfamiliar with it.

I heard a thump behind me and turned. A woman with short purple hair in a black leather jacket and short shorts was standing behind me in a crouch near a small circular pad nested within the base of the platform. It had a blue-and-white mechanism emanating concentric circles of white light. I started to greet her, but she ignored me, and jumped up and ran toward the Kingsmouth Sheriff's Office portal where she disappeared without a word.

I looked around helplessly. The copper automaton continued to pace around the platform, wandering from portal to portal, ignoring me. I heard a buzzing and watched a small mechanized drone flying toward the platform, ignoring me completely as well. It slipped through the Kingsmouth portal silently and disappeared. Was it some message delivery mechanism? I felt both annoyed and despondent.

I could see the headlines now: *Newsflash! Blodwedd Mallory stranded on Agarthan platform. Story at 11!*

Grrr. Just the thought of coming this far only to be stranded by my lack of knowledge annoyed me, and I felt anger at Sevenoir fill me all over again. I didn't know what to do. I approached the mechanism with the concentric circles of white light at the front of the platform carefully, edging toward it with the toe of my wet right shoe.

With a whoosh, the mechanism activated and my shoe flew off with a squelch, catapulted away from me toward a larger platform below, while my right leg lifted with the force. I fell backward onto my back end and elbows, electric shocks running up my left arm as I hit my funny bone.

My face turned red of its own accord as I scrambled to my feet, shaking out my arm. Thank goodness no one had been here to witness that moment of grace. It looked like the mechanism was some sort of launch pad down to the larger platform. My right shoe was now down there somewhere.

Well. That was it. It was clear that no one was coming to help me and I was *not* about to lose one of my good black pumps.

I walked back to the pile of my bags and grabbed them before stumping awkwardly over to the pad with my bare right foot and my left in the remaining black pump. There was no help for it. I had to try or be left standing on this platform forever.

I stepped forward firmly onto the jump pad and felt the concentric circles of light thrust me forward into the air like spring. I screamed as I was catapulted over the chasm of tree branches and endless space, my arms out gripping my suitcase and duffel bag for dear life as I was flung through the air.

I landed on the larger platform in a crouch, in front of an entrance to the room I'd seen from the portal inside the cave. I quickly stood up. A few people moved around this platform, running in and out of the large room in the tree, some of them landing in a crouch behind me. Scrambling forward to get out of the way, I spotted my errant shoe. I dashed over to grab it and, dropping my bags, slipped it back on my foot. A blast of steam startled me further, and I looked up nervously. There was a giant copper automaton positioned there behind me along the wall; its gears whirred as it stood guard next to the entrance.

Time to get my bearings. A few feet away I saw a short-haired woman in a black and white-checked miniskirt and jacket standing near the edge of the platform. I approached her cautiously, dragging my bags along.

"Excuse me," I said. "Can you help me find my way to London?"

She moved onto a jump pad and sprang away without answering.

I grunted with irritation. I was having a heck of a time getting any help here.

Another woman—this one dressed in an ornate costume consisting of a short black strapless dress, gossamer wings on her back, and black-and-white horns with an elaborate headdress on her head—stood nearby. She had a black lace choker and Egyptian makeup on her face. I wondered what the occasion was.

"Excuse me," I said again, hoping for some assistance this time. "Can you direct me to London?"

She nodded and indicated that I should follow her. She ran to the edge of the right of the platform to another jump pad, with me keeping up as best as I could, my bags in my arms. We sprung across the chasm to another large platform to the right, which I managed without screaming this time. This platform had the portal alcoves embedded directly into the trunk of the tree supporting it. She went to the third portal from the left and said, "Enter here."

I could see an image shimmering in the portal that looked something like a picture I'd once seen of the Tower of London. She'd brought me to the right place. I turned back to her as she was walking away and yelled out my thanks.

While I was turned, I looked across the wooden platform at the ocean of giant tree trunks extending in every direction into the distance and took a deep breath. I was about to realize my dream of going to London. I could still see the small alcove with the portal to Innsmouth Academy. It wasn't too late to turn around and go back.

But that wasn't in my nature. With a ripple of light and a sizzling tingle, I stepped through the portal into London.

The portal let me out under an overpass for light rail near a cab parked at the curb, startling the hell out of its driver, who had been minding his business waiting for his next fare.

"Sorry!" I said as I looked over my shoulder for traffic, then stepped out onto the street. I could see a sign on the overpass that read "Borough of Ealdwic, London." Based on the correspondence I'd had with Miss Plimmswood, the lady who owned the flat I'd be renting, this was the right place. I walked through the arched brick overpass.

Ahead of me two police vans were parked blocking the entrance to the borough beyond. I could see a theater marquee that said "Albion" in bright white lettering on the right side of the street. Sirens rang in the distance, and I could hear the dull roar of traffic. I approached the police officers standing in front of a barricade behind the vans and asked them how to reach Temple Hall.

"Sorry, can't let you through without authorization," the police officer on my left said, holding up his hand. He had on a bulletproof vest and was carrying a submachine gun of some sort. I was confused as I thought police in London didn't carry any arms beyond a nightstick.

I dug through my backpack and pulled out the letter from Richard Sonnac I'd received inviting me to London last fall. I held it out to his partner.

"I don't know what that's supposed to be, but it's not—"

A sandy blonde-haired woman with a chin-length bob and a black trench coat stepped up beside me and showed the officers her badge. "Alright lads, Detective Inspector Shelley, she's with me." She took my arm and brought me through the barricades into the borough. We stepped a few paces away from the officers, and she leaned into me and said, "Do us both a favor and don't go flashing that letter around out here. The boys on the cordons haven't been briefed. As far as they're concerned, this is all just 'heightened awareness' after the terrorist attack in Tokyo."

I nodded my understanding.

"But I don't deal with the bureaucracy, I deal with the truth. About the secret London. About the Templars."

D.I. Shelley looked me up and down skeptically, taking in my bags, and added, "I'd say, 'I hope you know what you're getting yourself into,' but you have no idea. Even I only get as involved as I have to, for the sake of us little people."

She stepped back to the cordon barricade and called back to me in a louder voice. "You've seen it on the news? The Tokyo incident? That's what happens when your new crowd lets things get out of hand."

Anger filled her face and D.I. Shelley stepped back my way, pointing her finger at me. "Not here, not on my watch. That's the deal. That's always been the deal."

At my look of alarm, she relented. Perhaps she realized this was all incredibly new and confusing to me. "You'll be safe inside Ealdwic. Go see one of the prophets prophesying up the road, by the tube station. They'll fill you in on the kind of crazy you've got ahead of you. Best be prepared."

D.I. Shelley walked away from me back to the cordon a second time, yelling "My sincerest condolences!" over her shoulder.

I sighed and turned back toward the street in front of me, which was narrow and made of cobblestones. I could now see the theater clearly on my right. It was called the Albion Ballroom. I noted that bands were scheduled on the weekend nights. That might be fun if I ever had a social life again.

On the left side of the street was a high wrought-iron fence, enclosing a city park. On the right, two- and three-story buildings that looked like shops with apartments above them lined the street—May Queen Market, the placard on the theater said.

Perfect! My new flat was No. 5-F May Queen Market.

Small cars, much smaller than I was accustomed to seeing in the U.S., were parked on both sides of the street without care for direction or traffic laws. Luckily, I wasn't going to be driving here anytime soon as far as I knew.

London was five hours ahead of Maine from a time zone perspective, and it was late afternoon here. I needed to find my new apartment before it got dark. I saw a small sign on the front of a building with a blue door and approached to read it.

"Are you lost, dear?"

I looked up to see an older woman with short, white hair wearing a jaunty brown hat with a blue flower standing on the sidewalk next to the door. She'd spoken in a warm, pleasant voice that was a lovely change from the welcome I'd had from the police. With a light pink jacket, a white and red polka dot blouse, and a brown plaid skirt completing her ensemble, she looked like a wonderful, crazy old aunt.

"I might be," I said, glad for the friendly voice and bit of help.

"New to town?" she nodded.

I smiled wryly. "Is it that obvious?"

She leaned over, putting a hand to the side of her mouth, "The bags were a dead giveaway. My name is Miss Plimmswood, and I'm the landlady here."

I set down my bags and shook her hand happily. "I've come to the right place then. I'm your new tenant, Blodwedd Mallory."

"Well then, come along Miss Mallory, and let's go look at your new flat together." She turned and entered the blue door. I picked up my bags and followed.

Inside was a small foyer with a stone staircase on the right leading to the second floor and a mail area with boxes on the wall on the left. We marched up the stairs, me still lugging the bags, to the second landing. I looked hopefully at the doors to the flats there, but she rounded the corner and started up the stairs again to the third floor. I sighed and resumed climbing.

"The deposit for the flat is £150. I've just had it cleaned and painted."

I stopped in my tracks and blanched at the cost. I hadn't factored a deposit into my plans. I had a few hundred dollars in my checking account but hadn't had a chance to convert any of it to the local currency. My mother had taken care of arranging for the rent to be paid.

Miss Plimmswood, looking back over her shoulder, gave a light chuckle. "Oh, you won't find anything much cheaper than that here, my dear. That is if you fancy a roof over your head and a door that locks at night."

"Perhaps you can point me in the direction of a bank when we're done," I said sheepishly. "That is if you'll give me some time to get the deposit to you."

She nodded in agreement and stepped out onto the third-floor landing, taking out a large keyring from underneath her jacket. The keys clanked and clattered as she sorted through them.

"Ah, here it is," she exclaimed, pulling out what looked like an ancient skeleton key. She thrust it into the lock on a door marked 5-F on the left side of the landing and pushed it open.

I stepped up and peered inside.

A small, but cheerful, living room greeted me. The space was furnished with a futon couch, a small armchair, and a coffee table. A bold, multicolored rug lay on the wooden floor beneath them, and a floor lamp sat in the corner. A set of dark wood bookshelves lined the back wall. I'd look forward to filling those when I had a chance. The ceiling was sloped down toward the window that looked over May Queen Market, following the contour of the roof. There were two doors visible in the corner across from the front door.

"This door leads to the bedroom," Miss Plimmswood said, stepping into the flat and walking across the room to open the door on the left. "And this one," she said, pointing to the door on the right, "leads to the kitchenette. The water closet is accessible from the bedroom. It has a tub with a hand-held for a shower."

I peeked into the bedroom. Along the back wall near a small window was a bed with a metal head- and foot-board. A modern-looking wooden wardrobe, Ikea perhaps, was directly inside the door propped against the wall. The bed didn't have any sheets, but the mattress looked firm and clean. On the far side was a door, which I assumed was the bathroom Miss Plimmswood had referred to.

Well, at least it was a step up from my old dorm room. It was practically a luxurious space in comparison to that.

I stepped fully inside the bedroom and smelled the faint scent of fresh paint drying and noted the clean wooden floors and window sill, and straight, smooth walls. It might have been a relatively small flat, but the space was well cared for, and I liked Miss Plimmswood. I could do worse.

"This will be great," I said, setting my bags down on the floor in front of the wardrobe with a smile.

"Excellent, dear," she said. I walked her back to the front door, and she explained how to get to the nearest bank while she took the old skeleton key off her key ring and handed it to me. I shook her hand again, and Miss Plimmswood said good-bye, closing the front door behind herself, leaving me alone in the flat.

What a whirlwind of a day!

Exhausted, suddenly, by the sheer newness of it all, I turned the lock on the bolt, walked back into the bedroom to the bare mattress of the bed, kicked off my shoes, laid down, and fell asleep.

CHAPTER SIX

Tests

June 15, 2012

I AWOKE REFRESHED the next morning. It was time to explore a little and present myself at Temple Hall.

I dug through my suitcase and found a clean blouse. It was wrinkled from being in the case all night but still better than the one I had slept in. I finished the rest of my morning routine in the small bathroom, then grabbed my backpack, and stepped out of my new flat, locking the door carefully behind me, ready for the day's adventure.

D.I. Shelley had suggested I check out the street prophets and Miss Plimmswood had directed me to a bank called Bartleby & Daughters just off Redcrosse Circus, on the way to Temple Hall. Two items for my to-do list today.

May Queen Market looked quite as I'd left it the day before, with people coming and going. I wandered eastward, noting a pub called The Horned God on the corner by a roundabout just a couple of buildings up from my flat. That was handy. I was looking

43

forward to trying some English beer before too long. And, since I was in England, not the United States, I was old enough to buy some.

On the left was Ealdwic Station, a stop on the Underground. The road curved north after the roundabout and turned into Antiqua Way, and I followed it past the station, noting a fish and chips place, a small Post Office, and a barber shop on the right side of the street. I was pleased with my choice of flat rentals. There were lots of convenient shops near it that would be handy as I learned my way around.

Just past the station, there was a small square with some kind of mural in the bricks, where a few people had gathered. A strange looking man stood atop a wooden box there, his back to the park behind him, wearing a sock puppet on his left hand. What was with the English and these eccentricities?

It occurred to me that this was probably one of the street prophets that D.I. Shelley had referenced, and I decided to step closer to him to listen.

"Too late to start recycling! Hehe!" the sock puppet raved in a squeaky falsetto. It was fashioned as a tiny king, wearing a gold crown and carrying a small scepter.

"Who is this?" I asked a man standing next to me in the crowd.

"This here's the Fallen King and his puppet, miss," the man said with a smile. "He's a barmy one, he is."

The puppet continued its rant, as the gathered people pointed at it and laughed. "To go to raves to save the gorillas! To cash out those Anansi shares! There's a storm coming, mondo storm. Paint your glass houses shut!"

I felt nervous at the puppet's words. They seemed to echo an all-too-familiar theme about the coming of dark days. I found the performance gloomy and weird.

The puppeteer—the Fallen King—was no less strange. He had a long, bedraggled overcoat with a red and green winter scarf that looked uncomfortably warm for the late Spring weather. His head was covered by a red hood-type of hat plastered with fetishes and pins, and he wore tiny round spectacles that hid his eyes over a scruffy beard and mustache.

The Fallen King looked out over the assembled crowd, catching my eye briefly, before continuing in a deeper, smoother voice, gesturing wildly to punctuate his sermon. "You don't have to take his word for it. This is a warning from the sun. It says it's old and tired and scared of death. It says you've lived as young gods for too long! Spoiled children who only need to wish for something and it'll come true!"

He looked conspiratorially at his puppet, then turned once more and bellowed bombastically at the crowd. "Well, those days are gone now and won't come here again! Hahaha! Sorry! I'll show you how it all goes down, through the medium of unreliable narration. A vision of the future. This could be your lucky day!"

"Tomorrow and all the ones after...not so much," The Fallen King continued in a much lower voice, turning back to the puppet. "It's a hot, wet day. You ever notice how the apocalypse always comes on a wet day?"

I jumped as thunder rolled in the background, competing with the nearly constant police sirens. An afternoon storm was moving in. I felt weird. Uncomfortable. The little square smelled like ozone, too many people, and old urine. The noise of the sirens was making my head hurt. I shook it lightly to try to clear my thoughts and scratched my neck. It had begun to itch madly while the crazy prophet ranted.

"There's the smell of warm air and stale piss. The atmosphere is electric. I mean actually electric, sparking off the tracks, lifting and snapping your hair." His voice was mesmerizing. I could feel myself becoming separated from reality. I stumbled on the cobblestones where I was standing.

"A voice over the speakers that you don't hear. You itch. The Black Signal sounds...Lights out," he concluded.

I tumbled unconscious to the pavement.

I came to on a cold tile floor. My ears were ringing, and I shook my head in confusion. Where was I? I looked around in a dazed panic, struggling to focus my eyes. Groggily, I pushed myself up on my elbow to survey the scene.

Oh gods. I was back in the dream, in the entrance to the subway platform in Tokyo, on my back against the tile wall that I'd hit before waking up a couple days ago. Why was I here again? One minute I was listening to the Fallen King and the next thing I knew I was here. What had just happened? Was this a dream or not?

"Get up, Sarah!"

Adrenaline spiked as I realized I was not alone. Rose, Mei, and Alex were here too and still thought I was their friend Sarah.

Right.

Ugh, I really wanted to know who Sarah was and why she was here in the subway because she kept bringing me here in these dreams.

We were on a landing between escalators headed down to a subway platform below, and they were preparing to fight. I scrambled to my feet and grabbed the shotgun beside me on the floor, as the team prepared to open fire on the Filth-infected.

"Don't let it get on you," Rose cautioned, her white toque bobbing with emphasis. "Don't even breathe in."

"It's reacting to us...like it knows we're coming," Mei said with alarm, as she pointed at the escalator stairs below us.

Filth covered the floor of the landing in pools. A swarm of Filth-infected people started running up the escalator stairs from the area below, their feet pounding on the metal. Mei swept the katana in a wide arc, cutting at the monster closest to her. Rose blasted down the escalator with both barrels. I pumped my shotgun and began shooting at our attackers, as they screamed and growled and hissed at us. I shut down the parts of me confused by the everyday clothing and focused on their tentacled, tar-covered heads as I found my targets.

"This stuff can't think," Alex growled as he let loose a ball of flame. "It's a cancer. Cancer doesn't know you're coming, it just is."

We cleared the landing and started down the escalators ourselves to the next landing. Another metal gate blocked our entrance to the platform itself. I realized the group of monsters we had just killed had been locked between the two gates and that it was entirely possible there was a far larger group of infected below. I swallowed hard at the thought. Even if this was only a dream, it was very real.

Mei worked on the gate lock while we caught our breath.

"New plan: fight chaos with chaos," Alex announced. "Keep the bastards at a distance then take them out."

Mei stopped working on the lock and looked over her shoulder at him with disbelief. "That's your plan?"

"Well, it's *a* plan," he grumbled.

Rose turned to me. "When the gate opens, you've got point, Sarah. Make every shot count."

I opened my mouth to ask what point was, but Mei swung the gate up, and the group charged down the last set of stairs. I moved quickly to catch up to them, shotgun at the ready.

"Incoming!" Alex shouted.

Screaming started as we moved forward and a half-dozen survivors who didn't appear to be infected yet ran shrieking by us and up the stairs we'd just gone down. I pointed the end of my shotgun away from a woman in business clothes as she pushed past me, terrified and running for her life. A horde of infected followed close behind them. Mei jumped forward to engage them. Alex and Rose fanned out in hopes of creating a wall of protection for the survivors to escape.

I stepped forward to Rose's right and opened fire on the nearest Filth-infected man. He collapsed when my shot hit him in the chest, filth oozing out of the wound and forming a puddle beneath him. I sidestepped around him and moved toward my next target.

There was hardly time to think! Adrenaline thrummed through my body as wave after wave of the Filth-infected attacked us. I backed up as one got too close to me. Alex finished him off. I nodded thanks and jumped over the puddle of filth left by his body, to engage the next.

There was a break in the waves of attackers, but the floor was covered in a viscous black ooze from the bodies of the Filth-infected we'd killed. Dozens of transformed people, from all walks of life, lay dead on the floor, their bodies mutated by the infection. There were women and men, dressed in everything from business casual to street clothes, in the group of corpses.

Bile rose up in my throat. This was different than killing familiars back at Innsmouth Academy, which, while they had a body, had never been truly alive. Well, at least not in their incarnation as familiars. These people had families, jobs, children, siblings, and parents that loved them. I stood in stunned silence at the scene. Dream or not, this felt real.

Mei wiped the sweat off her forehead with her arm, gauging my reaction. "We're gonna need to use some heavier powers," she cautioned me, then turned to the group. "Don't hold back, all right?"

Alex ran a hand through his hair. "I was pacing myself."

She shook her head at him. In the distance, we heard raw hissing screams coming from deep within the subway tunnels, echoing on the tiles of the platform. Alex and Mei looked at each other in alarm.

"Listen, Sarah," Rose said urgently, grabbing me on the shoulder, as Alex and Mei faced the direction the sound was coming from. "You have to find Zuberi. We'll hold them here. Make a stand."

My heart skipped a beat and fear welled up within me. I didn't know anything about this place, where to go or how to even survive, and Rose was asking me to leave the group? Moreover, I didn't know who Zuberi was or what he even looked like. The screams within the tunnel were getting closer, and the noise tore at my ears.

I looked once again across the platform at the maimed bodies that had been twisted and torn by the Filth and realized there was no choice. If I stayed here and we were all overwhelmed, it would be over. If I moved forward, just maybe I could find Zuberi and locate a way out for us.

Pumping my shotgun, I looked gravely at Rose and nodded. Stepping around the bodies, I hurried across the length of the passenger platform away from growls and screams of the incoming attackers. I made my way up to the far end and looked over to where the tracks lay.

Across the tracks, a chain-link fence with a gate closed off the other side of the platform. If I could just get through that gate, there might be a way up and out of here for us all. Maybe their friend Zuberi was somewhere in that area. I hoped he wouldn't think I was infected and shoot me when I found him.

I jumped down onto the tracks as Alex, Mei, and Rose began to fight the next wave of Filth-infected and ran over to the chain-link fence. I started to fiddle with the lock on the chain when suddenly a massive Filth-infected hulk—it looked like a bodybuilder on steroids only pitch black, its eyes glowing red in the dim light—charged the gate from the other side, bursting through. I jumped back and ran to the bottom of the platform from where I'd come, as far out of its reach as I could get, before opening fire with my shotgun.

It roared and ran toward me, pounding the ground with an enormous swipe. Filth flew up from the tracks where its gigantic fists landed. I scrambled back and fired again, aiming for its chest. It was a big target, and I was at uncomfortably close range. I hit it full on, but it didn't drop. Instead, it swung a fist at me, clipping my left arm.

My mouth dropped open in shock at the intensity of the pain that burned up my arm, turning it numb, as I cried out in pain and shock.

Run! My brain screamed at me as the hulk lunged forward again.

I turned in terror and ran full out back across the tracks, tossing my shotgun up on the platform I'd come from. I scrambled up, pushing with all my might against the tile ledge with both hands and kicking my left leg up to gain purchase. I grabbed the shotgun and turned around to face the filthy hulk once again. It roared in frustration and jumped straight up to pound the ground. Dirt and Filth splashed up like an evil wave.

My left arm still ached from the force of its indirect blow. Needles of pain tingled in my hand as the feeling returned to my limb. I shook it out. I couldn't afford to let this thing get close to me at all. A direct hit from it would be disastrous.

Putting the shotgun to my shoulder, I aimed carefully, and the gun barked, hitting the monster with a raging shot in the chest. The impact of the shell knocked the hulk back slightly, a fountain of black goo splashing from the wound. It roared in anger and stalked toward me across the tracks.

Not good. That was a massive, direct shot, and it hadn't really hurt it at all. Definitely not good. I pumped the shotgun and the chamber clicked dry.

Really not good. I panicked. I had no idea how to reload this thing!

Fumbling in the pockets of Sarah's jacket, I found more shells, but I still didn't know how to load the gun. I looked up. The filthy hulk had turned and was headed toward the end of the platform about 10 feet away to a pile of wreckage. As I stared at the monster in disbelief, it began to climb up the rubble to reach me. It was still coming!

I looked down at the shotgun, panting in fear.

Come on, come on! Think, Wedd. How do you load this thing?

On the body of the shotgun I spied something that looked like a place to put in a shell—there was a knob on the right side with a slide that opened to expose a chamber. I looked at the cartridge in my right hand. It was a kind of orangeish-red plastic on one end and metal on the other end. Brass, my brain supplied. Putting shells in the wrong way was probably bad.

Oh shit. What was the right direction? What if I put them in the wrong way? Was it possible to die in a dream? What if this wasn't a dream?

Crossing my mental fingers that I was loading them correctly, I inserted five shells with the brass ends toward the grip of the shotgun, then pulled the slide closed.

The filthy hulk monster jumped up onto the platform just as I slid it shut, and I pumped the shotgun. *Yes!* That seemed to work, but now the hulk was less than five feet from me. It was too close for me to avoid another blow from its fists while I aimed. I jumped down on the tracks and backed away trying to create some distance again. The hulk roared with anger, and to my right, I could hear the Filth-infected people scream in response from the other end of the platform. My heart beat wildly in a primal reaction to the noise. I hoped Mei, Rose, and Alex were all right.

I pulled the shotgun up to my shoulder, aimed at the filthy hulk, and fired over and over at its chest until there was a gaping cavity there, oozing black filth. It toppled dead to the floor of the platform, dissolving into a puddle of sludge.

Relief filled my body, and I bent over at the waist, panting, to recover.

Once I'd caught my breath, I counted the empty shells on the ground in front of me. I'd used every shot. I reached in my pocket and paused to reload a second time. My hands shook as I loaded five new shells into the slot.

Glancing back over my shoulder, I tried to see how Alex, Rose, and Mei were faring, but I couldn't see them through the swarm of tentacled, Filth-encrusted bodies covering the platform.

I needed to get help! I picked my way back across the tracks and moved through the broken gate of the chain-link fence to assess my path forward. Access to the platform on the other side was completely cut off by the train car pulled up on the tracks. I looked into the black of the subway tunnel. That wasn't an option. There was no telling what horrors were hidden in the darkness there.

Looking at the train cars visible from the lights of the platform, I saw a pile of rubble that just about reached the sliding doors on one of the cars. The entrance to the car was standing open, so I ran down the tracks, scrambled up the wreckage and pulled myself into the subway car.

At the front of the car, a dark-skinned man with round spectacles, long gray dreadlocks, and a tan leather jacket crouched to the left of a wounded man—a soldier?—leaning up against the front of the compartment. The soldier was wearing a black-and-white uniform with a stylized "O" on the chest and was slumped over in pain.

The black man stood up from where he was crouched and looked at me.

"Ah, the cavalry has arrived."

I awoke on the cobblestones of the square to a young black woman shaking my shoulder. I jumped with a start and scooted back on my heels against the wall. She crouched beside me, dressed in a green army jacket with dog tags around her neck, but she looked friendly, once I calmed down enough to take her in.

"You look like you've just seen the end of the cosmos, mate," she said.

That was an understatement! My brow furrowed. I didn't know what had just happened. Had I actually been in Tokyo or was I just dreaming? I shook my head in confusion. Why did I keep ending up there? What was that Filth stuff?

The young woman offered me a hand and yanked me to my feet. "I know the feeling. We're on the edge of it, and it's time to play your part, seen?"

My mouth opened and closed as I struggled for the words to answer her. I found I didn't have any, so I shrugged.

She nodded sagely, then smiled at me. "Me and you, we're blood now, yeah? Templars for the win and that."

I stared at her like a deer in the headlights as thoughts continued to swirl around in my head about what I'd witnessed. Nausea pooled in my stomach. I felt a deep uneasiness and a burgeoning conviction that I hadn't actually been dreaming, that that the events I had witnessed were happening in Tokyo right now.

Gaia help us if they were.

"Never mind. Looks like you've got some training to do before you're ready for your first kill."

Memories of killing the Filth-infected and the hulk flashed in my brain, and I blinked at her in confusion.

She put her hands on her hips and looked at me sternly. "Look, when you get your wits about you, you'll want to do what your letter says. Go speak with Sonnac at the Templars gaff. Not far. Can't miss it. Honest. It's unmissable."

Richard Sonnac! That's right. I was headed to Temple Hall. My heart raced with excitement, and I rubbed my hands. I was on my way to Temple Hall.

She shook her head at me with exasperation and walked away before I could get her name. Belatedly, I realized I hadn't ever even responded to her with words. I called out my thanks, but she didn't turn around.

I watched her go with a sigh. A missed opportunity there. She knew about my letter, she looked about my age, and she was a Templar, too. It would be good to have someone of whom to ask questions. I promised myself that I'd try to find her later when I wasn't so discombobulated from the Tokyo experience.

I spied a coffee shop on the corner called Moca Loco and swung inside, giving a short prayer of thanks to Ms. Usher and the £20 she'd given me when I left Innsmouth Academy. I desperately needed a shot of caffeine to finish clearing my head. I ordered the shop's namesake drink and stepped back out on the street, cup in hand. I continued north half a block, before turning left on Ealdwic Square, which eventually turned into the start of Redcrosse Circus. I wasn't far now from my destination, but I could also see armed guards in front of Bartleby & Daughters bank on the left. Although I wanted to take the young Templar's advice and head straight for Temple Hall, I figured I better swing into the bank before it closed and get some money exchanged.

After speaking with the teller and exchanging my currency, I headed back out to the curving street, walking past a large clothing store called Pangea and some sort of government building on the right. A variety of tall, narrow old buildings stacked in a neat curve formed the circus on the left. They appeared to be under construction and scaffolding covered several of them. One even had a double-decker bus parked out front. In the distance, I could still hear police sirens and noted that the day was cooler from the earlier storm.

Suddenly it was real. I was in London, and I was finally headed to Temple Hall. I felt a thrill of pride that I'd made it here myself, despite that crabby Sevenoir who left me at the Agartha portal without a clue. As I rounded the curve, Temple Hall stood before me, with an arched gateway enclosing the front of the Temple courtyard.

The sun split through the fluffy gray clouds in the sky above the rotunda of the white stone hall like an omen. The building itself looked like a fortress, emphasized by the neatly uniformed guards standing at the arched gateway. Cordons had been erected blocking vehicular access to the Temple Court. The guards were talking to a couple of police officers. Beyond the gateway, I could see the front of the hall adorned with long red banners bearing white shields with red crosses hanging to either side of the entrance. A large public fountain shimmered in the foreground. I looked around for a rubbish bin and found one near a guard on the left side of the arched gateway.

"State your business," he challenged me.

"I'm here to see Richard Sonnac," I answered.

"Ah, new blood I see. I suppose you look like the best of the new batch," the guard said, eyeing my outfit. I looked down at my wrinkled blouse doubtfully. "Right then. Show us your letter."

I reached in my backpack and pulled out the vellum envelope, stamped in red wax with the Templar seal. I closed the bag hastily as I realized my picture of Richard Sonnac was visible in the opening.

The guard gave me a nod and a wry smile, then stood back to let me pass. I walked through the gates and goggled at the sheer size of Temple Court. Ornate stone buildings stood on either side of the road. A fountain splashed and roared in the center of a cross-shaped pond. I walked along the walkway to the right of the pond toward the main entrance. Two more guards stood to either side, wearing red pants, black boots, and ornately trimmed uniform jackets in red, black, and white.

I stepped through the inner doors into a large foyer. Before me, up another three steps, were three open stone doorways, the largest in the middle, with two smaller to either side. Two more guards, a man and a woman, stood at attention there, next to tall cauldrons burning with flames. Beyond them, I could see a large open courtroom, with a Templar cross embedded in the floor. The floor of the foyer I stood in was made of tightly seamed slabs of white marble, and there were tall red wooden doors to the left and right sides. Thankfully, the door on the right stood open.

I turned and walked toward it and into what appeared to be an office, the floor covered by a red carpet with a gilded four-armed cross. The Templars certainly did not want anyone to miss the theme around here.

A small ornate fireplace sat on the far wall with an enormous painting of Saint George slaying the dragon above it. Similarly large oil paintings adorned the other walls I could see. The scale of the room was ridiculous for a single office, but tall floor lamps stood along the walls, adding a warmth to the light of the place, which primarily came from a crystal chandelier hanging down from the 20-foot ceiling. There were chairs and end tables, and even a wooden globe, filling the space.

My eyes were drawn to the desk, finely made, but small in comparison to the room, which sat along the west wall. A handsome black man, with closely cropped hair, in a tailored brown pinstripe suit sat at the desk reviewing some paperwork. My heart skipped a beat. At last, here was Richard Sonnac.

He looked up and spied me standing there. "Come in. Come in."

I approached his desk.

"I'm very pleased you can follow directions on the back of a card. It is the basis for us getting along famously," as he said with a dry smile. I was thrilled by his lovely English accent and grinned like an idiot.

He stood up and walked toward me, gesturing at the room. "Of course, with an establishment like this, we're practically in the Yellow Pages under 'Crusaders.'"

He reached out and shook my hand. "Richard Sonnac."

"Wedd…uh, Blodwedd Mallory," I responded, stumbling over my name and cursing myself for my nerves. Were my hands cold and clammy? Oh, Gaia, I hoped my hands weren't cold and clammy.

"So," he continued. "You heeded our call to arms."

"Yes, sir." Annoyance filled me at my shaking voice. I had waited so long for this that I was incredibly nervous.

"And what do you want?" He looked at me expectantly.

What did I want? What did he mean, what did I want? I gave him the only answer I had.

"I'd like to become a Templar, sir."

A smile spread across his face, and he nodded. "Very good. It's critical that the candidate asks. It's a requirement of your initiation. Only the first test, but you've passed with flying colors."

He spread his arms wide. "This organization will require much of you, I'm afraid. It's important that you understand what you're getting into. You have questions. I can furnish you with answers. Some answers."

Sonnac pursed his lips and looked at me. "To begin with, you haven't strayed into some atrocious Dan Brown airport paperback. We are not the 'Knights Templar.' That particular appellation went out in the 1300s, along with pageboy haircuts and burnings at the stake."

He turned away from me and paced a bit around the room as I ran my hands surreptitiously down my skirt to dry them. "No, we run a 21st century—well, let's say a 'forward-facing' organization, but one with its strength in the ancient bonds of tradition. In loyalty. In blood. And, to be perfectly frank, in a sizable private army."

Sonnac turned back toward me, gesturing as if to demand my understanding. "Our firm guidance is needed to save the world from itself. We are at war. Might will make right, and it will fall upon us to judge the correct application of might. It falls upon you as a soldier of the Templars. Show me that you have the will, and we can teach you the way."

I felt a fierce pride fill me at his words. I definitely had the will!

"Your invitation to join us is for two key reasons. First, your family has a history of serving us. That in itself makes you a candidate worthy of consideration." Sonnac continued, moving back to his desk. "But more importantly, you, like some others you will meet here at Temple Hall, were chosen by Gaia. That has given you remarkable powers. Powers that need to be honed and controlled."

Looking down at a paper on his desk, he quirked an eyebrow, and then looked back at me, adding, "At least, to a less disastrous effect on property values."

My face went red. I hadn't ruined anything at Innsmouth Academy permanently that I was aware of. Although it did take a lot of wax to get the scorch marks and cracks out of the wooden floor of the Media Room.

"I will discuss a date for your initiation with the Grand Master and let you know when it has been scheduled," he said. "In the meantime, there is a private training area which we have reinforced for members and candidates. You may spend your time there until the date is set."

He pointed at a second doorway to the left, then sat down at his desk and returned to his papers.

My face fell. I was dismissed.

I fiddled uncomfortably for a moment as my heart ached. This was not the grand meeting I had envisioned with Richard Sonnac in my fantasies about the future. I looked back at him sitting at his desk, engrossed in his papers, and fought back tears.

•

Taking a deep breath, I got my emotions under control, scolding myself silently for foolishness. I was here after all, and I would get a chance to prove myself worthy to become a Templar.

With that bit of hope to sustain me, I turned back to the door I had entered, only then noticing that D. I. Shelley was standing there at the entrance. I smiled at her, and she gave me a curt nod as she entered Sonnac's office.

I moved through the new doorway and stepped out into another marble-floored hall. To my right were two large red wooden doors carved with roses, hung inside a tooled stone frame that looked like a Greek temple. They made me feel very small. Two more uniformed guards stood before them. They didn't acknowledge me as I awkwardly pushed at the heavy doors and entered the training room as I'd been directed.

I stepped through the doorway into the room and looked around myself in confusion. This didn't look like a gym. It looked like a nightclub.

Directly in front of me stood a large wooden bar, with a marble counter and nearly a dozen stools in front of it. The back bar was lit glass, and I could see a variety of bottles of spirits as well as neat rows of glassware lining the shelves. The floor in front of me was covered in a thick, luxurious red carpet.

I did a double take and looked back over my shoulder at the door. Was I in the wrong place?

"Hi there," called out the bartender stationed behind the marble and glass edifice, dressed in an impeccable Templar uniform. "Come in then. Don't dawdle."

I stepped forward and looked right and left. The carpeted area was filled with tables and chairs on both sides of the bar, with small table lamps adorning them. The bar area appeared to be the raised portion of a split level surrounded by a wooden railing, and I could see steps down to a marble floor below it.

"Am I...?" I asked tentatively.

"This is the Crucible. You're in the right place," the dark-haired bartender responded as he polished a crystal tumbler with a white towel. "Everyone does that when they come in for the first time. I take it Sonnac directed you here to train?"

"Erm, yes."

"You'll want to talk to the master-of-arms down there then," he said, pausing to point his thumb over his shoulder. "Better head on down. The Brig doesn't like to be kept waiting."

I nodded and strode across the carpet to the stairs. I stepped down on to the marble main floor and approached a tall older man wearing a tan button-down army shirt and brown pants, a mechanical brace supporting his right leg. He turned to me, and I could see his right eye was covered with a black patch.

"Christ almighty," he said with an Australian accent and a scowl as he looked me over. "We've got our work cut out for us."

I could see four shiny medals attached to his chest, two silver medals with red and white ribbons, and two gold with solid red ribbons. This was beyond a shadow of a doubt the brigadier in question.

He watched me as I walked up, his scowl deepening, making the grooves in his forehead stand out. I could see a scar intersecting his right eyebrow and disappearing behind the patch. His hair was brown but closely cut, and he appeared to be in his mid-50s.

He pointed his finger at me. "The Crucible is my house, and in my house my word is law. Forget your mother's teat, from now on this is your home. This is where you learn to stay alive."

I swallowed hard. What had I done to deserve such an ear bashing?

"Now, what's your name, soldier?" he asked.

"Blodwedd Mallory," I responded in what I hoped was a crisp tone.

"Blodwedd Mallory," he said, lingering over my last name. "Your mother is Lisbette? Elizabeth Mallory?"

I nodded, pleased that he knew her.

"Hmm. She's a good agent. Your father…" He turned away from me and wandered over to a weapon case. "Have you ever used a blade?"

"No, sir."

He looked back at me, surprised. "What then are your weapons?"

"I have blood magic," I began, as he nodded.

"From your mother."

"And chaos magic."

The brigadier looked at me in astonishment. "No physical weapons training at all?"

I shook my head.

His face clouded over like a storm. "That is why the Illuminati should not be in charge of training anything," he yelled. "This is an outrage. Nearly 20 years old, I should think, and never picked up a blade?"

I shook my head again, warily. "I just turned 18, sir."

He gritted his teeth and got himself under control, before speaking in a somewhat calmer voice. "I am Brigadier George Lethe, and I am responsible for your martial instruction. You've come here an empty slate. You have potential, that's why you were recruited, but that potential needs strict guidance. Normally I give the recruits their choice of weapons, but not you. You will begin training on blade work immediately."

My mouth flopped open, and I closed it with a snap.

He limped back to the weapons crate and dug through it, pulling out a blade and a shotgun.

"Since your magic comes in two flavors of combat, we'll make sure you have the same in your weapons training."

I looked at him blankly.

"Melee combat, like blade work or chaos magic," he yelled, then pointed to the shotgun. "And ranged combat, girl, like blood or shotgun. You need both to have choices, depending on the fight you're in."

Brigadier Lethe set the weapons back down on top of a closed crate, then moved right into my face and leaned down, "You want to be close up for some things."

He stepped back and gestured at a long target range behind him. I could see the floor marked at intervals—10 meters, 20 meters, 30 meters—and at the back of the wall was a grotesque body strapped to a large wooden X. "And further away for others."

I looked with alarm at the creature hanging there, crucified. It was pale skinned and unnatural, with two arms and two legs like a human, but not like a human; it had a wide gaping mouth full of sharp teeth and a leather band of some sort covering its eyes. Widening my focus, I saw there were at least five more, secured at the end of each lane of the range. I was stunned to find monsters like these inside the vaunted marbled halls and turned to Brigadier Lethe with a question written on my face.

"Those things are called rakshasa," he explained. "They're basic hellhounds. We keep them chained. They used to make such a mess of the new recruits. You'll use them for target practice, to get accustomed to shooting your shotgun."

At my further look of doubt, Brigadier Lethe chuckled darkly. "Don't worry, they don't feel a thing, and they're unworthy of your mercy."

"Will I still practice my blood and chaos magic?" I asked. I couldn't imagine not working on my magic after four years of practice. I'd only recently come to like blood magic.

"You'll practice it all here," he answered. "From now on, this is the most important room in the world for you. It's a place where you can try out all your new-found power without risk of hurting yourself. Go on, get started. I'll offer some guidance along the way."

I set down my backpack, walked over to the black crate, and picked up the blade he'd pulled out, and pulled it from its sheath. It was a plain looking traditional type sword with a grip and pommel, as well as a metal cross guard. It had a long blade with two edges and a shallow groove in the middle. I touched the top edge of the blade carefully with my left thumb, catching my breath as the edge cut into the skin slightly. This was no practice weapon!

And it was heavy—at least for my unaccustomed arm. It must have weighed three pounds or more, and it didn't take long before the muscles of my arm complained about holding it. I slashed the air tentatively.

"The pointy end goes in your opponent," the brigadier called out behind me.

I made a face. Very helpful guidance. Not. I turned and looked back at him.

"Put that one back in its scabbard, soldier. We'll start next week with some strength training and footwork before you try to work with a sharp blade. It's too easy to cut off your limbs if you're not ready for it."

Brigadier Lethe pointed to his leg in the brace. I suspected he was pulling mine, but the past day had been strange enough that I wasn't sure. He walked over to me and picked up the shotgun.

"Let's start you on this for now, shall we? What do you know about shotguns?"

"I shot one the other..." I stopped, confused. I hadn't actually shot one, had I? The Tokyo subway had all been a dream, I was pretty sure, despite how real it had felt.

"Well, we'll start with the basics then," he said, holding the shotgun with care, but so I could see all the parts. "This is the hand stock; this is the barrel. This is the safety. You'll want to make sure that's on at all times unless you plan to shoot it, to keep you from blowing someone's head off. You Bees are resilient, but even you might struggle to regenerate a head. Also, it's good practice never to put your finger on the trigger until you're ready to fire."

Lethe held the shotgun hand stock in his left hand, and the wooden grip in his right as he demonstrated, with the barrel pointed at the ground. I guess I had been right about that part in my dream.

He reached behind him to the weapons crate and took out five shotgun shells, explaining an unmodified shotgun could typically hold three to five rounds. He demonstrated loading the gun, telling me that this particular model was a "pump action." He oriented a shell, so the brass end was facing toward the grip, I noted with satisfaction, and inserted it in the loading port. Pocketing the remainder of the rounds, he pumped the hand stock to finish loading the cartridge.

"You'll want to pull the gun up to your shoulder to fire it," he continued, turning the gun to the range to demonstrate. "Make sure you keep the butt tight there. Otherwise, the kick will hurt."

He flipped off the safety with his thumb and fired a shot down the range. The gun boomed, the noise enormous, but strangely enough my dream had prepared me for that as well. I recalled the sound of both Rose and me firing in the relatively small area of the subway station.

"Earplugs are a good idea, if you want to hear when you're my age," Lethe added, "Although I suppose you Bees can just regenerate your eardrums."

He flipped the safety back on and handed me the shotgun and a shell. "Here, walk out there to the 10-meter line on the range with me, and we'll have you try it."

We walked out in the wooden lane that reminded me vaguely of a bowling alley toward the line marked 10 meters. I shuddered as I got a closer look at the Rakshasa hanging on the wall. That was one ugly monster.

Holding the gun as he had shown me, and trying not to shake, I double checked the safety and put the shell into the loading port, brass end back. Then I slid the hand guard back toward the grip, pumping it to load the shell.

"Good. Now, bring it tight against your shoulder—Watch the barrel! Don't just be swinging it around willy-nilly."

I gulped nervously and re-focused on what he was saying.

"Look down the barrel to sight your target. You'll want the Rakshasa in this lane, soldier," he added dryly. "When you're ready, flip off the safety and pull the trigger smoothly, keeping the shotgun level."

I squeezed my eyes shut and pulled. Boom! The gun kicked up, the barrel raising by a few degrees, hitting the back wall above my target.

He tsked at me with irritation. "You have to keep your eyes open when you fire. And pull the trigger more smoothly, so you don't raise the barrel on the follow-through. You'll be fixing that divot you just made later."

Nevertheless, Lethe had me try again, insisting that I keep both eyes open to ensure I could see my target as I fired, particularly if it was moving, pointing out that most of the demons I encountered in the future wouldn't be handily secured to a wooden X.

That seemed like good advice. I carefully loaded the shell, pumped the shotgun once, pulled it back to my shoulder, and took a calming breath. Then, carefully, so carefully, I pulled the trigger back smoothly. Boom! The shotgun barked again, but this time, a hole blossomed on the body of the Rakshasa, blood running from the wound. Gross. And cool.

I lowered the barrel and flipped on the safety before looking over my shoulder at him, a smile on my face.

"Much better," Lethe praised me. He pulled a shell with a purple casing out of his pocket. "Now, let's try a specialty shell. This one is full of depleted uranium. It's twice as dense as a lead shell and makes a hell of a hole in your target. It can shoot through the side of a tank if you need to. Move back to the 30-meter line. I don't want to have to explain to Dame Julia why some poor unlucky sod in the next room keeled over dead from your stray shot."

He explained a few more techniques, then left me to it. I practiced shooting with a dozen or so shells of different types as well as techniques for single targets and groups of assailants.

When I finally ran out of shells, I walked back to the central portion of the practice hall to ask him for more, placing the empty training shotgun back in its case. Brigadier Lethe was in deep, animated discussion with a tall, austere-looking older woman wearing a very formal red-and-black Templar uniform, complete with a high collar, a cape, and a plate-mail shoulder guard.

She looked unamused by the topic of their conversation and kept glancing over at me and scowling.

"Wedd, come here," Lethe called me over. "This is Dame Julia Beatrix Tyburn. She's the Agent Special Assignment Supervisor. You will answer to her at the completion of your training."

I approached them both and offered a handshake to Dame Julia. She looked at my hand, and her scowl deepened, so I dropped into an awkward curtsy instead. What was the proper etiquette for meeting a dame anyway? They didn't teach that at Innsmouth Academy.

"Is this some sort of attempt to fraternize?" she enunciated in a severe tone which was as cold, I thought to myself, as her steel shoulder guard. "Well, I won't stand for it. Never mind me, you'd do well to worry a little more about yourself. How you dress, how you carry yourself. I mean, who are you?"

My face flushed red at the admonishment. I wanted to defend my choice of clothing, but figured discretion was the better part of valor in this instance.

"This is Elizabeth Mallory's daughter, Julia. She presented herself here today," Lethe explained in his Australian drawl, as Dame Julia continued to pin me in place with her scowl. "I'm going to see to her weapon training before I turn her over to you because…she has none."

Lethe revealed my lack of weapon knowledge with a tone as dry as a desert. The way the conversation was headed was starting to alarm me, and I looked at him in consternation. Would I be found lacking and unworthy of becoming an agent?

Dame Julia's head whirled back to Lethe, and she peered at him with the scrutiny of a hawk surveying a mouse.

"What do you mean, 'she presented herself'?" Dame Julia demanded. "Sevenoir was assigned to collect her and bring her to us."

Lethe shrugged in return.

She turned to me. "Well, girl. Did he bring you here or not?"

I faltered not knowing how to respond while she looked at me impatiently. I didn't have any great love for the agent who had dropped me off at the Agartha portal, but I also didn't want to throw him to the lioness. In the end, I decided the best answer was the unvarnished truth, expressed as objectively as I could manage.

Dame Julia's face darkened with anger as I related my tale.

"Well, we shall see about that!" she intoned imperiously. "Carry on here, George. Get this girl the training she needs post haste." With that, she whirled on her heel and marched up the stairs and out of the Crucible.

My face crumbled as I watched her go, and I felt the cold burn of acid in my stomach. Not just one, but two dismissals by high-ranking Templars on the same day? This was not turning out to be the triumphant entrance to Temple Hall that I had hoped for at all.

What if I washed out and they decided I didn't have what it took to a Templar? Where would I go? What would my mother think? I'd been so confident that I'd be a shoo-in here after successfully capturing the wraith back at Innsmouth Academy. Instead, I was treated like a child with no skills.

Brigadier Lethe paid no mind to my reaction. He rubbed his face and chuckled. "Sevenoir better run for the bushes. There'll be no love lost between the two of you for a while, I suspect."

I made a sound of protest. Sevenoir? I was the injured party here! He was the jerk who left me at the portal, and seemingly against his orders. All that struggle to find my way through Agartha…I wanted desperately to complain to Lethe about my experiences so far, and the downright unfairness of getting here only to be treated like a child. That, I realized, would have the opposite effect of what I intended. Complaining would show that not only was I immature, but that I could not roll with the punches, and neither of those was the impression I wanted to leave with Brigadier Lethe.

I quelled my frustration at potentially being blamed for Sevenoir's trouble. I didn't need to be distracted from my goal, which was to prove my worthiness to become a Templar. I was resolute. It was time to get back to it. I would use every opportunity to show my fitness for the job.

"What next, sir?" I asked Lethe, standing at attention.

Brigadier Lethe quizzed me for about 15 minutes on the things I'd practiced on the range before deciding that was sufficient training for the day. I didn't let it show, but I was relieved. My ears were tender from the shotgun retorts, and my left arm and right shoulder were sore, but I felt pleased with my progress. And, since I now knew a little more about shotguns, if I went back in that dream again, I could better help Rose, Mei, and Alex clear out the subway.

My stomach growled loudly, and I realized it had been a while since I had last eaten.

"Okay, soldier. Report here on Monday at 0800 to start your blade training," Brigadier Lethe said, dismissing me. I thanked him, gathered my backpack, and headed up the stairs toward the big red doors.

"See you later, miss," called the bartender, still wiping glasses with his white towel as I walked by on the thick red carpet. I waved to him and stepped back out into the main hall.

65

I contemplated whether I was supposed to go back to Richard Sonnac's office yet today, but decided he wouldn't be ready to see me until my training was concluded. Based on what Brigadier Lethe had said, it hadn't even really started yet. That was disappointing, but I was resolved to learn what I needed to know to be an effective agent.

I didn't know yet what to make of all the experiences I'd had today. Richard Sonnac, Dame Julia, Brigadier Lethe. None of them were quite what I'd expected. I bit my lip. The day had been full and exciting, but it was a far cry from the triumphant pageant of homecoming I'd worked up in my fantasies over the years, and I struggled to control my discouragement.

Oh, how I missed Ms. Usher, Gypcie, and Carter. I felt a long way from Innsmouth Academy. I needed to buck up if I was going to be successful.

Stepping out to the large courtroom of the main hall, I could see a variety of uniformed guards stationed near doors or patrolling the floor. Temple Hall looked much the same as when I'd entered earlier today. This was a 24-by-7 operation, and I decided that it probably looked similar regardless of the time of day or night.

My stomach growled again, so I resolved to head back to my flat and make a plan to get some supper. Maybe I'd get some fish and chips from the shop I saw earlier.

The front door to The Horned God stood cheerfully open as I walked by after grabbing some fish and chips to go, and I could hear the chatter of patrons inside as they imbibed the local brews. Above the door, a placard read "Horned God Est. 900 AD," which simultaneously blew my mind and filled me with disbelief. There wasn't a bar even remotely that old in the U.S.

I was sorely tempted to go inside, but I decided to look around a little more. I continued on the walk past the south-east side of the pub, passing an old movie theater, a butcher shop, and a bakery on the corner that sold "Cheese: Cheshire, Leicester, proper Cheddar, Wensleydale, and Blue Stilton."

What was "proper Cheddar?" In fact, I had no idea what half of those cheeses were, but decided to try them at the first opportunity.

An antique shop and a small florist specializing in orchids made up the balance of the nearby shopping attractions. Not a McDonald's or Old Navy anywhere to be found. I was thrilled. I felt like I'd stepped 50 years into the past. Kingsmouth had been quaint, but this was fabulous!

A side alley cut back toward May Queen Market, so I headed that way but realized that I had stumbled onto the back patio area of The Horned God in the process. I apologized to the short-haired waitress stationed there for wandering in carrying my own food, but she waved it off and invited me to have a seat and a drink. I ordered a pint of "St. Swithin's Famous Stout" and sat down to eat my dinner at an empty, nearby wooden picnic table that had a patch of afternoon sunshine.

This was the life! I took a big bite of the crunchy, deep-fried breaded fish fillet I'd unwrapped. It was a long way from powdered orange drink and fish pies, at any rate. I felt the stress of the day fall away and settled back to look around more closely.

The back brick wall of the patio area had a giant painted mural of Pan, or some satyr, complete with a bright green beard. Ivy grew up the wall, framing the mural in a pleasing combination of nature and artifice. An oak tree grew in the middle of the flagstone patio, providing more beauty as well as shade on hot days.

"Ho there, Blodwedd," Miss Plimmswood called from my right, as she approached from the May Queen market side, her eyes twinkling. "I see you've found one of the very best features of your new flat. Can I join you for a cup of tea?"

I motioned her over gladly, and she flagged down the waitress to bring her drink. I ordered another pint at the same time.

"So, tell me," Miss Plimmswood inquired, sitting with me at the table and taking off her hat with a flourish, her short gray curls bouncing, "how was your first day in Ealdwic?"

Glad for someone to share my experiences with, I launched into the tale, regaling her with my encounter with the Fallen King and his puppet, although I didn't tell her that I'd fainted, or about my dream, for fear she'd be concerned, or worse, think I was crazy.

"He is such an oddball duck with his cloth friend," she tutted, shaking her head. "He's an outlandish puppet, and the little doll is peculiar too. You get all sorts around here. All sorts."

I wasn't sure what to make of her reply, so I asked her how long she'd been in the area.

"Oh, most of my life, dear. My work brought me here from Wiltshire as a young woman, and I suppose that was so many years ago now that this is home."

The afternoon light was beginning to wane by the time the waitress brought Miss Plimmswood her "tea"—that was a mug of whiskey if I'd ever seen one, but since I was about to start on my second pint of stout and was feeling a little blurry from the first, I was in no position to judge.

Miss Plimmswood asked me about my life on Solomon Island, and I told her about my time at Innsmouth Academy. That made me immediately homesick, and I vowed to write Gypcie a letter just as soon as I had the chance.

I also wanted to find out if Miss Plimmswood knew anything about the Templars, but I was reluctant until I knew more about what was proper to share with members of the public, so I bit my tongue and asked instead about what work she'd done that brought her to Ealdwic.

"Oh, I'm long retired, dear," she said, with a wave of her hand. "And you must call me 'Plimmy.' All my good friends do."

Tears welled up in my eyes without warning. I dashed them away quickly with the back of my finger. I was overcome by her kindness and a little embarrassed at my emotional reaction.

"And you are homesick, I see." She clucked her tongue in sympathy. "You're a long way from home. It's to be expected. Things will get better once you're settled into the flat. I'll lend you some sheets for your bed until you can buy some, and, when you have a free hour, you can pick up fresh food from the Haitian Market stalls and canned goods from Annapurna. It's a grocery shop just around the corner. You can't just live on fish and chips, you know. What would your mother say?"

What *would* my mother say? Miss Plimmswood's gentle concern reminded me of her and was just what I needed to right my worldview. It was nice to know I wasn't completely alone in a strange new city. We finished up our drinks shortly thereafter and left The Horned God. True to her word, she lent me a set of sheets and a blanket from her own supply—she lived in the ground flat of the building next to mine.

I trudged up the stairs to my new apartment, bedding in hand, unlocked the door with the old skeleton key, and set about getting settled in. That included dashing off a letter to Gypcie about my adventures so far. I wondered how things were going for her in New York.

CHAPTER SEVEN

Londinium

June 16, 2012

UNLIGHT CREPT in my flat windows the next morning, waking me. The weekend was here and with it a chance to do a little shopping and some more exploring around Ealdwic. I hopped out of bed and realized with despair that I didn't yet have a means of making coffee or even some English breakfast tea.

Time to get up and get out, I thought. I could take Miss Plimmswood's—Plimmy's!—advice and head down to the Haitian Market she'd mentioned yesterday. I didn't have a lot of money, but enough to buy a few staples.

I jumped into the shower in the tiny bathroom of my flat and then completed my morning ritual, selecting jeans and sneakers with one of my favorite tops. It was red with a cool Asian-looking print and was cut out in the center front to show my middle. I emptied out my backpack of everything but my wallet, my ritual knife—known to magic users as an athame—and my spell foci, then pulled it over my shoulder and headed out the door. I didn't think I'd be doing any chaos or blood magic today but better safe than sorry in a new place.

Plimmy said that the market was over behind Aethelburga Row on the street called Pagan Hill, so I stepped out on the May Queen Market and flipped around the front of the pub. Just past Burnt Offerings, the bakery I'd seen last night, was the street I was looking for.

I tucked into the bakery first and bought some baguettes and Stilton at the suggestion of the shopkeeper—"Just chop up a nice onion to put on the loaf with it, dear"—then, after putting my purchases in my pack, I stepped out of the shop and turned left on the cobblestone road and went under a rounded brick overhang.

A staircase with stone steps led down to an area filled with exotic sounds and smells. In front of me, I could see some shop fronts, including the one Plimmy had recommended, but on the left was what looked to be an open-air market filled with stalls. That must be the Haitian Market area.

I was unresolved about buying from the stalls before I knew a little more about the area so I turned around and headed back up the stairs to the landing with the storefronts and entered a local grocery store called Annapurna that had displays of fresh fruits and flowers out front. The signboard above the store indicated they offered everything from incense to phone cards, which just about matched the variety of my needs.

Grabbing a small basket, I selected the items to fill my pantry: fruits, veggies, a few cans of vegetables and soups, and, of course, ground coffee. I even picked up a tin of Earl Gray tea. I hadn't really drunk much tea back in Maine, but when in Rome...

The shopkeeper rang up my purchases, and I filled up my backpack until there wasn't room for much more. I headed back out to the landing and looked at the Haitian restaurant at the south end. I could smell fried food, and my stomach rumbled. I hadn't had any breakfast yet.

I stepped inside to the counter and ordered myself a black coffee. I was contemplating the rest of the menu, particularly the "Kanaval Kabrit" until I realized that was prepared goat meat. I chickened out and went for the twice-fried plantains to go with my coffee, instead. I sat down at a table near the window to enjoy my *ad-hoc* breakfast and congratulated myself on trying new things. The fried plantains were crunchy, like a thick potato chip, and came with dipping sauce. The kabrit and the head cheese would have to wait for another day when I was feeling more adventurous.

While I ate my plantain chips, I watched the passers-by. This was a vibrant neighborhood with folks from all walks of life, but it was weird not knowing anyone. I searched the faces for some familiar aspect, but to no end. At one point, I could have sworn I saw a pair of bunny ears—I would have even been glad to see my erstwhile escort among the strangers—but I lost sight of them too quickly to be sure.

I drank the last gulp of my coffee and briskly headed out the front door of the restaurant thinking I'd head back to my flat when a high-pitched coughing sound caught my attention.

"Slow down, child. Why you rush so sharp-sharp? Delay yourself."

I whirled around to see an older Haitian woman in a green and red smock dress and green flip-flops sitting in a white, wicker wheelchair with a red and white striped umbrella trying to get my attention. She had a crucifix around her neck, a red turban on her head, and was smoking a cigarette. She waved me over.

I raised my chin and stepped over to where she was seated in the corner between the Haitian restaurant and the House of Chalk Voodoo shop.

"Temple Hall has been here for a thousand years," she said, exhaling a plume of smoke from her nose. "It will perhaps stand a little longer, while you take time to breathe in the magics."

Introducing myself, I learned her name was Mama Abena, the proprietress of the Voodoo shop. My eyes darted over to the shop's signage. I wondered if this was what my friend Renee had practiced in New Orleans. In addition to various religious supplies, the shop offered readings, rituals, and Voodoo spells for sale, with the caveat to the latter: "Use at your own risk!"

Right. Those wouldn't be on my shopping list this week.

"What part of London is this?" I asked her, gesturing around me. "This area seems to be beneath the city itself."

She spread her arms wide. "This is the Darkside, not the London you are learning, the London of brick and mortar. This is her heart, her soul. Let her speak to you through the wind in the trees, the smoke on the air...and the prophets on street corners," Mama Abena punctuated her words with a wave of the cigarette, smoke following her gesture. "All you need to do is listen."

I winced. I'd had my fill of the prophets on the street corners recently, as I thought back on my experience with the Fallen King. Of course, I considered further, maybe she meant herself. She no doubt had knowledge of the city, including its history and secrets.

She inhaled deeply and blew out another cloud of smoke. "The Templars, they tell you about the power, the magic, and the glory. That is why you're here."

How on Earth did she know that?

I nodded minutely in acknowledgment. "That's right."

She scooted forward in her chair, her face serious, and stood up, closing the space between us. "The bees, they are anxious. They feel the storm coming."

I looked at her in alarm. *Did she mean bees or...Bees? And what storm was she talking about?* My mind flew unbidden to my dreams of the Tokyo subway and the Filth-infected people there.

Mama Abena chuckled at my reaction and pointed at my face. "I see by the scar on your nose that you wants to be a hero. To go fight all the bad things. But no one is born a hero, child. They gots to learn, and the teaching, it come from all places. Not just the Templars. Not even the blessing of the bees."

Now she had my full attention. "What do you know about the blessing of the bees?" I asked warily.

Standing up from her chair, Mama Abena looked across the cobblestone courtyard for a moment before turning back to me, her eyes piercing mine. "I know the truth. And, the truth, it does not come with a fancy office or a tailored suit."

Looking down quickly at my own clothing, I was pretty confident that she wasn't accusing me of wearing a tailored suit. I felt my face flush red with embarrassment and a little anger at her words, as I visualized Richard Sonnac in his brown pin-striped suit

73

in his lavish office. She waved a hand in front of my face, drawing my attention back to the courtyard in front of her shop.

"The Fallen King, now he has neither, but appearances deceive. His words hold deep truth," she said, touching the area over my heart with her hand. "Remember this well."

She turned around and sat back in her chair, her body plopping onto the cushion as she held tightly to its arms. She seemed tired out by the brief time she spent standing. She looked up at me gravely.

"As for me, I tell you a little truth. It is not about glory or power. Do not run blindly into this war," Mama Abena urged me. "Open your eyes, and you will find what you search for. Just like the powers of the Earth found you."

Then she leaned back against the wicker chair and closed her eyes, offering a final benediction. "Ibi so, ibi so."

I thanked Mama Abena and stepped away, considering what she'd said. I knew I was a little drunk on the Templar nectar, but what she said made sense. My powers didn't come from the Templars. They came from Gaia. Maybe I could prove my worth by doing a little investigating of the mysteries on my own. I decided to follow her guidance and go visit the Fallen King again. Maybe this time instead of freaking me out, he could illuminate her strange words and London's secrets.

I stopped briefly by my flat on the way to put away my purchases, then swung my backpack on my shoulder, headed out the door of my flat, down the stairs, and back out on the street toward Ealdwic station and the Fallen King's domain.

As I rounded the corner past the station, I stood for a moment, watching the prophet entertain the gathered crowd. This guy did seem to have a following. The square was full of a half-dozen or so people listening to his end-of-the-world shtick.

Gathering my courage, I approached him once again.

"Knock knock!" he called to the crowd. "No takers? Ah, fair enough, I'm not convinced I can remember how the rest of this one goes."

He looked at his puppet then back to his gathered audience. "Ah. The gist of it is that the planet doesn't like you. Ha-ha! Don't expect to be on her recycled Christmas card list."

Oh, boy. More of this. I put my hands on my hips and scowled at him.

"Oh, I know," he said, acknowledging me. "Snap judgments are hurtful. She's only had a few millennia to get to know us. It takes time for a person's true personality to come out."

He gestured broadly to the square we were standing in and then at Via Antiqua behind us. "Ask the Romans, they had a good run. Laid this pretty paint-by-numbers under your feet, and that road too. Ask the stones. Lot of blood and sick and kebab sauce split on those stones."

Gross. He was no doubt right, but I didn't want to think about what might be spilled on the stones.

"They turn up in the strangest places, these Romans. So ask their stones, lay your head down on them and go the whole *milia pasuum*. Not right now, you'd look crazy, and I'd be done for inciting mass hysteria. Again," he finished wryly.

Whatever. I wasn't laying my head on the stones for anything. I didn't care what secrets they held. I scowled up at the Fallen King.

"Here's what they'll say," he said, drawing out the crowd's anticipation. The gathered listeners leaned forward visibly, waiting for the punchline.

"Nothing!" The Fallen King laughed heartily at their crestfallen reactions. "Sorry! Their whole empire meant nothing."

Several people muttered angrily and turned to leave. One woman pointed at him and laughed aloud. I pursed my lips in irritation. This was the great prophet of Ealdwic, providing sage answers to all of its secret questions? His revelations left a lot to be desired in my book.

I scuffed my shoe against one of the cobblestones and looked down. There was a faint image of a mural in the stones. What was so special about these stones? Could the mural really be a relic from Roman times, right out here in the middle of the street, unprotected from the ravages of foot traffic and weather?

Huh. Maybe there was something to what the Fallen King said.

The cobblestones were a dirty tan, but the image seemed to hold a circular mural of some kind of animal. It was too faint to make out. I examined the edge of the decoration, which filled most of the space of square we were standing in, and could just make out the faint impression of words. Was there a Latin inscription here?

The Fallen King carried on with his rant, but I ignored him as I stepped around the mural slowly, looking at the inscription on the stones. There was "maximus" on one stone. That meant something like "big," I think.

Making a full circle around the mural, I finally pieced together the whole phrase: "sub maximus arbor ille flevit dixit inferius sicut superius."

Not that it did me any good. My Latin was mediocre at best. I was pretty sure "sub" meant under, and "arbor" meant tree. That would make the first part "under big tree"? Maybe "inferius" and "superius" meant lesser and greater? What did the whole phrase mean?

So much for my great investigation to prove my capabilities at being an agent. Stymied in the first half hour by a lack of Latin. Ugh.

I was going to have to figure out where to find a Latin dictionary before I could learn any more. I knew the Templar Library was somewhere in the Court. It was more famous than the Innsmouth Academy library, and I definitely planned on visiting it at some point.

I could run up there right now. Was it open on a Saturday? Would someone let me in? I thought back to my adventures with Gypcie at the Innsmouth Academy. She had chastised me time and time again about running into things half-cocked, with no clear strategy. Was this one of those times? Argh. I didn't know what to do.

My shoulders slumped. I was pretty sure I needed to think this through a little more carefully. Maybe I could ask Brigadier Lethe about the Library on Monday, but without alerting him to my little investigation. I gritted my teeth. Waiting was not my strong suit. Why didn't I have a cell phone? Google would have the answer to this.

I looked up at the Fallen King, still preaching, and realized that behind his make-shift pulpit lay the entrance to Ealdwic Park.

With resignation, I decided that I'd go explore the park instead. It was something to do today that was unlikely to get me into too much trouble. The investigation, like my initiation, would have to wait.

I stepped around the gathered crowd and moved through the ornate, wrought-iron gates into the park. It contained the expected greenery: trees, shrubs, and grass. It seemed to be a large square park, the size of a small city block. In the center was a wooden stage made out of old pallets and boxes. Someone had created an ad-hoc "castle" that acted both as scenery and backstage area and had spray-painted "CAMELOT" in large red letters. Red cloth banners, intended as pennants, hung around the castle and stage proper.

It was sort of impressive in a thrown-together way. I imagined that Shakespearean troupes did performances here in the summer evenings. A couple of people sat on the side of the north end of the stage, so I moved to the southern end to afford them their privacy. Looking south, I could see my apartment window and the Albion Ballroom. This was a small borough, but it might as well have been Trafalgar Square for all the people I knew. I looked back around at the edge of the stage and noticed a massive oak tree growing behind it. It towered over the park, lending shade to most of it. If there was ever a big tree needed, this was the one.

Still feeling a little sorry for myself, I decided to sit for a bit under the tree on one of the boxes that comprised the stage. Ravens cawed in the tree branches, scolding one another. In the distance, I could hear a light-rail train passing by on its tracks above the city. A gentle breeze blew, and the leaves whispered overhead. I could smell the damp soil beneath the Spring lawn. It reminded me of making my way through the crevice in the rock to the Agartha portal.

Which made me think of Innsmouth Academy and Gypcie and Carter. And Ms. Usher and Renee. And even Headmaster Montag. Before I knew it, tears were rolling down my face. I was homesick, and I was throwing myself a pity party.

Abruptly, the cawing of the ravens stopped, and the park went still. My breath caught. What was this? I wiped the tears from my eyes as I strained to listen through the unnatural silence.

Then, the sound resumed. The wind picked up above me, diving down from the branches and whirling around me. I could actually see the air movement in a golden light, flowing like a party streamer. The magical breeze pulled at me, tugging on my blouse and hair, urging me to follow where it wanted to lead. It drew me in a southeastern direction, back out onto the May Queen Market, past The Horned God and the fish & chips place. When I got to the small Post Office, the pull changed, dragging me down a small alley, ominously named "Warlock Stairs."

As advertised, down a set of stone stairs the alley led, and I followed. The breeze pulled and pushed me toward its destination, gold streamers flowing past my face and down, down. I passed another small shop on the left and went down another staircase. The streamers took a left turn into a high tunnel made of brick, with an arched ceiling overhead. Was this part of an old Roman aqueduct?

More likely it was a modern-day sewer, I mused, as I continued to follow the streamers. So much for not jumping in blindly. But this was too wild to ignore. I couldn't turn back now any more than I could throw my picture of Richard Sonnac in the trash.

A deep hum filled the tunnel, the sounds of the city itself above me. Water dripped from the ceiling and plopped onto the brick pavers every few seconds. It was damp, but not wet, so I continued my pursuit of the streamers. The tunnel sloped down before it let out in a wider area. Here there was a small river of water flowing, but a walkway had been created above it with metal grates fastened at the edge of the tunnel walls. Probably for city workers to access the tunnels, I thought. I stepped out onto the grate nearest me carefully, but it seemed stable, so I continued along chasing the golden streamers.

What was it that they wanted to show me?

I turned left again into another small side tunnel and jogged after them a few yards. The streamers came to a stop before a door, and the wind stopped pulling at my hair and shirt.

Was this where they wanted me to go?

I could hear the noisy racket of a portable generator behind the closed door. I was probably about to give some poor city water employee a startle, but I wasn't about to give up now.

The door was locked.

Argh. Stymied again.

I turned away, disappointed. All that magic, just to be led to a locked door? I stomped my foot in frustration and started to trudge away. A small wicked voice in my head mentioned that it wouldn't stay locked for long if I hit it with a little chaos magic.

Hmm.

I hunched my shoulders and looked around. No one was here to see me. I shouldn't do this but…I couldn't stand it. Gaia's magic had led me in, and now I wanted to see what was behind the door!

Moving back to the entrance, I reached into my backpack and pulled out my Chaos focus. I concentrated on it for a moment, focusing my Will, then cast some entropy at the lock. A couple of sharp jabs with my fist to deconstruct the lever and bang, the lock sprung, and the door swung ajar. I put my Chaos focus back in my pack, pushed open the door and went in, pulling it closed behind me.

Stepping through the threshold, I could immediately smell dust and dirt, and feel a dryness which was strange after all the water in the tunnels. Large commercial lights and a water pump sat inside the door. I could see that someone had excavated the old brick wall of the shaft, revealing an older stone tunnel beyond.

I paused. This looked purposeful, like some kind of archaeological excavation. I knew that London was actually the modern name for the Roman settlement Londinium, which was built in the same spot two thousand years ago. Over the years, people had piled their household garbage, building rubble, and animal waste and built the modern city on top. There were digs all over the British Isles to uncover the hidden history.

Could that be what this was? I would be in all sorts of trouble if someone caught me down here, but I pushed that aside. A Templar agent wouldn't be afraid to investigate a mystery. Besides, I was too engrossed with what might lay ahead.

I stepped through the makeshift threshold and onto the wooden pallets the archaeologists had laid down to secure footing into the dig. The entrance led to tunnels dug out of the earth and stone, reinforced in spots with chicken wire to prevent sloughing. The excavators had suspended wires along the sides, connected to modern lanterns. Boxes and scaffolding stood along the walls. Down and down the tunnel wound until it opened into a sort of amphitheater.

A stone facade of a Roman building—some kind of temple?—had been dug out of the dirt and muck. Five tall Corinthian columns stood at the top of a graceful set of stairs. Behind it, a square doorway signaled the start of the building proper. I stepped inside and discovered an electric lamp that pointed toward another breached wall behind it.

This area had not yet had the extent of excavation and renovation. I picked my way across the rubble. The older building still stood and looked like I could enter it. Giant spider webs covered the passage, and I shuddered as they stuck to my face and hair. I didn't want to know how big the spider that made that web was. At the end of the passageway was another set of stone stairs, leading even deeper underground. These again appeared to be part of the older building. Flaming torches were fastened to the wall in antique sconces. Curious. How come there weren't electric lights? How were they even burning? Who lit them? And, they were lit, illuminating the stairwell.

I saw movement to my right and stifled a shriek.

Oh. My. God. It was a freaking familiar. Hadn't I dealt with enough familiars already after coming from Innsmouth Academy?

Argh. I stomped my foot in sheer irritation.

Familiars were an all-too-common magical construct, with pale, animated bodies that could perform simple tasks for the person who made them. Their bodies were acquired—stolen by some enterprising grave robber—and prepared by taking a small, spiked chisel to the corpses' brains to destroy the former personality and then imbued with the creator's Will to animate them. We had learned to make them at Innsmouth Academy by coating them with a reagent to preserve them, which made them very shiny.

This one was not shiny, but instead dull and dirty. Its skin was also darker than the ones I was accustomed to seeing, like it was made of old leather. It was hard to guess how long it had been down here. The hostility of the academy's familiars fresh in my mind, I reached into my backpack for my chaos focus and prepared to fight, my heart racing.

Chaos spells at the ready, I watched it for a few minutes. It was wiping an area of the wall over and over, like a faded and forgotten caretaker, lingering over its task. Finally, I calmed myself and realized that it was paying absolutely no attention to me. It didn't give a damn what I was doing. And, most likely, it would leave me alone as long as I didn't try to stop it from doing what it was doing.

Hmm. Did that mean its creator was still alive somewhere? At least, it seemed, something still had it under control.

Fair enough. I'd let sleeping dogs lie.

Leaving the creature where it was, I put my chaos focus back in my backpack and headed down the stairs. In front of me at the bottom was a round circular hole in the floor, covered by an ancient iron grate. I guessed that it had provided ventilation or aqueduct access to the original building, similar to the access tunnels above, but I was not about to walk across this centuries-old grate to see if it could hold my weight. I edged around the side and progressed deeper into the structure. I was quite far below the Earth at this point, and it was quite cool, like a natural cave. Shivering, I regretted my short-sleeved blouse with the open midriff.

Two more lingering caretakers wandered the hall toward me, making their customary hisses, squeaks, squeals, and squawks. They were yawning and humming away, the little buggers. Yep, these were definitely someone's familiars, but they seemed to be a more docile variety than those that were running amok at Innsmouth Academy. One of them walked past me up the stairs. The other dug in a pile of rubble in the hall in front of me. It seemed distressed like it was trying to put the rubble back where it belonged. I glanced up, noting that was up in the ceiling somewhere.

Oh great. I was deep underground in a collapsing Roman temple with a bunch of animated maintenance monsters. And there was another massive spider web covering the hall. Who knew what manner of creepy crawlies scuttled and slithered around down here?

Yuck!! Maybe Gypcie did have a point about me jumping into things without thinking them through.

Why was I here again? I scowled at the caretaker. That's right. I was investigating on my own, and I was not afraid of spiders, snakes, or familiars.

More torches ahead illuminated a closed set of doors and what appeared to be a T-juncture to a hall. The lights flickered, teasing me with the secrets the temple might hold.

Excitement leaped inside me. Nope. I was not turning back now.

I stepped to avoid both the caretaker and the spider web, hopping over and around the rubble to advance to the juncture. I spotted a recessed circular mosaic of small tiles in the center of the floor and got down on my knees to take a closer look at it, positioning myself so I didn't block the dim light quivering from the sconces. The shadows were deep, so I moved my face close to see what was pictured there.

Ugh! My lip curled at the horrid looking face as it revealed itself to me from the shadows, fashioned in the center of the mosaic, decayed and gaunt, but with curly golden hair and a lighter yellow halo or sun rays of a sort behind its head. Holes gaped in the eye sockets of the face, and an actual sword had been stabbed down between its teeth.

The whole effect of the image of the face was skull-like, but with an unsettling touch of youth in the golden hair. Below the image, I could make out the name "Sol Invictvs," inlaid with small tiles to look like a scroll.

This was probably that guy's temple back in the day. Yeesh. I hoped he wasn't still in here somewhere.

I looked more at the recessed bevels of the mosaic. They looked like they could move up and down. I reached down and touched the sides of the mosaic. I could feel small scratches on the inner bevel of the stone that framed the face. I touched the socket holes where its eyes should have been. Were those holes intended to hold something? Shuddering, I removed hands and dusted them off.

I shook my head at myself. My imagination was running away from me. I'd seen too many Indiana Jones movies.

Still, the face was puzzling. Stepping back into a crouch, I pulled the sword out of the mosaic's mouth, and then immediately decided that it had looked better with the blade in. Some craftsman two thousand years ago had taken the time to insert tiny tile teeth into that mouth with a rectangular slot between its lips.

Creepy.

A passage I remembered learning from the Book of Revelations crawled unwelcome into my mind, "And out of His mouth goeth a sharp sword, that with it He will smite the nations."

I looked at the sword I'd pulled out. This sword didn't seem to be in any shape to smite nations; it was broken beyond repair. And wrong pantheon anyway. The architecture and style suggested this was a Roman temple, not a Christian one, as far as I could see.

Still, a chill ran down my back.

I shrugged it off and moved over to a nearby torch for more light. Holding the sword up to the flame, I could see the hilt of the blade had a glyph engraved on it that looked like the planetary symbol for Mercury, the god of thieves and tricksters. Well, that confirmed Roman deity worship. Mercury was also the god of communication and words, I realized with a shudder. I might not be out of the woods on that smiting thing. I wondered when the sword had been placed in the mosaic's mouth and to what end. Curiouser and curiouser.

I broadened my view of the area. As I suspected, a hall extended to the east and west of the mosaic, although it was not well lit in either direction. To the north of it was a set of ornately carved stone doors. I could see a seam that indicated they opened, but who knew when that last was. The whole area was cool and musty and lit only by the few torches high up on the walls. The floors were in shadow.

I stepped around the side of the mosaic toward the doors in front of me.

CLANK!

I looked down and stifled a scream. On the floor was a metal shield, attached to the very decayed skeleton of a Roman centurion, its skull covered in a bronze helmet with cheek guards. It had been hidden in the shadows. And I'd just kicked it.

My heart raced. I couldn't tell what scared me more, the skeleton, or the noise. I was in so much trouble if someone caught me down here. The centurion looked long dead, but I was certain a fully dressed skeleton in situ was a pretty significant archaeological find. I was contaminating the area just being here. Why was it even still here? What kind of shoddy archaeologists would leave such a find exposed to the elements?

Shaking my head in irritation, I pushed on the stone doors. Nothing happened. Judging by the dust on the floor in front of them, they hadn't been opened in years, maybe millennia. Wiping my hands on my jeans while juggling the broken sword, I turned back to the mosaic and jumped in fear as I saw a naked body moving down the hall behind me. Adrenaline shot through my body.

Stupid. Freaking. Familiars.

I took a deep breath to calm down. I was unnerved. I needed to consider if I was going to continue.

Should I leave?

No. I couldn't stand the thought. Mama Abena, the Fallen King, and the grand tree in the park had all conspired to send me here. I'd investigate a little further, to see what I could find. Besides, hadn't I wanted to join the Templars to have adventures? I was having one right now.

But if I was going to stay, I definitely would need a better light source. The modern lanterns up the stairs were all attached to power cables. They wouldn't work. The torches down here all looked to be affixed to the walls in sconces, and I didn't think I was up for any vandalism to go with my breaking and entering.

How were they even lit? Their flames burned steadily, but there didn't seem to be a definite source fueling them. I crossed my fingers that they stayed that way.

Squinting my eyes, I looked right and left down the hall. In the flickering gloom, I could see there was another giant spider web at the east end.

Eww. That settled it. West it was.

I picked my way down the hall to the west. Rubble and dust covered the floors, but the walls themselves were a marvel, at least from what I could see. Shadows from the flickering torches bounced off the walls highlighting the stone columns that lined them on both sides. Every five feet or so there were arched alcoves with a flat bottom that looked almost like shelves as if they had at one point housed statuary or some other ancient Roman trinkets. Now they were barren and dusty, showing their age.

Another branch led to the north off the west hall, but it was caved in about 10 feet back. Two more dead Roman centurions lay desiccated on the floor, and two of the caretaking familiars were digging at the stone around them.

Were they trying to bury them?

My stomach turned at the sight of their ragged and grisly fingers, torn from the attempt. One of the soldiers held an ancient sword—was it called a gladius?—in its skeletal hand, similar to the one I'd pulled from the mosaic. I approached and slid the blade away from its owner, being careful not to attract the attention of the digging caretakers. The blade on this sword was still intact, but it had no glyph etched into the hilt that I could find. I put the broken blade with the glyph in my backpack beside my chaos and blood foci and held the intact blade at my side. I felt a little safer doing so, although I hoped Brigadier Lethe didn't ever hear about it. He'd make me get a tetanus shot just for holding it.

Turning back west again, I moved deeper into the hall. About halfway down in an alcove shelf on the left side, I spotted a torch. Success! There was my light source. I picked up the torch and lit it from a wall sconce to my right. That was better. At least now I could direct the dim flickering light toward what I wanted to see.

I contemplated the purpose of this temple as I moved further down the hall. There were no windows at all, nor any gaps in the walls that might once have been open to the daylight. I looked above me at the ceiling to see if there was an opening there, but the torch ruined my ability to see that far.

It was possible this temple had always been underground. The wall sconces indicated that it had needed to be lit. I thought back to the Ritual Magick class I took my junior year at Innsmouth. I remembered that there was a whole cult of Roman ritual practice based in underground, cave-like temples. I couldn't remember what those temples were called for the life of me, but I knew they had been used for initiation mysteries.

Lost in thought, I continued picking my way through the rubble until I realized I had come to the end of the west hall. To the left, there was again a passageway north, but it was caved in. To the right was an open doorway curved at the top and carved from the same stone, with columns and ornate details framing it. The room behind it was devoid of the wall torches and, as a result, pitch black.

Taking a deep, steadying breath, I contemplated turning around. I listened for a moment. The underground temple was quiet as the grave, except for the occasional screech and chatter of the naked caretakers. It was starting to get on my nerves.

Should I turn back? I stood there, hesitating.

Bah. I couldn't do it. I'd come this far. I had to know what was there in the dark.

I stepped over the stone threshold and moved inside. From my view at the doorway, I couldn't see much. Just a broad stone floor. The room was much wider than the hall—30 feet or so across. I moved further inside, the shapes of two large stone pillars supporting the ceiling coming into my view. I could hear the moans of the familiar caretakers in front of me and readied myself for a startle when they came into view.

The remains of a squad of Roman centurions lay moldering on the floor beyond the pillars. Five caretakers surrounded the bodies. They appeared to be mourning, the one nearest me on the right, swaying back and forth with its face in its hands. Shuddering, I stepped around the remains and continued moving deeper into the room. The fifth caretaker bent over the last corpse, inspecting it and sniffing its body like a dog.

A set of stone stairs rose out of the darkness before me, and I increased my pace to put some distance between myself and the wailing caretakers. Rubble covered the stairs on each side, and I craned my head up to see if see the source. The ceiling was too far away for the light of the touch to reach. All that I could see above me was darkness. I turned around and looked back toward the entrance. I could see the faint movement of the caretakers as well as the rounded doorway and the flickering torchlight beyond.

Steeling my nerves, I faced the other direction again and started up the stairs. The open floor area narrowed here. The rubble had filled it as the ceiling sloughed down over time. I was aware that the room might collapse on me and hurried over and around the piles.

I could see another, taller stone staircase ahead and hurried toward it. Another caretaker shot out of the darkness. I jumped and swore under my breath. It ran in a roughly circular path, down the stairs, around me and back up. Was there was something at the top?

No. There wasn't. I got to the top of the stairs only to find still more open floor. This room was huge. I could see that the floor itself became more refined here. Etched tiles replaced the stones.

The caretaker ran in front of me. I tripped and did a somersault across the tile floor, dropping the sword and my torch.

Shit.

Thank the gods it didn't go out. I picked up the torch and searched around for the sword I'd dropped. I picked it up and oriented myself away from the rounded doorway of the entrance in the distance. Ahead on the floor were still more dead centurions — another squad — and behind them a tall, rounded alcove with a broken stone pillar, or pedestal altar, within it. An unlit sconce was mounted on the wall behind it.

At last, I'd come to the end of the room. I walked over to the altar. Laying on top was a golden coin. I picked up the coin, listening for evidence that someone or something didn't want me to do that. The caretaker continued charging around its circuit, paying no attention to me.

Hmm. That coin seemed odd amid the rubble. Did it have a purpose? I slipped it into my pocket and turned around. The distance now to the shadowy shape of the entrance was plain. This room, whatever it was, was as long as a football field. The ceiling was still obscured, even after I had mounted two sets of steps. I could see there some type of braziers to the right and left of the floor. Was this some sort of rostrum from which a ritual would be conducted? I wasn't sure.

And, I'd had about enough of the creepy walk through the darkness. My curiosity had been appeased, and now I just wanted to get back to the relative safety of the torch-lit hallway. I resisted the urge to stab the running caretaker as he ran around me for the umpteenth time and headed back to the doorway in the distance. I considered climbing some of the rubble to get a better look at the ceiling but decided that was too foolish even for me.

Finally, I stepped out of the room and breathed a giant sigh of relief. I was glad to get out of that cave of darkness.

I made my way back down the hall to the circular mosaic and looked again at the face there. I knew that the ancient Greeks had placed coins, called obuli, over the eyes of the deceased to pay its passage to the Underworld.

Skull face. Check. Deep underground. Check.

On that hunch, I pulled the golden coin from my pocket and looked at it in the shadowy hallway, holding the coin up to the light of the torch.

On one side seemed to be Caesar's head in profile, with the words "Sol Invicto Comiti" written around it in a semicircle. On the other side was a figure with a staff wearing what appeared to be a flaming crown. Beside the figure was the Cheshire-cat smile of a crescent moon. I looked at the size of the coin, then looked again at the mosaic. I reached down and put it over the left eye-socket hole of the skeletal face. The coin fit.

Alrighty, then.

Where was the next coin? It was time to face down the giant spider web at the end of the east hall, I guessed. This hall looked much the same as the western side, and I made my way to the end, keeping a wary eye out for the web spinner. Rubble and sticky webs filled most of the juncture. I didn't see any spiders in the wreckage, but the smell of something burning reached my nose.

Through the rubble, I could see another rounded doorway leading to the north. The area behind this doorway, however, was not dark at all. In fact, it was brighter than anything else I'd encountered down here. I laid the torch I had been carrying on the stone floor and stepped forward over the threshold. Flames shot up through metal grate on the floor, and I jumped back with alarm.

Gah! What fresh hell was this?

After a few seconds, the flames stopped so I stepped again into the room to have a look. Red-hot coals filled space below the grate. Was there some sort of natural gas system down here providing the fuel? That might explain the torches in sconces that seemed never to run out of fuel. There was another grate to my left as well, but with safe floor space beyond it. Was this some sort of test? A gauntlet of sorts for initiates?

I decided to put the old sword I had been carrying into my backpack, struggling to fit it in among my foci, my athame, and the other broken blade. It didn't quite fit, so I left the pommel sticking out of the top and set the backpack down by the doorway, away from the smoking grate.

I watched the second grate carefully. The flame lasted a second or two, then died down. A few seconds after that, smoke began to rise, and the flames started up again. The heat coming from them was remarkable. I did not want to get caught on a grate when they started up again. I watched and counted, and watched and counted until I was sure I had the timing down. Then, as the flame extinguished, I took a running jump across the grate and landed on the far side.

From the safe section of floor, I could see two more grates— longer and more narrowly spaced in the next part of the room. I could also see a set of doors to the right of where I'd come in that I hadn't noticed at first. Should I go forward, or go back and try the doors?

Ugh. Of course, I'd go forward.

I crossed the first of the two long thin grates. From the tiles between them, I could now advance to a barred window of sorts. I looked in the room, across the smoke and waves of heat. Another lingering caretaker stooped inside, scratching at the wall. I could see a stone pedestal altar behind the caretaker, with a faint glint of light reflecting from something on top of it.

Bingo! There was my other coin.

Positioning myself, I waited until the flame dropped in the second grate and jumped to the stone flooring beyond it. The passageway seemed to sneak around the corner to the right, so I stepped forward again, timing my approach to avoid the flame.

It shot up behind me like a rocket. My knees buckled, and I swayed on my feet. I swallowed hard, my throat dry. I was starting to get woozy from all the heat. It was time to get the coin and get out of here.

On the other side of that grate was a small set of stone stairs in the lower area I'd seen through the barred window.

Three more grates to go to get there, all of them in close succession, and all with differently timed flames. Here was a challenge. It looked like it might still be safe to stand between them, but it would be hot.

I stepped across the first grate, hearing the crackle of the flames as they surged up. The second grate had already started to smoke, so I waited there, my eyes burning. The smoke here was terrible. I covered my mouth and stepped across the second grate as the flames died. But, I lost my balance and started across the third and final grate as it had begun to smoke. I was committed.

Using all my strength, I launched myself at the stone beyond, but not before the flames plumed, scorching my jeans and singeing my hands.

Damn it. That hurt.

I landed on the far side near the pedestal altar and patted myself down as best I could, my hands smarting, to make sure I wasn't on fire. This was like being in the middle of a bonfire.

I looked up and started. There was the familiar caretaker I'd seen from the other side, scratching at the wall. I had totally ignored it as a potential danger. Luckily, like its companions, this caretaker continued to ignore me as well. It smelled a little well done, its skin a very dark-roasted brown.

My stomach lurched at the thought of it here for centuries, slow cooking.

Eww.

Time to get out of here. I grabbed the second golden coin from the pedestal altar, but in my haste, it slipped through my fingers and bounced away.

Shit! Where did it go?

I looked around the floor in alarm trying to see where it had dropped. I needed that coin!

Behind me, the flames seethed up through the grate, and I stepped closer to the pedestal to avoid the heat, although I was grateful for the light they provided.

Damn it! I couldn't see the coin anywhere. I knew in my heart that it was critical to solving the mosaic's puzzle. The flames behind me died down, and I turned around to see if the coin had fallen the other direction.

There on the top of the grate lay the coin. Relief filled me that it hadn't fallen through the cracks down to the banked fires below. I reached down and quickly grabbed the coin with my right hand as the grate began to smoke, indicating the flames were about to shoot up again.

Agony consumed me, and I jumped back with the coin in my hand. The skin of my palm smoked as the superheated coin seared my flesh. I screamed in pain and shook my hand trying to dislodge the coin from my palm. It peeled away and fell to the floor in front of me, smoking. The smell of burned skin and soot filled my nose, as the flames roared again through the grate.

Holding my right hand in my left, I bent over and sobbed.

As soon as I could bear it, I looked at the damage to my hand. In the center of my palm was a deep angry red burn, blisters starting to swell in a circular pattern around the edge. The center of the wound looked far worse. The skin there was black, with white charring, and I couldn't feel that area of my palm anymore.

I don't know how long I stood there, sobbing and looking at my damaged hand before I realized I was going into shock. I was starting to sway on my feet and needed some help.

I'd come down here by myself, I realized. No help was coming for me.

A healing spell would help, but it was so hot in here I was starting to feel faint. I had to get out of this oven. But I couldn't leave without what I'd come for. Besides, I'd left my backpack with my athame back at the entrance. I needed that to cast a healing spell.

Coughing, I reached down to where the coin lay and picked it up with the bottom of my shirt, wincing at the residual heat in the metal as it radiated through to the abused fingers of my left hand. I slipped it into my little jeans pocket on my hip and squirmed with the heat as it transferred from the coin through my jeans to my skin. My right palm ached terribly, and I raised it upright to keep swelling down.

There was a carved lever to the right of a set of doors at the back of the area. I hoped that these doors were the same set I saw when I crossed the first grate. Using the unburned side of my right arm, I pressed the lever forward, then hissed in pain as I scalded the skin there as well.

But, I was in luck. The doors swung open, revealing the entrance to the gauntlet. I scurried up the stairs and out of the heat, grabbed my backpack, and headed back up the eastern hall toward the mosaic and the temple entrance, sighing with relief as the ambient temperature dropped.

A few feet outside I dropped my backpack again and swayed, gathering my Will. My dropped torch still lay where I'd left it, smoking and guttering on the stone floor.

It was time for a healing spell. I was running out of energy to cope with the pain. Gingerly I dug into my backpack with my left hand to locate my blood focus and athame, a painful challenge with everything I had stuffed inside. Finally, I upended the bag, dumped everything out on the stone floor, wincing at the noise, and grabbed the athame.

With resignation at inflicting yet more misery on myself, I poked my finger with the ritual knife until a drop of blood welled up. I focused best as I could amid the agony of my burns, and cast a small mend spell.

Golden healing light flowed through me. I sighed in relief as the pain of my minor burns eased. My right palm was a different matter altogether. It still ached like a mother despite the healing spell. I needed to see how much damage was still left.

Grabbing my torch from the floor, I held my palm up to its light. Branded in the center of my right palm, the damaged skin showing the detail in bright red relief, was the head of Caesar in profile, complete with the victory crown and "Sol Invicto Comiti" inscribed in a semi-circle on my flesh.

I gaped at the brand for a moment before I noticed that the ends of my right middle and ring fingers also had ridged impressions from the trauma as I picked up the superheated coin.

On the pad of my middle finger appeared to be a permanent flame-wreathed head of Sol and a lunar crescent covered the pad of my ring finger. I'd been so overwhelmed by the pain in my palm I hadn't even noticed those burns. The coin had also burned most of the fingerprints off those two fingers in the process.

Well, shit. This wasn't good.

A tear leaked from the corner of my eye, and I wiped it off with my left hand. My palm still throbbed. The mend spell was too limited to heal the damage of the deeper burns. Chewing my lip, I decided to cast a more significant healing spell while I sorted out what to do about my new scars.

Pinching my left pointer finger to get the blood flowing, I recited the incantation to cast a redemption spell. My right ring finger tingled as I finished the spell. The bone-deep ache of my palm ceased, and the skin there lost its charred hue as the heat of the burn evaporated with the spell, and my body healed itself.

I ran the fingers of my left hand across the ridged imprint on my palm and fingertips. I would be carrying around a permanent souvenir from this adventure it seemed. I also whispered a small plea to Gaia to help me when my trespass was discovered since I'd be carrying around the evidence of it.

At least I had the coin to show for all my trouble.

I put my things back in my backpack and hurried to the center mosaic. Laying the torch down to the side of the mosaic, I dug the coin out of my hip pocket and put it on the mosaic's right eye socket.

Once again, it fit like it belonged there, but nothing happened.

"Gods' damn it!" I swore aloud and stomped my feet.

Surely the flesh of my right hand was sacrifice enough to get a little success? I couldn't go back empty-handed after all this. I scowled as I realized the irony. I'd never be empty-handed again.

I looked at the mosaic and rubbed my head in frustration. I had hoped that this was a puzzle I could solve. Maybe I was wrong.

Still, there was the slit in the mouth area that had held the broken sword. I opened my backpack again and took out both swords and examined them.

Would the sword I retrieved from the centurion work? I slid it down into the slot. The sword fit in the hole, but nothing happened. I looked at the broken sword and particularly at the glyph that had been secured to the hilt. Was that the key to this puzzle?

I pulled out my athame again and pried at the Mercury glyph on the broken sword. With a little effort, the glyph popped off. Now I needed something to secure it to the other sword. I looked around for something that would work.

"What in the bloody hell are you doing down here?" A man's voice boomed behind me.

I just about jumped out of my skin. Whirling around, I saw Sevenoir coming down the main stairs behind me, the rabbit ears bouncing on his head.

"I have been looking for you for hours," he yelled, his face red with fury, batting the giant spider web out of his way as he moved up the rubble-filled hall toward me. "What are you doing down here?"

My face went hot and my fingers cold as I struggled to come up with a plausible excuse for my trespass into the Londinium excavation. Finally, I decided the truth was my best defense and explained to him what had happened with Mama Abena, the Fallen King, and the tree in the Ealdwic Park.

"And so, when the energies led into the excavation, I just sort of followed." I shrugged my shoulders and gestured at the halls around us.

Sevenoir looked torn about whether to believe my explanation or throttle me, although his face was a lighter pink shade now, rather than full-on magenta. "So, you've been exploring an ages' old Roman Mithraeum that not only is an English Heritage-protected site but is also probably in imminent danger of caving in on your head? I can't believe the door wasn't locked."

I flushed bright red, then decided to ignore the last part. "Well, when you put it that way," I groused, pouting, before explaining further.

"I've been trying to solve the puzzle of the Sol Invictus mosaic." I pointed to the tiles at my feet and showed him the Mercury glyph in my left hand, and explained my efforts to collect the golden coins so far. I went light on my description of the eerie darkness of the hall on the west side and the scarring burns I'd gotten traversing the flames on the east.

Sevenoir looked at the coins I'd laid there in the mosaic and scratched his forehead. "So you think by somehow affixing this glyph to the other sword you'll be able to trigger whatever mechanism is in the mosaic?" he asked.

"Right," I nodded. "And hopefully get these doors in front to open."

"You have no idea what's behind those doors."

That was true, but I figured the statement was a trap. I hadn't really thought about what I'd do if something dangerous were behind them, which he no doubt would take me to task for. I decided to punt with some distraction.

"The lingering caretaker familiars down here have all been docile and benign," I explained. "They've ignored me the whole time."

Sevenoir grunted skeptically at that. He tapped his chin, thinking.

Why was he down here looking for me anyway? He'd been looking for me for hours? Why? Figuring this might be a good time to go on the offensive, I asked him.

"Just trying to keep you out of trouble." Sevenoir cracked his knuckles and ground his teeth. "I saw you head off at a trot from Ealdwic Park down Warlock Close and figured I better check out what you were up to. It never occurred to me you'd break into a dig and go skulking around in the dirt and rocks. I spent hours chasing up and down the sewer tunnels looking for you."

He took the bunny ears off his head and shook the dirt and spider webs out of them with disgust before placing them back on his head.

"So will you help me?" I asked.

"Help you? Get further into trouble?" he snorted with derision. My heart fell.

It must have shown on my face, because, rolling his eyes, Sevenoir waved a dismissive hand at me. "Let's see what you've got there."

As I explained what I was trying to do, Sevenoir examined the glyph and the broken blade, then held out his hand for the other ancient gladius I'd retrieved from the remains of the centurion. He produced a leather thong from around his neck, and after removing the Saint Jude medal from it, handed the blade and glyph back to me with the makeshift strap.

I looked at him with a raised eyebrow as he tucked the medal into his jeans' pocket.

"Saint Jude," he quipped. "Patron Saint of Lost Causes."

Ah.

"Should have left it on," I responded, dryly. "I could use the help."

Taking the leather thong, I wrapped the Mercury glyph to the gladius hilt tightly, then carefully slid the sword into the mouth socket of the tile face, completing the image. With a deep rumble, the stone doors in front of the mosaic slipped open, revealing a torch-lit chamber and a fire team of three more dead centurions inside and a stone marker beyond their bodies.

"Well then," Sevenoir said. "This was unexpected."

Our previous argument forgotten, we both stepped forward into the room, avoiding the centurion corpses, to the stone pedestal. It appeared to be engraved with something.

Oh great. More Latin.

I tried reading the engraving aloud: "*Consequuntur Veneris Alter, Alter Mercurii Cursus, in Infimoque Orbe Luna Radiis Solis Accensa Convertitur.*"

Nothing happened.

I sighed loudly. This was the end of the road, apparently, until I could get to the Temple Library.

"Your accent is atrocious. However do you manage spell work?" Sevenoir sniped at me.

"It hardly matters," I mumbled, "since I don't know what it says."

Sevenoir scowled at me. "It says, 'Him, as his companions, Venus and Mercury follow on their different courses; and in a sphere still lower the moon revolves, lighted by the rays of the sun.'"

He looked at me in inquiry to see if I recognized the quote. I didn't.

As if accepting the inevitable, he sighed heavily and added, "It's from the *Somnium Sciponis*, the story of Scipio's dream of the music of the spheres in Cicero's *De Republica* and it describes the Roman views on cosmology."

Sevenoir pointed at the inscription. "Look here, it's missing the first part: *'Deinde subter mediam fere regionem sol obtinet, dux et princeps et moderator luminum reliquorum, mens mundi et temperatio, tanta magnitudine, ut cuncta sua luce lustret et compleat.'*"

At my blank look, he rolled his eyes and continued. "That means 'Beneath this, the Sun holds nearly the midway space, leader, prince, and ruler of the other lights, the mind and regulating power of the universe, so vast as to illuminate and flood all things with his light.'"

I stared at him, my mouth hanging open.

"Didn't you have to read Cicero in that prep school of yours?"

"Not in the original Latin! And I certainly didn't memorize it. I haven't read it since I was 14."

He arched his eyebrows in a manner that showed me exactly what he thought of that.

I thought furiously, attempting to recover. "Still, it's about the sun, Sol Invictus, just like the name on the mosaic."

He nodded in agreement.

We both looked further down the narrow passageway, which was lined with columns. On each column was a sconce, most of which were burning with lit torches, affording visibility. Some of the columns were knocked askew, and others were broken, having suffered the same degradations of the passing of millennia as the rest of the temple.

In the middle of the pairs of columns sat big bronze braziers, which were still full of wood, ready to be lit. Whatever this room's purpose was, it absolutely held the semblance of ritual space. I quickly counted the braziers. There were six of them.

At the end of the space was another set of closed stone doors. Sevenoir and I walked the length of the room to get closer. The doors, we could see as we approached, were engraved with a round image of the Earth as viewed from space, showing clearly the continents of Europe, Asia, and Africa, albeit in inaccurate ancient proportion.

"Interesting," Sevenoir commented. "In the ancient view, astronomy and astrology were geocentric, not heliocentric. There were seven classical planetary bodies; in order from the Earth, those were the moon, Mercury, Venus, the sun, Mars, Jupiter, and Saturn."

"So if the image on the doors is Earth," I said, pointing to the engraving, "would the braziers represent the planets?"

I stopped with disappointment as I realized the problem with that. "But, there are only six of them."

"Perhaps the pedestal is meant to represent Saturn," he said. "It was a marker put here to signify order, to create the pattern that represents the structure symbolically. Certainly, the inscription is well suited to that."

"So we have braziers which burn, and an inscription that indicates an order for the placement of the braziers," I concluded. "Shall we light them up?"

Sevenoir's eyebrows lowered, and I could see him struggling against the desire to go forward and solve the puzzle. He shrugged his shoulders helplessly.

I laughed with glee and ran all the way back to the mosaic to grab the torch where I'd left it.

"One thing that bothers me," he said, as I returned with the lit torch. "The ancient Romans believed the Earth didn't move, and yet this is clearly a doorway, liminal space to something deeper inside. A sort of Earthgate."

"But what is deeper inside the Earth?" I asked.

"I think I might know," Sevenoir got a glint in his eye and motioned me to get started. "You'll want to start with Venus. It was the first mentioned in the inscription and would be the third planet from the Earth."

I counted back three braziers from the doors and put the flaming torch to the ancient wood. It caught fire with a whoosh.

"Now Mercury," Sevenoir said. "Come back this direction one brazier."

I lit that and looked at him for the next step.

"OK, now the last planet mentioned in the inscription, the Moon. This one, right in front of me," he advised, pointing.

I lit the brazier as instructed and waited.

Nothing happened.

"Ugh. We're so close. I just know it," I cried. "Wait, you said there was a missing part to the inscription, and it was all about the sun. Also, this temple is dedicated to Sol Invictus!"

He nodded at me, pleased. "I think you're right. Light up the fourth brazier to represent the sun."

I walked swiftly down the passageway to the fourth brazier and lit it. The flames leaped, and behind me, I could hear stone scraping across the floor. Sevenoir jumped out of the way as the doors flung wide.

"Ha!" he crowed as he looked inside.

Beyond the stone doors lay a chamber, the walls and floor once again constructed of stone. At the back of the chamber was a small raised dais, steps leading to it on all sides. At the top of the dais, I could see the telltale roots and leaves framing a golden Agartha portal.

"That is what lies deep within the Earth," Sevenoir said with satisfaction, pointing at the portal. "Agartha. We've found an Earthgate to Agartha."

Next to the portal stood an ancient rusted custodian, a giant mechanical robot similar to what I'd seen standing sentry in Agartha on my way to London. This one, however, didn't look like it had moved in years.

"Could it be this temple was built here to protect the portal?" I said, wonder in my voice. "Who else knows about this?"

"At a guess," he answered. "No one has been in here in two millennia besides us. Let's hope Dame Julia takes that into account when she takes her riding crop to our hides for being down here in the Mithraeum."

We stepped into the room, marveling at the glowing portal.

The rusted custodian, which had been slumped over, whined to a start and straightened up, its hinges squealing with disuse. It stepped forward, moved down the dais stairs, and began tromping towards us aggressively.

"Whaaaat?" I said, scrambling back, sudden fear making my voice rise an octave.

"Oh, bloody hell," Sevenoir swore. "It has been here protecting the portal for 2,000 years and probably thinks we're intruders."

The custodian was at least 20 feet tall, so it closed the distance in remarkable time. We scattered as it pulled back its metal arm and took a swipe at us. On either side of the room were little alcoves filled with three columns each. I ducked behind the nearest column on one side of the room, as Sevenoir did the same on the other. I pulled my blood focus out of my backpack and quickly pricked my finger with my athame. Focusing my Will, I cast maleficium at the giant metal guardian.

My attacks bounced off of him harmlessly as he stomped across the room toward Sevenoir.

"I can't seem to hit him," I yelled at Sevenoir.

"He's probably got some kind of protection subroutine," Sevenoir yelled back. "All the Agartha custodians do."

He pulled out his pistols and, leaning around a pillar, unloaded on the custodian. I ducked behind my pillar as the bullets ricocheted around the high-ceilinged room.

"Stop that!" I screamed, crouching for cover.

I heard a muffled grunt and a stomp as the custodian took a swing at him, having followed Sevenoir around his pillar.

"Run for the portal, Wedd," he yelled.

I scrambled up and ran up the dais stairs toward the portal. As I came within five feet of the glowing circle, my body lifted off the ground, and my arms opened of their own accord. A golden glow suffused my body and I could see my anima draining off into the portal.

"What is happening?" I cried.

Sevenoir peeked around the pillar he was currently dodging behind to avoid the custodian.

"It looks like…" he grunted as the arm of the custodian slammed down on the pillar he was standing behind, shaking dust from the ceiling. "It looks like the well is using your anima to charge itself. Can you move away from it?"

Struggling because I was floating in midair immobilized like a little kid in a puffy snowsuit, I kicked my legs and upper body to attempt to move away from the portal. Slowly I made progress away, but I was a sitting duck if the custodian decided to take a swing at me.

The noise stopped, and the custodian dropped again to its knees.

"It seems its motor has malfunctioned," Sevenoir said with relief, as he jogged over from where he had been hiding. As he neared the portal, he too lifted off the ground.

"Shit."

"Oh my gods…Were you not paying attention?" I growled at him, as I continued to struggle to the edge of the portal's grasp.

"Well, I guess I'll help play anima transistor too," he said wryly.

With a screech, the custodian stood up again and turned toward us.

"Gods damn it!" I spat out the words, renewing my struggle to escape the pull of the portal.

With a big stomp, the custodian stepped forward and clattered across the room, its gears grinding and squealing, as it lurched into range. I struggled forward another inch and dropped to my feet on the stairs, as it pulled back its arm to swing at Sevenoir.

Not knowing what else to do, I ran over and kicked its metal leg with all my might, trying to draw its attention as Sevenoir struggled to free himself.

"Hey, you big lug! Come pick on me for a while."

Whining, the custodian's upper body swiveled toward me, changing the trajectory of its swing toward me. I ducked and ran back to the relative safety of the pillars, and began playing cat and mouse with the giant metal guardian, as it pursued me around them. It didn't move particularly fast, but its legs were so long, it could cover a lot of ground with one stride. I did my best to make sure I stayed out of the range of its giant fists, as it swiped at me.

One solid fist connected with a pillar with a crash. The pillar rocked, causing a small avalanche of dust and rocks.

I looked up with alarm. Fearful that repeated blows to the pillar would cause the ceiling to fall, I ran for the center of the room, baiting the custodian toward me, away from the pillars and away from Sevenoir, who was still pinned into donating his anima to the drained portal. He squirmed and struggled to get free, much like I had.

The custodian crossed the room in two strides and pulled back its arm for another swipe when its motors malfunctioned a second time, and it dropped into a crouch. I ran back toward Sevenoir.

"Don't get too close!" he warned.

"Copy that." I agreed, breathlessly. "How much juice do you think that thing needs?"

"I don't know, but I'm feeling it," he said, his face tight with strain.

"Assuming we can fill it up, it should open to Agartha, right?" I speculated, as I bent over, hands on my thighs, to catch my breath.

"That makes sense," he grunted and with a twitch dropped to his feet, escaping the portal's pull. "You go again. I'll keep the custodian occupied for a while."

Assuring myself he was beyond the pull of the portal, I stepped into the edge of its range again, rising into the air, as the flow of my anima to the source resumed. I concentrated on not resisting its pull, letting the portal have my anima. I wondered what would happen if I ran out.

The custodian rose to its feet a third time and started to stomp toward me. I squeaked in alarm, but Sevenoir was on it and dashed in front of the goliath, waving his arms and yelling. They jockeyed across the room, Sevenoir feinting and dodging out of harm's way as the giant robot swung at him time and time again.

I was starting to feel faint, but the custodian's motor was not failing this time, so there was no opportunity to change places with Sevenoir.

Stars popped before my eyes, and the room started to take on a gray tinge. I sure hoped this wouldn't result in anima depletion. I had experienced that once before and was in no hurry to do it again. A buzzing noise filled my ears, and I could feel my consciousness slipping away. Sevenoir ran toward me yelling something, but I couldn't make out the words. He grasped my legs as the custodian tromped up the steps of the dais behind him.

With a burst of light, the pull of my anima stopped, and I fell limp-limbed from where I was suspended, my head spinning. Sevenoir caught me as I fell and hoisted me over his shoulder in a fireman's carry, scrambling out of the way of the custodian.

Instead of turning to pursue us, the metal guardian continued its march up to the portal, then stepping through, it disappeared.

Sevenoir put me gently down on the far side of the dais and urged me to put my head between my knees as I struggled to recover from the near faint.

"Keep your head down until it passes," he cautioned me. "It'll keep you from blacking out."

"What happened to the custodian?" I asked, weakly, as the world stopped spinning.

"The portal must have regained enough of a charge to reconnect with Agartha," he said. "So, the custodian returned to where it belongs. I'll have to talk to the Stationmaster about getting it checked. I've never seen one of those things go rogue before. And, I frankly hope I never will again."

I shivered and nodded my head in agreement, which made my stomach lurch. I realized this little adventure had taken hours and I was both hungry and thirsty. It had been a long time since I had my coffee and plantain chips. I said as much to Sevenoir. He told me to rest, and pulled out his cell phone and made some calls. I marveled at the technology able to connect through the hundreds of feet of dirt and rubble underground, but he winked and mouthed the words "anima powered" when I asked him about it.

Within 15 minutes, a small army of uniformed Templars had joined us in the underground temple and began cordoning off the area with "Do Not Cross" tape. One of the agents was bearing a Bingo! Cola, a sandwich, and a bag of chips for me—the English call them "crisps," I learned. I was thankful and exhausted. Sevenoir walked over to the agent-in-charge and got into an intense discussion with her. Even curiosity and concern for my standing couldn't bring me to move from where I was sitting, enjoying my food. I'd have to pry it out of him later.

When I had eaten and recovered sufficiently, an agent walked with me back up the stone stairs of the temple, out through the excavation tunnels, out of the sewers to the twilight illuminating Ealdwic's streets, right to the blue front door of No. 5 May Queen Market, where he bid me adieu. I trudged up the stairs, unlocked my door with the old skeleton key I had tucked in my backpack, and, after securing the door behind me again, I stumbled into my bedroom and collapsed on my bed to sleep. There would be time enough later to deal with the consequences of my discovery.

CHAPTER EIGHT

Allies

BANG, BANG, BANG.

A sharp knocking filled my small flat, startling me from sleep. I looked around, groggily. What time was it anyway?

I needed to put a clock on the list of things to purchase apparently. I could see a faint tendril of light coming in my bedroom windows heralding dawn. Good grief. Who could be knocking for me at this time?

Since I hadn't bothered to get undressed before collapsing on my bed—when? Last night?—I climbed off the bed and shuffled out into the living area to the door.

"Who's there?"

"Message for Blodwedd Mallory from Richard Sonnac," an all-business male voice boomed from behind the closed door.

I flipped open the lock and cracked the door. A tall, uniformed Templar stood at the threshold. I opened the door wider and gestured for him to enter, but he shook his head and handed me a sealed letter instead, then nodded and turned on his heel and marched down the third-floor stairs.

Pushing the door closed and latching it, I looked at the envelope in my hand. It was too dark to read anything still, so I flipped on the light, wincing as the bulbs illuminated my tiny flat. I broke the wax seal on the back and hurried to open it. I took out a small card.

Ms. Blodwedd Mallory
No. 5-F May Queen Market
London, England UK

Mr. Richard Sonnac
Temple Hall
London, England UK

June 17, 2012

Dear Ms. Mallory,

Your presence is requested at Temple Hall at 7 a.m. sharp on Sunday, June 17, 2012. Formal business attire is advised. Don't be late.

Regards,

R. Sonnac

Argh! That was this morning. Business attire? What time was it, anyway?

Panic set in and I ran around my flat in a flurry. What was this about? I wracked my still sleepy brain, and then I remembered what I had done yesterday.

Right. That was probably it. Uh oh. I was in deep trouble.

My stomach cramped, and I wrapped my arms around my middle as dread filled me. The chickens of my ill-advised adventuring yesterday had come home to roost, and now I was being called to account.

Stupid, stupid, stupid! I knew better than this. I had worked for these past few months to not be so headstrong, so impulsive, and what did I do the first day out on my own?

I groaned and rubbed my face. Well, there was nothing for it but to face the consequences, if that's what this was. First course of action, find out the time. Grabbing my keys, I locked my apartment and flew down the stairs, out to the sidewalk and ran next door to Plimmy's home, and knocked rapidly.

She opened the door a few moments later in her housecoat. "What is it, dear? You look upset."

"I just got a notice for an appointment this morning, and I don't have a clock yet," I explained breathlessly.

"It's just past 5 a.m. Would you like to come in for a cup of breakfast tea?"

I shook my head. What I really needed was a cup of Plimmy's *special* tea. "Thanks, I wish that I had time, but I've got to get ready."

Miss Plimmswood gave me an understanding smile. I apologized for my abruptness and then turned and ran back up all three flights of stairs to my flat.

After showering and putting my hair up in its usual bun, I dug through my small wardrobe and came up with the black skirt and a red button-up dress blouse — they were the closest things I had to business attire.

Unfortunately, I didn't have a Templar uniform to wear but hoped the red shirt would signal my loyalties. I grabbed a conservative black jacket and my black pumps as well. I didn't know what I was going to be walking into but decided that I would do my best to meet the expectation for my dress.

Jogging through the cobblestone streets of Ealdwic, I made it to Temple Court as quickly as I could. As I approached the main stairs, I was stopped by the guards stationed outside. Someone would come for me, they indicated, when the time was right.

Turning away from them, I wrung my hands. I was a nervous wreck, my mind filled with worry at the summons. Was I about to be disciplined? But the letter had come from Richard Sonnac. Could it be my initiation? I had a sick feeling in the pit of my stomach that it wasn't why I'd been called to Temple Hall.

The weather outside was as dark as my mood. Despite it nearly being summer, the sky was overcast and gray, and a brisk wind blew. I could smell dampness in the air. No doubt there would be rain later. I was glad of my suit jacket because fear of what was to come was making me shiver. My hands were damp, and I clenched them to attempt to warm them up as I paced in front of the building until my feet started to hurt.

Eventually, the guards signaled me over and instructed me to follow another uniformed guard into Temple Hall. We mounted the outer steps, walked through the arched threshold and into the greater hall. I followed the guard closely, my heels ringing as we walked across the marble floors. I looked up at the giant rotunda, gray light filtering through the glass, and marveled at the centuries of history reflected by the space. The four-armed cross was carved on every column and set into the marble floor so that none could mistake the weight of tradition here.

The guard led me to a large set of doors on the right side of the hall, beyond where I knew the Crucible lay. We stopped before them, and he knocked briskly. The heavy door opened and I was ushered in past him into a large room, embellished in a similar style. The floor was covered in a thick red carpet, and in the front of the room was a tall ornately carved judicial bench of dark wood. The room was lined with chairs on each side, like a courtroom.

Seated there was a panel of three uniformed Templars, Dame Julia in the center. The others were unfamiliar to me. Richard Sonnac stood near a table at the left of the front of the room. Along the left wall were two frightening looking figures. One was wearing a neat brown suit with a lighter brown waistcoat and a red tie. His hands were covered in red gloves, and his face was hidden behind a white full-faced mask. The other stood on his right side and was dressed in a full set of plate combat armor with a deep red hood emblazoned with the four-armed cross in white on his forehead. His face was obscured by a cross-visored helm underneath the hood.

Fresh worry flooded my body. My throat was dry, and I swallowed hard to keep my composure. I stumbled slightly, my heel catching in the deep carpet, as I approached the bench.

"Ms. Mallory." Grim-faced, Richard Sonnac gestured for me to sit at the table beside him.

"Proceed with the opening statement, Richard," Dame Julia intoned from the front of the room.

Sonnac stepped out from the table and approached the bench, gesturing to the room and then back to me. "This is an informal proceeding. We are here to evaluate the...events that took place yesterday in the Mithraeum dig located in the Ealdwic municipal tunnels under Darkside."

He turned to face me, and I felt myself shrink in my seat at his attention.

"Ms. Mallory, please describe for us your actions and mindset that encouraged you to break into the locked archaeological dig, bearing in mind that your behavior not only reflects upon me as your sponsor for candidacy to become a Templar but on the venerable Templar organization as a whole. Understand that we have already taken testimony from Sevenoir on the matter."

The weight of the panel's gaze fell upon me, and Dame Julia gave me a skeptical glare. Resolutely, I cleared my throat and stood up. I might have been exploring without authorization and perhaps even criminal in breaking and entering, but I wasn't a coward or a liar. I would accept the consequences of my actions.

Taking a deep breath, I launched into the story, from my encounter with Mama Abena in the market, to the Fallen King's strange words, and the gusts of mystical wind from the park that drew me down into the sewers in the first place. I explained my thought processes upon seeing the face in the mosaic, which emboldened my further exploration. I described my startle at Sevenoir's appearance, and my beseeching him for assistance in solving the puzzle that ultimately revealed the rusty custodian and the entombed anima well, being careful to absolve him of any responsibility.

"So you decided it was within your own mandate to pursue this course of action?" Dame Julia questioned me when I had finished.

Chagrined, I admitted that I honestly hadn't given it sufficient thought at the time. I had been caught up in the mystery and had, once again, dived in headfirst without considering the broader implications to my desire to become a Templar.

"I want to know what made you realize the mosaic was a puzzle lock." A dark-haired middle-aged woman on the panel at Dame Julia's right asked me. My mind went blank at her question, and Dame Julia turned to scowl at her.

"She clearly showed initiative and intelligence, Honored Dame," the woman retorted in response. "The Oxford dig team has been struggling to open that door for weeks. Ms. Mallory figured it out in the course of an afternoon. We want our agents to have these qualities and not be a bunch of mindless drones."

"But, they also must have discipline and show forethought and strategic thinking," the man at Dame Julia's left responded. He looked like a business executive or political candidate, with carefully coiffed silver hair. "Ms. Mallory, I must admit I find these qualities to be significantly lacking in your judgment in this instance."

I hung my head. "That is true, sir. I struggle with forethought in particular."

He chuckled, not unkindly. "You are not the first nor the last candidate for whom that is the case."

"Nor was Ms. Mallory specifically prohibited from exploring the area around Ealdwic. She hasn't been here long enough to have been given any context around expectations for her role," the dark-haired woman added. "We can't blame her for what she doesn't know. It's our role to train her in those expectations."

"She broke into a locked door and did just as she pleased," Dame Julia said throwing up her hands in exasperation. "At a minimum, there are legal consequences for that!"

"I've spoken to the municipal board with regards to Ms. Mallory's breaking and entering," Sonnac said. "They are looking to follow our lead in this matter."

Dame Julia harrumphed and narrowed her eyes at me. "Very well. This panel will discuss the matter further and provide any further guidance to your sponsor within a few days. In the meantime, Ms. Mallory, I suggest you keep your nose clean and avoid any further behavior that might cast doubt on your worthiness to become a Templar."

I met Dame Julia's eye and nodded gravely. I had learned my lesson. No more running off on bootless errands for me.

"Thank you, Ms. Mallory, that will be all for now," Richard Sonnac said as he gestured to the exit.

I nodded, stepped out from behind the table, and made my way back to the tall doors at the far end of the room. I felt a prickle on my neck as I walked and glanced back over my shoulder at the imposing pair against the wall. With a jolt of apprehension, I noted that the helmed warrior was following me with his eyes and wondered why. I was left with the impression that something in particular about me interested him, something beyond the proceedings in the room.

June 18, 2012

Before I knew it, it was Monday again. I had spent most of the day Sunday after meeting with the panel in bed resting. Who knew the hangover from charging an agent anima battery and getting called up to account felt like the flu? By Monday morning, however, I was feeling right as rain and woke up early to get to the Crucible, ready to start my training, if they let me in the front door.

Luckily, the big red doors opened easily when I pushed them. I stepped in, ready to wave to the bartender when I heard Brigadier Lethe bellow at me from across the room.

"Ah, the prodigal daughter returns, I see. Decided you needed a little instruction before you hare off on your next solo adventure? So glad you could join us."

News had apparently traveled fast around Temple Hall. I grimaced. The bartender raised his eyebrow and gave me a rueful smile.

I trudged down the stairs to the practice area and approached Lethe half-heartedly to explain, but he waved away my excuses and instructed me to begin stretching before we started working on strength training. I stepped over to the stairs, thankful that he didn't seem to bear a grudge, and began stretching out my calf muscles. They complained loudly. It had been a while since I'd been to the gym.

"Breathe while you stretch," Lethe barked at me from where he was standing. "And do it gently unless you want to tear a muscle."

I spent the morning in a humiliating round of exercises that made it only too evident that my physical conditioning was a complete pile of crap. I'd done plenty of running around at Innsmouth, but my application of effort to actual exercise had been sorely lacking.

To hear Brigadier Lethe tell it, my stamina was nil, my muscles were all weak, my flexibility was "shite," and I was sure to get myself skewered as soon as I got into a "proper bout on a proper assignment." I complained bitterly in return that this was all new to me and that I could hardly be held responsible for things no one had ever taught me.

"Don't pretend you've never encountered a locked door before," Lethe yelled at me, clearly in Dame Julia's camp with regards to my adventure. "You had no business running off by yourself. You're weaker than a puppy, soldier. A blind man would kick your arse."

I scoffed openly at that but realized my mistake as Lethe pointed to his own eye patch. Then, he got a devious look on his face and turned away to make a phone call. I had a feeling it didn't bode well for me.

Other agents came in and out of the Crucible throughout the day to practice their weapons and spell work. I didn't pay much attention because I was too tired from the workout Lethe was inflicting. Currently, he had me practicing falls on a mat. I was damned sick of that and was about to tell him so in no uncertain terms.

As a result, I didn't see the blind woman approach until she was standing right in front of me.

She was tall, nearly six foot by my guess, and towered over me since I was not quite five-and-a-half-feet tall. She had snow-white dreadlocks, which she wore pulled back into a short ponytail. Her skin was dark brown, kind of a warm umber shade. She stood very straight, with her shoulders back, wearing a loose set of all-white workout clothing, and her eyes were covered by a blindfold.

"Wedd," Lethe said with a grin. "Meet SnowDrifter. She's going to help you work out for a bit."

Apparently, the all-white was a theme to match her name. Nope, this didn't bode well at all.

"Pleasure to meet you, Wedd," she said in a lyrical tone. It sounded sort of English, but I wasn't sure, because her accent was slightly different than what I heard around Ealdwic.

"You as well," I replied cautiously, trying to be gracious, yet wary of what was in store.

"Drifter here is from Wales," Lethe added. "But don't let that fool you. She's plenty tough despite it."

Drifter's face pulled up into a wry smile at his words, apparently accustomed to his manner. "Aye, and someone has to teach the English how it's done, we do."

She cocked her head toward me, listening. I moved subtly to the right on the mat, and she tracked me. I dropped my left leg back, and she mirrored me.

I now had a sense of impending doom. This was definitely not good.

"Now, when I first met Drifter, I made the mistake of underestimating her because she couldn't see," Lethe said. "I advise you not to do the same thing. Drifter, your job is to put Wedd on the floor. Wedd, your job is to stay off the floor. Good luck to you both."

Drifter nodded at Lethe. I looked at him and then back at Drifter.

"Ready, then?" she asked.

I nodded, then realized she couldn't see that and responded aloud that I was.

"Brilliant."

In the blink of an eye, she crossed the space between us and grabbed my right arm. Then, turning the back of her body in toward me, Drifter pulled me forward and off balance, bent at the waist, and rolled me over her hip where I landed with a slam on the mat, the wind whooshing from my lungs.

Lethe looked at me gasping for air on my back and guffawed. "Well, that went about as well as I expected. Drifter, good job.

Wedd, see if you can stay on your feet for a least five seconds next time."

I scowled at him as I climbed to my feet. Inspiration struck, and I edged toward the side of the mat, figuring that maybe I could run away from Drifter to avoid being thrown again since she couldn't actually see me.

"I'd advise you not to leave that mat," Lethe said dryly, noticing my movement. "She'll still find and throw you, but the marble floor will hurt."

He laughed once more, then moved away to talk to a short, dark-haired agent who had a question about a weapon in a nearby crate. I grimaced. The mat had hurt plenty.

"So, I see he's brought me here to teach you a lesson of sorts, eh?" Drifter asked me. "Complain or cause trouble once too often, did you?"

I grudgingly admitted that was the case.

"Done much close-quarters combat, then?"

I told her no and gave her a little background on my limited combat experience. We bonded over our shared love for chaos magic, and she told me a little bit about herself. I was amazed to learn that Drifter was a relatively new agent as well and had only just finished up her own training with Lethe. That said, she explained that she had a black belt in judo, which she'd earned well before ever swallowing Gaia's bee.

Ah. I'd had no chance whatsoever of staying on my feet. I said as much to her aloud.

"Quit chit-chatting and get back to it, you two!" Lethe hollered from across the room.

"Let's go through a few basic moves then, shall we?" Drifter offered with a bright smile.

By the time we were ready to knock off for the day, I was tired and sore, but more than that, grateful. Drifter had been a patient, effective instructor, although I longed to wipe the smug look off Brigadier Lethe's face. He'd been right to call her in. Because of her lack of vision, Drifter demonstrated the moves slowly and precisely, and described them in terms of proprioception, literally helping me get a feel for how to defend against an attacker standing in my personal bubble. When she attacked, it was a like a lightning strike, but the more we practiced, the more I was able to see the telegraph of her body, preparing for a particular move. By the end, I'd actually been able to avoid one or two of her attacks.

Sure, I'd been on the mat a lot, but I also had some confidence now that if I were attacked, I'd know what to do about it. I reflected between bouts of instruction and falling that I could have used some of this knowledge when I was battling the familiars lurking around Innsmouth Academy or in the temple, avoiding the rusted custodian. I couldn't wait to write Gypcie. I wondered how her training was going in New York.

I pulled my backpack onto my shoulder when Lethe yelled at me again. "Not so fast, soldier. Sonnac wants to see you before you leave."

My face grew bright red. Oh no! I thought I'd endured the rest of my consequences in today's training, otherwise known as the ego beat-down from Lethe. I was both mortified that Richard Sonnac wanted to talk to me more about it and terrified that the panel had levied a decision about my further training that I wouldn't like one bit. I covered my face with my hands.

Lethe coughed uncomfortably at this but urged me on my way. "Go on now," he said. "Bad news doesn't get better with age."

The bartender held up a bottle of whiskey at me, a question in his eyes as I walked past, but I shook my head. There was no balm for this. I needed to face the music.

I stepped out the doors into the marble-floored hallway and rounded the corner to the north door to Sonnac's office. I stood there a while in silence and watched him while he worked, pondering the right approach.

"Come in, come in," he gestured when he looked up from his desk.

Richard Sonnac set aside the papers he'd been reviewing and stood up, tugging down his slimly tailored suit. He stepped around his desk toward me.

"Your smooth transition into the Templars is among my top priorities," he began in a calm, even-tempered voice. "Certainly in the upper percentile."

He steepled his hands in front of his mouth, then added, "Should you be unsure of the correct conduct in any situation, come to me in the first instance. We can speak in confidence and largely without judgment. I will take pains to understand."

Contrite, I nodded, my face sober.

Sonnac considered me for a moment, then moved away from where I stood in the doorway and looked up at the painting of Saint George, which hung over the fireplace. "I accepted this position because I saw a new way for the Templars to achieve our old potential. Ours is an organization with no shortage of history."

He gestured up at the painting. "Some might say too much history."

Sonnac turned back to face me, a stern expression on his face. "But you are our future, Ms. Mallory. Don't squander it." His eyes pierced me to the quick before he returned to his desk and sat down.

He turned back to his papers. Once again, I was dismissed. This was definitely not the impression I had intended to make on Richard Sonnac. I hung my head in misery and turned to the door to leave.

"As you know, there are others," he called out behind me, "who do not regard your trespass as lightly. They think it's a bad sign of your fit for the organization. I have their agreement, for now, to give you another chance. This is information worth thinking upon in the future."

The world was moving in slow motion as I dragged myself back through the marble hall, headed for the large doorway that led to the front vestibule and out of Temple Hall.

"…utterly lacking in any sense of propriety or duty!"

I heard the woman's shrill voice echoing across the main court floor. Forgetting my self-pity, I glanced around to see if anyone could see me, then dodged behind a large pillar to check out what was happening.

At the far end of the hall, I could see Sevenoir's telltale bunny ears and platinum blond hair as he stood at attention in front of Dame Julia, who was clearly in a froth. Her voice was loud enough that I could hear it across the room. She was giving him a sound scolding.

At first, I felt some schoolgirl glee at hearing him dressed down, but very quickly felt ashamed as I realized that he was probably in trouble because of what I had done. Sevenoir didn't deserve criticism for trying to look out for me down in the Roman temple. Of the two encounters I'd had with him, that was the most helpful he'd been.

Around the court area, the other agents on duty were doing their level best to pay no obvious attention whatsoever to what was happening. I could make out words like "recalcitrant" and "ungovernable" and a particularly loud screech of, "You'd better take this assignment seriously, or else!"

I debated approaching to defend Sevenoir, but remembering Richard Sonnac's words, I decided that in this case discretion was the better part of valor. I whirled around and fled out the doorway and down the front stairs, not wanting to be caught eavesdropping.

June 19, 2012

As I walked into the Crucible the following morning, still smarting from the dressing down I'd received from Richard Sonnac as well as the soreness of my muscles, I was caught up short by an unwelcome sight.

"What are you doing here?" I blurted before I could catch myself.

Languishing on a stool at the Crucible bar was none other than my old nemesis and new partner in crime, Sevenoir, nursing a glass of whiskey (at eight o'clock in the morning!) and glowering at me.

He was dressed in a ripped, but stylish, pair of jeans, a white T-shirt and leather motorcycle jacket, wearing a pair of heavy-duty boots, his white-blond hair spiking out from his head like he'd just come from a Billy Idol concert. Ms. Usher had introduced Gypcie, Carter, and me to Billy Idol last year, saying he was required listening when she was a girl.

Around his throat was a spiked leather collar and, of course, the flopping white bunny ears sprung from his head like antennae.

I put my hands on my hips and gave him my darkest scowl.

"Could you lower your voice just a titch?" Sevenoir winced, his blue eyes bloodshot and tired-looking. "Hair of the dog this morning."

The bartender smirked and grabbed the bottle of Drambuie from the back bar and topped off Sevenoir's breakfast tonic.

I shook my head in scorn and bewilderment. Did he not care at all for propriety? For the dignity of the Templars? What was he doing here drinking—drunk?—at this time of the day? Some of us were dressed and ready to put our best foot forward.

"Let's get started, Wedd," Lethe yelled from the lower floor. "Daylight's burning."

I gave Sevenoir another dark look and marched by him with my nose in the air. Today, I was going to learn footwork, and I couldn't wait to get started. Thank the gods Miss Plimmswood had had some Epsom salt I could borrow last night. I'd soaked in the tub for hours and wasn't feeling too horrible given my workout the day before.

Using the stairs as a prop, I began to carefully stretch my sore muscles. My shoulders and back were in tight knots from all the "falling practice" the day before, but my legs didn't feel too bad. But, I took the time to stretch out my thigh muscles, my hamstrings, and my hips nonetheless, because I knew that I'd be using those muscles today.

"Today, we're about your footwork, soldier," Lethe announced, as I joined him when I finished my stretches. "Blade work relies on control, and control requires solid footwork. With proper footwork, you can maintain balance as well as sufficient distance from your opponent."

Lethe guided me into the stance in the middle of the marble floor, with my right leg forward and my left leg dropped back. My right foot was pointing forward with my left foot perpendicular. He had me lean forward slightly with my weight centered between my heels. After adjusting my stance in a dozen minute ways, he was finally satisfied.

"Good. Now, hold your right arm up and out. You'll practice the movement until you start to build muscle memory."

"Do I need a blade?" I asked, anxious to have a chance to feel one in my hand.

"Don't get ahead of yourself. You'll thank me later when your thighs are aching."

Back and forth across the marble floor, he made me move, forward and back, advance and retreat, as he watched, yelling: "Stop sticking your backside out. Quit trying to take the weight off your thighs!" or "Don't pick up your whole front foot when you move, just your toes. Then move your heel forward." Or "What, are you a horse, galloping across the room like that?" And, "Take discrete steps and keep your back straight!"

Back and forth, I went, for what felt like hours. Actually, it was probably only ten minutes. I wondered if a person could actually die from thigh pain.

"How will I learn how to use a blade doing all these dumb drills?" I finally asked, exasperated. Apparently, I hadn't learned my lesson about complaining the previous day.

Lethe arched his left eyebrow at me menacingly and told me to get my arm up and keep practicing. I shut up and focused again on moving up and down the floor in a line. It was then that Sevenoir decided to catcall from the bar to "cheer me on." I was torn between wanting to laugh and wanting to punch him in the face.

"Go, go, go, get him!" he shouted, like a World Cup announcer calling out an attempt to score a goal. "Oh, bother, you missed. Better luck next time."

"Ah, you got him! Skewered him right through the heart!"

"Point to the red-headed girl. Wedd, one. Demon, zero."

"And the match is on. It's exhilarating footwork we're watching from newcomer Wedd Mallory. Up and down the floor she goes! The crowd goes wild!"

It was absurd but entertaining, and after a while, I began to enjoy his play-by-play, as it distracted me from the pain in my thighs. Brigadier Lethe ignored Sevenoir entirely, and before I knew it another few minutes had passed.

"That's good, soldier. Take a break and walk it off." Lethe called finally, raising his hand for me to stop. As I walked off the ache in my legs, he shouted up to the bar. "Sevenoir, get your arse down here. It's clear you want to help out."

Sevenoir waved a hand in protest. "No, no. I'm good, General. Having a fine time spectating right here from the stool."

My mouth dropped at Sevenoir's cheek.

"That wasn't a request," Lethe barked. "Get down here double time, or I'll get Dame Julia to drag your ass down here."

Sevenoir stood up, drained his glass, and then tipped it to Brigadier Lethe.

"To argue with a man who has renounced the use and authority of reason, and whose philosophy consists in holding humanity in contempt, is like administering medicine to the dead," he said, adding, "That's Thomas Paine, for the dilettantes in the crowd."

"Soldier, shut your mouth and get down here or I'll show you some pain," Lethe barked again, but there was no real anger behind his words. Then lowering his voice just for my ears he said, "Sevenoir is a good agent. He's angry right now and acting out, but he brings his game face in a real fight. You'd do better to not pick up his habit of flapping his jaws at authority, though. It gets him in a world of hurt."

I nodded tightly and watched as Sevenoir sauntered our way at his leisure. Lethe asked him to assume a blade stance opposite me on the marble floor. We began to skirmish, sans weapons, using only footwork and feints to mimic actual combat. I wondered how Sevenoir could move so gracefully with a belly full of Scotch. It didn't seem to affect him, however, as we moved back and forth on the floor. I practiced the pattern Lethe had instructed, advance, advance, lunge, recover, repeat. For his part, Sevenoir just danced out of my reach, mockingly. He looked like a swan. I felt like an elephant stomping around on the floor, my muscles aching. I was quickly running out of steam.

"Don't take your eyes off his torso, Wedd. Learn to anticipate his moves by watching his body. That way when your opponent has a blade in hand, you won't be distracted by the sharp, pointy thing," Lethe instructed me.

Finally, Lethe called an end to the footwork practice and came over to give me some more instruction. I was exhausted, bent over at the waist, panting and tired, trying to recover my breath as I listened, but couldn't help noticing with irritation that Sevenoir walked up to resume his seat at the bar. Didn't he have anything better to do with his time?

"All right, take an hour for lunch and be back here. We'll work some more on shotgun this afternoon, soldier," Lethe said.

A break! I nodded and grabbed my backpack, groaning at my sore legs as I marched up the stairs to the entrance. I was famished. I'd been thinking of getting a ham sandwich from Carroll's Delicatessen, which was located right off the square where the Fallen King preached. I wasn't looking for trouble, just a quick and satisfying lunch, and the advert on their awning said they catered tea parties for Queen Elizabeth. I figured I'd give it a try. Here was hoping that it wouldn't cost a queen's ransom.

I walked carefully down the steps from Temple Hall as my thigh muscles screamed, and waved at the guards stationed at the entrance as I stepped out into Temple Court heading for the gateway onto Redcrosse Circus, and broke into a light jog.

I made good time down to the square. The usual crowd of onlookers pointing and laughing were there taking in the Fallen King's end-of-the-world shtick. I was just about to enter the delicatessen when I saw him pause and look directly at me.

"Do I seem foolish to you?" The Fallen King asked. "Here in my rags, my filth, my little puppet, gibbering to whoever will give me the time?"

He raised his hands over his head as if he were invoking a deity. "I am the Fallen King. The end of the path. You are the Fool—the zero, the nothing, straining at the precipice, the little dog yapping at your feet. You are nothing. Nothing but an idea, a starting point in Gaia's great dream. Ripe for seduction, ripe for destruction."

He leaned over and gave me a beady, intense look. "You, Wedd. The screech owl will make mincemeat out of you."

I felt a cold shock run through me as he called out my name.

"Do you remain huddled on the edge? Stroll blindly to your doom?"

I turned back to the door of the delicatessen to hurry inside to avoid further confrontation or another fainting spell.

"Or do you leap forward to what comes next..." he yelled as the door to the shop closed behind me.

Inside, the young woman behind the counter greeted me. I ordered my ham sandwich and waited nervously while she filled my order. I was simultaneously weirded out and irritated that the ragged prophet caused me such anxiety.

How would I ever be able to face down foes on a mission if a dirty man on a wooden box chased me away?

Still, I definitely wasn't looking forward to going back out there for more and wondered if the delicatessen's business had fallen off since he began hanging out there. The shop girl finished ringing me up and handed me a sack with my sandwich. I thanked her and turned back to the door, but I couldn't make myself go back out to the square. I chewed my lip and looked out the front windows for the right time to make a break for it.

It was then I saw a familiar spiky haired blond head, complete with jeans, T-shirt, and leather jacket sauntering down Antiqua Way, headed in the direction of The Horned God. There was Sevenoir! I rushed out the door and hurried to join him.

He looked up with a start as I ran up to him. "Where's the fire, Wedd?"

"Sorry. I was just a little weirded out by that creepy prophet on the box."

Sevenoir laughed heartily until he realized the depth of my upset. He asked me what had happened. I explained, best as I could, what the Fallen King had said to me.

"Never mind him. He says weird shite to everyone," Sevenoir placated me. "It's his job. Now, am I to understand you're planning to join me in a liquid lunch at the pub? Good girl."

I followed Sevenoir into The Horned God, which smelled of hardwood, old beer, and people. Dozens of patrons were in the pub for a noontime break. In the center of the main floor was an elaborate free-standing wooden bar area, complete with stools on each of the sides. It was carved from polished oak, the wood darkened from the touch of many fingers over the years. In the center of the bar proper, two bartenders served the patrons.

On the side nearest us, the bartender was a young woman with a short strawberry-blonde pixie cut. She had on a strapless green dress with gossamer, fake fairy wings springing from her back and looked like a younger, reddish-haired cousin of Kylie Minogue. Apparently, Sevenoir wasn't the only one with an affection for out-of-season Halloween costume pieces.

The back bar, or perhaps more accurately, center bar was also carved of oak, with shelves holding the many varieties of spirits the pub had for sale. Etched glass panes were inserted in the upper portion, which were backlit, and globed lights hung along the top railing, giving the room a cheerful atmosphere. Along the sides of the room were sectioned tables and chairs, affording the patrons comfort and privacy while they enjoyed their beverages.

All in all, it looked like a quintessentially British pub and an enjoyable place to spend some time. I pushed down guilty feelings at being here in the middle of the day. I wasn't used to how central pubs were to English life yet but realized that for a Londoner, there was nothing strange about going to one for lunch.

Sevenoir strode directly to the center bar. He waved to two patrons seated at the front of it and joined them, lifting a hand to get the bartender's attention. I realized as I walked closer, that one of the patrons was none other than the girl who'd helped me find Temple Hall after I passed out in the Fallen King's square the first time. Sevenoir introduced me to her and her companion, then ordered himself a pint. Her name was Zamira Vata, and the older man beside her with a thin mustache, wearing an off-white linen suit with a green shirt, was another Templar agent named Konrad Engel. Zamira recognized me as well from the previous Friday and greeted me warmly.

"Bloody hell, who decided to make London the capital of the secret world? They'll be out of Stella soon at this rate," Zamira commented with irritation, surveying the crowded pub, as she motioned me to grab a stool next to them at the bar.

She and Engel appeared to be old pals and batted back and forth at each other verbally a mile a minute, discussing everything from the current management of the Templars to the politics of the Council of Venice. Sevenoir chimed in occasionally with a droll comment or a scoff. I wondered briefly if I'd be chastised for being seen in the same vicinity as the three of them since they didn't seem to have any particular awe of the organization I was trying so hard to find my place in.

"Want a beer?" the bartender asked me. It was hard to hear her over the dull roar of the tourists and locals as they laughed and chatted in the nearby booths. The pub seemed pretty full for a lunchtime crowd.

I shook my head no, and I asked for a cola instead, then opened my bag, and began to eat my sandwich. I wouldn't be good for anything this afternoon if I had a beer with my lunch. I took a bite, and Sevenoir glanced over at me suspiciously. What now? I stopped chewing and looked back at him questioningly. Was he concerned I was eating my sandwich in the pub? The waitress from the other night had said it wasn't a problem.

"I despise the sound of other people eating," he explained briefly. "But I can't hear you." I nodded my understanding and took pains to continue to chew quietly.

Beside me, Zamira launched into what seemed to be a long-standing argument with Engel.

"What I'm saying is that there aren't really any shades of gray in this Secret War. It's us against them, bloods, and the last soldier standing wins the war and rewrites history."

Sevenoir looked over at me again and rolled his eyes. He'd heard this discussion before, apparently. Engel contemplated her statement for a moment, then asked, "I see. So what about those who fight on our side but for different reasons?"

"There's right reasons, and there's wrong reasons. We're right, they're wrong," she said.

"Oh, how comforting to know the New Templars have got it all sorted," Engel said, his German accent and slight slur of the words making it difficult to understand him.

"Shades of grey only does one thing, mate. It makes everything charcoal."

"Mhm. In your world, then, the Illuminati and the Dragon, they are our enemies?" he asked.

"Well, we already fight them, yeah?" Zamira stated.

"No, no, no. We play with them, following carefully established written rules that leave no one dead, only slightly disoriented and no worse for wear. I would not call this a conflict between mortal enemies."

"Right. So we tolerate them, but that still don't make them in the right," she said with irritation.

"And already you are making compromises, Fräulein Vata. Hmm? Shades of grey? Hmm? You see how slippery the road?" Engel said with satisfaction.

Zamira crossed her arms over her chest. "Smartass."

Engel chuckled and turned to me. "And what about you, Fräulein Mallory?"

I gulped down the bite of my sandwich before answering. "I just got here this week to start my training."

"Another new Templar," he said, slapping his forehead. He turned in his seat to Sevenoir, who had just purchased his second pint.

I was puzzled by his reaction. Engel was obviously a Templar too, so why did he seem less than excited about adding to the ranks.

"Aren't you glad that there are people interested in joining?" I asked.

Engel put his pint on the bar and turned to me. "It isn't that I despise your desire to become a Templar, Fräulein. You simply don't understand much yet. As I've been trying to tell Fräulein Vata, when you dig under the red, green, and blue uniforms, you find fanatics who are led around by the noses by three factions that are not as different as they may seem."

He stood up, warming to his topic.

Zamira rolled her eyes and put her hand on my arm. "Oh, now you've done it. We're about to hear the lecture."

"The Templars would have you believe they're different than the Illuminati or the Dragon. There is bad blood between the organizations that in some cases goes back centuries. But the disputes are political, not substantive. Our leadership has never forgiven the Illuminati for worming their way into the New World, even though their origins are revealed by the pyramid you see on their uniforms. The Dragon, on the other hand, is a wild card. They are unchallenged in the Far East, and their particular brand of Zen chaos is spreading like a virus to every liberal bleeding heart who prefers meditation to ritual."

Zamira shook her head and threw up her hands. "See what I mean?"

Engel ignored her, picked up his pint, and took a swig. "But underneath it all, the organizations themselves are like triplets, separated from their mother's breast. They are more alike than not. They thrive on creating dominion through imbalance. We Templars may pride ourselves on our conviction to do right, but we are also intolerant and have a zeal for the work that borders on the religious."

Engel pointed a finger at me. "But you young Bees are becoming quite the fly in the ointment in the old balances of power. Make no mistake, Fräulein Mallory. All of the factions are very clear that history is written by the winners. And so, winning becomes more important than anything or anyone. And what better way to win than to fill your ranks with agents who don't die anymore?"

I could feel my face warming as he spoke. His words filled me with confusion. How dare Engel say such things about his own faction? Where was his loyalty?

He looked at my red face and chuckled. "I see Fräulein Mallory is cut from the same cloth as Fräulein Vata. They're both a couple of idealists, Sevenoir, as though there were still ideals to strive for."

Sevenoir made no comment and tipped his own glass back for a swallow.

Engel gestured at me with his glass and leaned over to me conspiratorially. "Now I am an embarrassment to our organization, but once I was a diplomat."

I narrowed my eyes and crossed my arms across my body, fuming. That he was considered an embarrassment to the Templars, I had no doubt.

He shook his head and wobbled a bit on his stool. "As if Templars could wage diplomacy other than by jackboot." He and Sevenoir clinked pint glasses at that statement and Engel took a deep swallow of his beer.

"Just 'cause you've become old and bitter don't mean you have to take us all down with you," Zamira retorted, pointing to herself and me. "Everything is changing mate. It's not just the Templars anymore; it's the New Templars, independent of heritage, skin color or gender."

Engel clucked his tongue back at her, shaking his head sadly. "Oh, the naiveté of youth. It is heartbreaking. My heart is literally breaking apart. Listen, you can hear it."

"Oh, fuck off, Konrad," Zamira said, laughing.

"Right then," Sevenoir said, emptying his pint glass and setting it on the bar with a bang. "It's time for Wedd and me to be off unless we want to feel the wrath of Herr Lethe." He gave a stomp and an exaggerated salute to our two companions and turned on his heel, heading out the way we'd come in. I quickly drank the rest of my cola, said my goodbyes, tossed my sandwich bag and wrapper in a rubbish bin, and ran out of the pub after him.

I had to scramble a little to catch up. Sevenoir had set a brisk pace back to Temple Hall. I was careful to move to the right when we walked past the courtyard where the Fallen King lingered.

"Why do you do that?" I asked him when I caught up and stepped alongside.

"Do what?"

"Hang out with someone like Konrad. Do you pay no attention to the impression you leave people with about the Templars? There were all kinds of people in the pub. Talking to someone like him…It's like you don't care about being a Templar at all. Like you're not Templar material."

He looked at me dumbfounded for a nanosecond, then threw back his head and laughed heartily. The rabbit ears wobbled, and he quickly moved his hand up to stabilize them, running the drama of the action.

"You…you…you've been here all of, what, three days, you've caused a tremendous uproar by sneaking down into a locked temple ruin, and you have the gall to try to instruct me on how to adequately represent the Templars?"

He was laughing at me still, but with open irritation now. "How little you understand, and yet you want to judge. My ancestor Hugues de Payens was the co-founder and first Grandmaster of the Order of the Knights Templar. I am Templar material quite simply *by breathing*. You, on the other hand…" He stopped and gestured dismissively at me while quirking his eyebrow.

Suddenly, I was overly aware of the people on the street watching us and of the odd pair we made, standing out in the intersection of Antiqua and Ealdwic Park. Sevenoir in his Billy Idol ensemble and rabbit ears, and me in my gray and maroon fleece hoodie, over my leggings and bright red sneakers, arguing in the middle of the street.

Paralyzed by shame, I couldn't respond. I was so confused, but I felt weirdly responsible, like a little sister chasing an older sibling down to call them in the house for dinner. I didn't like it.

He shook his head in disgust at me. "Mind your own bloody behavior and leave me out of it." Sevenoir took off again down the street, double time. Sighing, I jogged after him.

As we entered the Crucible, Brigadier Lethe yelled at us and pointed at his watch. "Really pushing it to the last few moments, I see. Wedd, what did I tell you about following Sevenoir's lead? When I say one hour, I mean one hour."

Sevenoir took his customary stool in front of the bar, but I could tell by the set of his shoulders that he was angry about what I had said.

"Made it with one minute to spare," the bartender said to me on my way by, giving me a thumbs up and a wink. Now, at least I understood why Sevenoir had set such a brisk pace on our way back from The Horned God. Thank goodness we were one minute early instead of the other way around.

I set my bag down and joined Lethe on the practice floor and schooled my face in what I hoped was an expression of patient interest, while I awaited his direction for the afternoon's practice.

Inside, however, I was in turmoil. I felt bad about what I'd said to Sevenoir. Despite my frustration with his cavalier attitude and his incomplete assistance to me at the Agartha portal, overall he'd been helpful and even sort of protective down in the underground temple. I certainly was glad to see him after the Fallen King accosted me again. He'd even introduced me to his friends. In return, I had called him out in the middle of the street. Shame flooded me. I owed him an apology at least.

Also, he had a point. Was *I* Templar material? I thought I was. It had been my goal for so long to come to Temple Hall that I was a little set adrift now that I was here. Certainly, I wanted to prove myself worthy of being a Templar, but what did that mean exactly?

If I asked Brigadier Lethe, he would no doubt say that meant shutting my mouth and practicing hard in the Crucible. I had been doing that, sort of. Dame Julia would probably say it meant keeping up propriety and tradition and not running off on cockamamie adventures. I realized that subconsciously my criticism of Sevenoir probably came from a desire to do that, but trying to control him was wrong of me. I could only fix myself.

What would Richard Sonnac say would prove me worthy of being a Templar? That would show I wasn't squandering my chance?

I contemplated that as Lethe reached into a weapon case and handed me a practice shotgun and a dozen shells, and sent me down to the ranged target practice area. I put in my earplugs and practiced carefully, but my mind continued to spin as I thought about what I'd said to Sevenoir. By the time I ran out of shells, I felt lower than a piece of gum on the bottom of a shoe. I owed him an apology as soon as I could get a minute alone with him.

"Where is your head, soldier?" Lethe asked from behind me. I jerked with a start as I hadn't heard him approach.

Lowering the barrel of the shotgun, I turned to him and took out my earplugs and put them in my hoodie pockets. "What do you mean?"

"Your form is improving, but you've been practicing that shot for the last 10 minutes. Nothing wrong with that, of course, but you've got something else on your mind."

I hung my head. Tears of shame started to well up, and I took a deep breath to hold them back. I didn't want to cry in front of Brigadier Lethe. "I just want to be worthy of being a Templar, sir," I responded, my throat tight.

"And you're worried that you'll be found wanting?" he asked gruffly.

I nodded. "I also said something to Sevenoir that I'm ashamed of," I admitted.

"Hmm." Lethe stroked his chin thoughtfully for a moment, then his face fell back into its customary scowl. "Well, that's enough practice for today. Gather your things and get yourself sorted out. Next time your body is on this floor, I want your head here too."

I thanked Lethe for his time and hurried to put the practice shotgun back in its case. I grabbed my bag and ran up to the bar, but by the time I got there, Sevenoir was nowhere to be found.

My shoulders slumped.

The bartender looked up from where he was washing glasses. "Do you need a drink?"

I shook my head no and turned to the door.

"You might be able to find him at The Horned God," the bartender said. As I looked back around, he gave me a wink. I realized that Sevenoir might have told him what had happened.

"Is he mad at me?"

"Sev? Nah. He's an all right chap, Sev is. He takes a lot of guff for his style, but when the chips are down, he's the right one to have in your corner. He's on assignment. He won't have gone far."

I wondered what Sevenoir's assignment was, but figured it was time for me to take his advice and stay out of his business. I was also a little embarrassed that I didn't know the bartender's name yet, but thankfully he had a name tag that usefully supplied that information.

"Thanks, Jake. I appreciate your help," I said, giving him a smile.

"That's the spirit. You'll be fine," he counseled me as I waved goodbye and headed out the big red doors. "I'll see you both here again tomorrow."

I walked back to my flat briskly, thinking I'd drop off my stuff and change into something less "I've been at the gym all day" to go out looking for Sevenoir. I hoped Jake was right, and I'd find him perched on a stool in The Horned God pub.

I spied Miss Plimmswood—Plimmy!—as I made my way back to 5-F May Queen Market standing in her favorite spot next to the railing by her front door. I greeted her and invited her to come with me The Horned God for a cup of "tea." I figured it would be nice to have moral support as I tried to find Sevenoir.

She agreed. I left her there waiting while I dashed up to change into jeans and a nice shirt. I had a pair of purple jeans with gold stitching that I loved and hadn't worn yet that went perfectly with my favorite purple boots. I threw them on with a colorful blouse and went back downstairs to meet Plimmy. Going to the pub twice in one day was a record, at least for me.

We walked up the alley between my apartment building and the Albion Ballroom, which was just west of The Horned God, and grabbed a seat at one of the wooden tables in the courtyard area of the pub. I settled my backpack at the floor near my feet while Plimmy took off her hat and placed it on the table beside her. The waitress assigned to the area had her hands full with a rowdy table of tourists, so I offered to run inside and grab our drinks. Plimmy demurred, most likely I suspected to preserve the fiction that it was actually tea in her cup, but I was fine to just sit outside for a while and observe the comings and goings of the bar patrons.

"Are you looking for someone, dear" Plimmy commented after I gawked after a fair-haired man who'd just stepped into the pub proper. "Or at least more specifically than any young woman tries to catch the eye of a handsome young man in a pub," she concluded with a smile.

I felt my cheeks heat up at her appraisal. "I *am* looking for someone," I admitted, with a little shame. "I said something mean and kind of inappropriate to him today, and I wanted to apologize if I can find him."

"Oh, dear," she said, patting my hand. "What did he do to deserve it?"

At my shocked look, Plimmy laughed, then pressed her lips together controlling her mirth. "I don't mean to make light of something that obviously distresses you. Would it help to talk about it?"

Would it? I wasn't sure how much I could say without revealing I was training to be a Templar. Miss Plimmswood looked at me steadily with a kind look on her face, and I found that I wanted to tell her about it.

Oh, for the Gods' sake, Wedd, you're an open book, I thought with irritation at myself. *Gaia help you if you ever actually got interrogated if even your landlady can get you to spill the beans about everything.*

I reviewed the details of the interaction I'd had with him and decided that there really was no way for me to share it with her. I thanked her for her kindness in asking and said that I wasn't ready to talk about it yet.

The waitress came over and asked if we needed a drink. Plimmy ordered her tea, and after a moment's thought, I ordered one of the same. She arched her eyebrow at me. "You wouldn't prefer a pint of stout?"

I smiled mischievously. "I'm trying a new drink each time I come here. I haven't tried the 'tea' yet."

"Er, uh, yes," she agreed, her voice muffled as if she was trying not to laugh. "It's a bit strong, but perhaps you'll like it."

The waitress nodded and headed inside the pub to fill our orders. In short order, she brought back two teacups and set them in front of us. Plimmy paid the tab, once I made her promise to let me get the next round. Then she turned to me and leaned over conspiratorially.

"So tell me about this bunny-eared fellow I keep seeing following you around," Plimmy placed her cup down on the table with a twinkle in her eye. "Is he a beau?" I had just picked up the teacup and taken a sip. I couldn't help myself. I choked and sprayed what I suspected was Scotch whiskey across the table. I set the cup down abruptly and covered my mouth with my hand as I coughed to evacuate the liquor from my lungs.

"See," she said primly. "I told you it was strong!"

"It's not the…" I fanned my face and pounded my chest before continuing, "tea. It's the thought of Sevenoir as my boyfriend."

"Oh, his name is Sevenoir, is it? That's an odd name."

"It's his, um, nickname," I scrambled to explain. "I think his real name is Michael something Pain. And he is a pain. Well, at least, he was when I first met him. But wait, you said he's been following me?"

"I'm sure I'm probably imagining it, dear. Ealdwic is a small place, after all. Maybe he lives here in the vicinity. It's just that those rabbit ears are so…prominent. Why does he wear them?"

I told her I had no idea, and really I didn't. I suspected he wore them primarily because they were obnoxious, and therefore supported his obvious disdain for authority and order. That wasn't quite right either though, I thought as I remembered him stopping at the stop sign as he drove me to the Agartha portal and checking up on me down in tunnels. Thinking about that made me frustrated all over again, and it must have crossed my face.

Plimmy tapped her chin as she looked at me. "So, is this Sevenoir someone you work with?"

"He's been helping me learn my new job." My cheeks went red with the white lie. "Sort of."

"And what did you say you did, Wedd?"

Of course, I hadn't said. I was hopeless at this. Either that or Plimmy had the instincts of a bird dog.

"Can you excuse me for a moment?" I stood up in a rush. "I need to use the lady's room."

"By all means, dear." She smiled and picked her own cup back up from the table for a sip as I fled into the pub.

Inside, I regained some of my composure and was utterly irritated with myself. I was acting like Plimmy was some sort of spy trying to tease the secrets of ages from me. She was just a sweet old lady and my landlord. I really needed to get a grip. All this "Secret War" this and "end of times" that was starting to get to me. I glanced around the interior of the pub to see if I could spot the tell-tale rabbit ears, but no luck. I saw Zamira and Konrad Engel still chatting on the other side of the bar, and she threw me a quick wave when I caught her eye.

It was just as well I was in here under the pretenses of using the restroom. I had whiskey all over my hands. I asked a bouncer where the water closet was, and he pointed me to the door at the left of the stairs. Inside I scrubbed my hands and freshened up, before returning to the back patio.

I sat back down at the table and was determined to have a drink of tea without choking. I said as much to Plimmy, and she cheered me on as I took a robust sip.

At least I didn't spit it across the room this time.

"So here's the trick, dear," she said. "When you take the next drink, roll the whiskey around the sides of your tongue before swallowing it."

I followed her instruction, and the warm burn of whiskey coursed down the back of my throat. Hmm. It wasn't so bad that time. I drew the cup to my lips again and pulled in another gulp of the liquid heat for fortification.

"Well done!" Plimmy took another sip from her cup as well and sighed with satisfaction. "So, a lovely girl like you must have a beau somewhere."

Thoughts of the handsome Dragon agent that I'd dated casually at Innsmouth filled my mind.

"There was a fellow when I was in school," I ventured. "He is from New Orleans. His name is Renee Laveau. I think his great-grandma was a famous voodoo priestess or something."

"Indeed?" Plimmy's eyes got round as an owl's. "There is a very well-known Voudun practitioner with that last name. Tell me all about him."

I told her what I knew of Renee, about his dark hair and green eyes, that he was 25 years old, tall and fit, and that he'd been raised in New Orleans and attended school at Lake Pontchartrain. Oh, and that he was a Capricorn, born on the Winter Solstice. I shared tales of the things we'd talked about together over coffee in the few times we met and that I had not heard from him before I left Innsmouth Academy.

Plimmy listened with gratifying raptness, punctuating my story with the supportive comments and noises of a good friend. Warmth from her support and understanding filled me. I realized that I sounded like a school girl, but it was lovely to be taken seriously in regards to my feelings. I definitely still thought about Renee and missed him.

"So you were never able to tell him you were headed to London?" Plimmy ventured. "Oh, what a shame. I'll keep my fingers crossed, my dear, that he reaches out to your old school to try to make contact in the future."

I nodded my head with a wistful smile. Above us, a raven cawed in the tree on the pub patio, and the light rail whined past in the distance as it sped along its track. The faint strains of a dubstep song drifted out from the open door of the pub, along with the chatter of patrons.

"How about you, Plimmy? Did you ever fall in love or get married?"

"Me? Married? Oh heavens no!" She tittered, placing her hand over her heart. "I was always far too hard-headed to want a husband. As a young woman, I wanted to do what I wanted to do."

"But surely you fell in love somewhere along the way?"

"Yes," she acknowledged with a fond smile. "There was someone. *Is* someone. But, it's complicated, dear, to fall in love with a person whose career is more important to them than anything. And I would no more stand in the way of that than I would allow anyone to stand in the way of what I wanted. No, I am content these days with watching from afar."

"Well," I lifted my teacup in a toast. "Here's to spending time with those who warm our hearts when we can and thinking fondly on them when we can't."

Plimmy lifted her teacup and clinked it with mine across the table with a nod. "I'll drink to that."

We finished our drinks and headed back to our respective homes shortly thereafter.

I had been meaning to write Gypcie another letter, so I grabbed pen and paper, sat down on the futon in the living area of my flat and, settled in to dash off an update on my adventures so far. I hoped I'd hear back from her soon, but until I got a cell phone or access to a computer, I had to rely on the Post to provide the updates. I wondered how she was doing. I made a mental note to check the box tomorrow on my way to Temple Hall.

With a yawn, I sealed the letter in an envelope and addressed it. I gathered my supplies and put them back in a box on my bookshelves, then turned out the lights in the living room, and got ready for bed. Tomorrow would be another full day.

I was asleep as soon as my head hit the pillow. But tired as I was, my adventures for the day weren't complete.

I looked up to find myself back in a subway car, howls and screeches coming from every direction. I was back in Tokyo, right where the dream had left off.

The dark-skinned man with round spectacles and long gray dreadlocks stood up from where he was crouched next to the wounded soldier and looked at me.

"Ah, the cavalry has arrived."

I needed to figure out why I kept ending up back in this dream, this vision. I contemplated the man. This must be the friend Rose told me to look for. What was his name? Zuberi, that's right. I told him where I'd last seen Rose, Alex, and Mei—on the platform, surrounded by the Filth-infected, fighting their way through. He took in the information with a nod, then leaned back down to the wounded soldier.

"Even where Filth corrupts, Gaia's power endures. Take her power into yourself. Breathe it out. Will that your broken body is mended." Golden light poured from Zuberi into the soldier, healing his body. After a moment, the soldier started to move and stretch, then nodded at Zuberi.

I reached out a hand to the soldier and helped him stand.

"Good, good," Zuberi said, with a musical lilt to his words, as he surveyed the soldier's progress. "But even Gaia will be tested by what is to come."

Behind me, Rose, Mei, and Alex rushed into the subway car and slammed the door shut behind them.

Rose looked up at us, her hand pressed to her side as she panted. "Making a stand wasn't working out. I see you found Zuberi, Sarah. Good job."

Alex peered out the subway car window at the platform nearest to the car. "Yeah, about that...this side ain't looking much better, to be honest."

Zuberi stood and scolded them, "Now is not the time for argument!"

Mei turned to Alex and mumbled under her breath, but they were near enough that I could hear it. "Told you he would say that."

I shook my head, amazed anew out how realistic these visions— dreams?—were. The group all argued and bantered among themselves like old friends or a dysfunctional family together for a holiday dinner, and 'Sarah' was clearly a member. Surreptitiously, I gave my arm a quick hard pinch. It hurt.

Was this a dream or not? And if it wasn't, what was I here to witness?

Before I could contemplate it further, the doors at the top end of the car behind Zuberi opened, and we all ran out onto the platform to face the Filth-infected infesting it. Mei, Alex, and Rose all dove into the fight.

I stopped and took careful aim at one tentacle-headed man as he ran at me, his arms waving. The shot hit him squarely in the head, and he dropped like a sack in front of me.

"Well done!" Zuberi encouraged me.

We all fought as the Filth-infected attacked. As the bodies began to litter this platform, I realized that not all of them were strictly human-shaped anymore. Three more of the massive filthy hulk things ran toward us, and we destroyed them. I also saw creatures that looked like they had morphed into something with parts that were vaguely insect-shaped. Had these once been people before they were infected by a Filth parasite? I shuddered at the thought.

This was awful. Humanity was doomed if something like this Filth were to get out and infect a broad population. I hoped that this really was just a dream, and the bomb in Tokyo was contained as the news reports were saying. Gaia help us if it wasn't.

"Something's coming out of the ground!" Mei screamed.

I looked at where she was pointing, fear spiking in my body. A black cloud of Filth gathered at the far end of the platform and coalesced into a giant boar, taller than any of us at the shoulder, dripping in Filth, with glowing white eyes and strange markings on its body.

"What the bloody hell is that thing?" Alex yelled.

The boar pawed at the platform with its front hoof and began to charge.

"Watch out!" Mei yelled and jumped out of its path. We all scrambled toward the inside wall of the platform to avoid the massive pig. It roared past, leaving a trail of black slime in its path. It got to the far end of the platform, turned on its hooved legs, and trotted back toward us, its head lowered and tusks glinting with Filth.

I dodged behind a magazine kiosk to get out of its direct line of sight and tried to catch my breath. This thing would give me nightmares in my nightmares for weeks. It opened its maw and spewed forth a fountain of black goo, exhaling the void at us. We all jumped back to stay as far as possible from the Filth, while simultaneously trying to pierce its tough hide with our weapons. The six of us, including the soldier Zuberi had healed, were hitting the boar at point-blank range trying to wear it down.

Again and again, it charged us. We hid in corners and behind benches and pillars to avoid its bulk as it surged across the platform. Wounds littered its slimy black hide as we pummeled it with shots and spells, dripping ink-colored blood. There was no way to meet the boar face on. Its tusks and sheer mass guaranteed a bad end.

At last, Mei got in close enough to slash the tendon behind its front leg with her katana, and the beast roared and dropped to its knees. We rushed in and beat, stabbed, shot, and burned it where it sat, unable to maneuver. The boar collapsed on the platform, its life expended, and dissolved into a pond of black ichor.

But there was no time for celebration. We needed to get across the platform and start climbing out of the subway. We ran to the entrance on the far end of the platform. I ran up the stalled escalator stairs. The rest of the group tried to follow me, but the platform gate crashed down separating us. In the distance, I could hear the tell-tale growls and screams that indicated that more Filth infested were on the way.

"Go get help," Mei shouted at me, as the infected swarmed onto the platform behind us.

I hurried to the top of that flight of escalators and quickly looked left and right. I was blocked on the left from continuing up. To the right, there was another set of escalators headed down. I stopped and looked back at my trapped group of comrades, who had turned to face the incoming horde.

"They're not stopping!" Rose yelled.

"And they will not stop," Zuberi intoned in his deep, musical voice. "This is all to hold us back."

"Well, top marks for effort," Alex said, his words dripping with sarcasm.

"Look out! It's all coming down!" Mei yelled, covering her head with her arms.

That catalyzed me. I needed to get help and fast. There was nothing I could do for them where I was.

I dashed down the escalator stairs to the right but stopped in my tracks at what I saw there, the hair on my arms and neck standing on end. I struggled to draw in a breath as the muscles of my body constricted in terror and horrified awe.

The edge of the platform had crumbled off into a giant space-like void. A cosmic sort of red glow shined in, highlighting what remained of the concrete support pillars, rendering them two-toned in the half-light.

My mind boggled trying to make sense of it. What was I seeing? Was this the end of the universe? The floor of the platform that hadn't crumbled away was covered with roundish Filth pods and branches, overgrown like some terrible disease cells. I could see why Alex had called it a cancer. Whatever was happening, it seemed like this Filth was a symptom.

Two weirdly glowing giant moon-like objects hung in the starry expanse of the blackness, with space dust trailing away from them. Asteroids tumbled through the space near the platform edge weightlessly, spinning and turning as they passed by. A metro train subway car was suspended in mid-air, pulled up alongside the broken platform.

I edged, numbly, to the broken ledge of the platform, my guts churning with nausea and fear as I tried to see what was below. I was deep underground in the earth in Japan, not at the end of the galaxy. I looked down at the endless drop into nothing.

Below the broken platform loomed the vastness of space. My head spun, and I wobbled. My heart raced as adrenaline shot into my bloodstream, the unbridled fear stabbing me in the chest, and I stumbled backward. The pain shot upward through my neck to my brain, and I grabbed my head as I collapsed.

CHAPTER NINE

Enemies

June 20, 2012

I AWOKE THE NEXT MORNING, depressed by my dream of darkness and Filth. Then I thought about the fight I'd had in the street with Sevenoir, which depressed me further. Frustrated with myself at not knowing what to do in either case, I got out of bed and jumped into the shower to prepare for another day of training.

I arrived at the Crucible shortly before eight o'clock. Sevenoir was not yet sitting at the bar, drinking his breakfast. Plimmy's comment from the pub about him following me jumped into my mind at the sight of the empty bar stool. Why would Sevenoir be following me?

Nah. She had to be wrong about that. If he were following me, I wouldn't be having such a hard time finding him. I sighed, my earlier depression welling up again. I'd track him down sooner or later to apologize.

I made my way down the stairs while my mind wandered some more, reviewing the questions raised by my dream. What was the Filth? Was this what was really happening in Tokyo? Who was Sarah? Did I need medication and a therapist? I couldn't decide whether I should tell someone about it or not. And who would I tell? Sevenoir? Plimmy? Brigadier Lethe? They'd think I was crazy for sure.

"You're early," Lethe commented as I stepped down onto the marble practice floor.

I gave him a tired smile as I dropped my bag near the half wall separating the practice area from the lounge. Using the stairs, I took care to ensure my muscles were well stretched as the day's practice would entail more footwork. I'd learned the hard way just how many muscles that used on my lower body.

When I was done, Brigadier Lethe motioned me over, his usual scowl firmly in place. I'd begun to realize that was a natural state for him and so I didn't take it personally. I had enough on my mind already.

"I need to focus on some other recruits this morning, soldier, so practice advancing with a jump and lunge, and if Sevenoir decides to grace us with his presence, we'll have you do some work together."

Nodding, I gathered my things and moved over to the west side of the room, where there was a more forgiving practice area. The last couple of days had taught me that the marble was hell on my heels and knees, but Lethe had set up a sparring mat near the melee target practice area that had a little more give. Once I'd gotten over my aversion of being near the chained rakshasa demons, I'd started working out there.

I was on my third round of jumps and lunges when I noticed a tall, platinum blond man walking down the west-side steps to the practice floor. What was it with Templars and white hair?

At first, I thought it was Sevenoir rolling in from whatever debauchery he'd gotten up to the night before, but I got a look at this man's face and realized my error. He was handsome, but with a stern visage, wearing a long black overcoat that ended slightly below his knees, loose cargo pants, a black T-shirt, and a pair of sturdy-looking black boots. An ornate Templar cross hung around his neck from a chain. A five o'clock shadow covered his jaw, which only served to reinforce the impression I got that this was an agent who took his job seriously. If anything, he was the anti-Sevenoir and looked like an avenging angel, rather than a rogue Lothario.

"Ho, Drenneth!" Lethe called in greeting. "Good to see you in here. How did yesterday's skirmishes at the Fusang Projects in China go?"

He approached Drenneth, and they clasped arms, Lethe slapping him on the back. Drenneth responded in a deep rumbling voice, but I couldn't quite make out what he said.

China? Foiled in my attempts to eavesdrop, I turned my attention back to my footwork and focused, trying to apply all the guidance Lethe had given me. I worked on my step size and varying the tempo as he taught me. My footwork had improved as my muscles were conditioned to the legwork. I could sustain almost 20 minutes now without wanting to die, which was good because I would be getting a blade to work with any day now, and I could hardly wait.

I heard a footstep and looked up. Drenneth had moved over to a rakshasa near me and had pulled out a long practice katana from the weapon case and secured it at his left hip with a sash. His own sword, a vicious looking one-handed blade with a glowing red gem in the pommel and top edge serrated with spikes, was hung by its scabbard on a rack to the right of the practice area.

I was thrilled! Finally, a chance to see someone work with a blade. Abandoning any pretense at practicing my footwork anymore, I stopped to watch. While I watched, he began to methodically practice hitting his target with quick and precise strikes, striking downward first, then reversing direction and striking again instantly in an upward motion. My mind boggled at how quickly he could attack the bound rakshasa.

"What do you call that move?" I asked, intrigued.

Drenneth gave no response.

I tried again, a little louder this time. "Excuse me. What do you call that move?"

"I heard you the first time," Drenneth rumbled. "I'm practicing. You should be too."

My face got hot at his dismissal, and I felt disappointment well up. This day sucked. I just wanted to learn how to wield a blade! "I'm sorry for interrupting," I said in a small voice, and went back to my lunges.

He continued on with the quick strikes for a few more minutes as I advanced, jumped, and lunged, varying my approach each time, per Lethe's instruction.

"It's called *Tsubame Gaeshi*."

I turned my head at his voice and stopped my footwork.

"It's a technique from ancient Japan. The name means 'turning swallow cut' because of movement of a swallow's tail in flight," Drenneth explained, continuing to practice the move. He stopped finally and turned to me. "I've been using it for years, but one can always get better with diligence."

"Thank you for explaining. I hope to start learning blade work myself soon," I said gesturing at my legs and smiling wryly. "Hence why Brigadier Lethe has me practicing footwork."

"Footwork is key," he agreed, turning back to his target.

He began practicing another blade technique. This movement was so graceful, watching it was like watching water trickle over stones. It was mesmerizing. Part of my brain recognized that this was a more straightforward technique that probably took much less energy to use.

I realized I was gawking and once again turned back to my footwork. Advance, advance, lunge. Advance, jump, lunge. Again.

"Flowing strike."

I looked up at him, confused.

"That's the name of that technique. You use it to attack a single opponent. As opposed to 'crescent fang,'" he said as he moved forward until he was standing midway between two of the bound rakshasas and swung his blade in a crescent-shaped arc that hit both of them, "which you use for more than one. Very useful if you find yourself surrounded."

Drenneth turned back to me, his katana at rest in his right hand, the tip of the blade pointing at the floor, and eyed me speculatively.

"Both are simple moves that don't require a lot of preparation. They will buy you time to assess your opponent's strengths and weaknesses to prepare your strategy in combat."

He sheathed the sword, and crossed the space between us and, pulling the scabbard from the sash around his waist, he grasped it palm down near the middle, and handed the sheathed katana to me horizontally. "Here, you try."

I reached out eagerly for the weapon with my right hand, my scarred palm tingling.

Drenneth shook his head and gave me a slight smile. "Tradition requires you to put both your palms up to receive a katana. That is how you show respect to a teacher or anyone with more skill or power than you have."

I nodded my understanding and put my hands up as he suggested. He placed the sheath in my hands. It felt cool against my skin, and my right palm itched with the desire to hold the blade by the pommel. I resisted the urge and stood there patiently.

"I assume you've never actually used a katana before, correct?" he asked, and I acknowledged that I hadn't. "Okay, then. Let's start first with some basics of handling and drawing a blade. First, give it back to me the same way you took it from me, palms up. That is the correct way to return the blade as a student."

He took the sword back, pushed the scabbard back in the sash at his waist, then turned slightly to the left so I could watch him in profile. He pushed the hilt of the katana forward slightly with his left thumb. That, he explained, was called breaking the seal on the scabbard.

"In Iaidō, you draw the sheath forward with your left hand as you pull the katana out. The blade flips forward as you draw to point at your opponent. This is a fast, graceful draw that shows you mean business."

Drenneth demonstrated the maneuver. It was scary how fast he moved. He resheathed the sword, then did it again twice more slowly so I could see what he was doing.

"Don't ever break a seal unless you are prepared to fight. It is an open threat to someone trained in fighting with a blade."

Other open threats, he explained, included reaching across your body and grasping the hilt without actually drawing the blade, or pulling the sheath forward but not entirely out of the sash, to make it accessible for a draw.

Good to know! If I'd listened to my itching palm, I would have grabbed the scabbard from him and whipped the blade out without that instruction. I realized that there was an ocean of information here I had yet to learn, yet I was glad to begin to dip my toes in it finally.

"Iaidō is the practice of learning to be a warrior. It has standard forms, called 'kata,' which train the body to learn to use the katana as an extension of itself," Drenneth said. "It also trains the mind to develop 'mushin'—the single-mindedness necessary to face your opponent with honor and spiritual harmony in the face of death, or in our case, anima exhaustion. Think of it as a kind of yoga or tai-chi with a blade."

I was so caught up in Drenneth's lesson that didn't hear Brigadier Lethe approach until he spoke. "I see you're giving Wedd a bit of a lesson with the blade."

Hands on his hips, Lethe nodded his approval, then eyed me with suspicion. He had learned to read me pretty well in the past week. "Don't get too excited. You will start with a wooden practice sword in a few days, I think. For now, go over to the other side of the room and brush up on your blood magic and chaos spells. It won't do for you to forget those in the meantime."

I grumbled under my breath at being sent away, but grabbed my stuff and dutifully wandered back to the east end of the practice area, while Drenneth and Lethe continued to discuss other concerns out of the range of my hearing.

"So, do you want to go?" Zamira Vata asked me.

We were sitting out on the patio of The Horned God once more. Zamira had spotted me on the way in the door of the pub and had come over to join Plimmy and me for a drink. Plimmy was having her usual tea. I had reverted back to the St. Swithin's, and Zamira had a bottle of Stella Artois in her hand. We were discussing the Summer Solstice, which was happening early tomorrow morning right after midnight.

145

"Come on, Wedd. It's customary if you're new to London to spend your first solstice out at Stonehenge, howling at the moon," she said with a smirk as she set the bottle back on the picnic bench. "We'll get a special access visit, so we can go right in next to the sarsen stones. Nothing like that touristy tosh where you have to stay on the outside."

"Is Konrad coming?" I asked, warily. I liked Zamira, but I had no desire to see Konrad Engel again any time soon.

Zamira threw back her head and laughed aloud. "He's no fan of the wilderness, that one. Spent too much time in the pretty halls of politics, he did."

I looked over at Plimmy for guidance.

"Sounds like good fun, dear. A chance to run around with people your own age. I used to love the Solstice parties at Stonehenge," she said, a far-away look in her eye. "Who knows, you may run into some neo-druid types. I read an article in *The Independent* that said they make quite a showing there on the Summer Solstice to watch the sunrise and celebrate the longest day of the year." She got up and went over to talk to the patio waitress about getting us another round of drinks.

"It's settled then," Zamira said with satisfaction as Plimmy stepped away. "Be here at quarter to midnight, and we'll go together so we can be there precisely at 12:09 a.m. for the actual astronomical solstice itself."

"How will we get there?" I asked. I knew Stonehenge wasn't that far from London, out on the Salisbury Plain, near Wiltshire. It was about 90 miles from Ealdwic, I figured, which was at least a couple hours' drive, presuming that Zamira had a car.

"There's an anima well nearby. We'll just jump in when the time is right, no worries, and be there in the blink of an eye."

I nodded my head in agreement, although I had a strange feeling that there was something here I didn't understand. If this was a sunrise event, why were we going in the middle of the night?

"Oh and, wear sturdy clothes and boots. It can get dirty out there in the fields around the henge," she advised me. "I'll bring us a flask to share. And, uh, don't forget your weapons. Just as a precaution, yah? Nothing to worry about, but good to be prepared."

I arrived back at The Horned God just after 11:30 p.m. The pub was full of people, laughing and celebrating the beginning of summer. I spotted Zamira in her regular place at the bar and walked up to her. She tipped her pint at me then turned to the bartender and called for a bottle of St. Swithin's.

"You all set then?" she asked, eyeing my blue jeans, hiking boots, and leather jacket.

I took the bottle from the bartender and nodded. "Yep, I think so. I've got the rest in my backpack although I'm not sure why they're necessary."

"Never hurts to be cautious," she said with a wink, then nodded her head toward the front door. "Ah, there's Sev now. We're almost ready to roll."

I whirled around to see Sevenoir approaching us in his usual black T-shirt, jeans, black leather jacket, and bunny ears. "Oh."

"Ladies," he said as he approached the bar.

"I didn't...I didn't realize you'd be joining us tonight," I fumbled awkwardly, caught off guard. "I've been looking for you. I, uh, have something I need to say."

"Well, spit it out then."

My face flushed. This was not how I envisioned apologizing to him. I cleared my throat. "I'm, uh, sorry for what I said the other day. It was inexcusable. And, uh, thank you for helping me with the puzzle in the Mithraeum. I'm sorry if you got into trouble over it."

Sevenoir waved my apology away with his hand. "Ah, I got the broadside of Julia's tongue, but that's nothing new. So, you're joining us to do battle at the Stonehenge, eh? Your training must have progressed well in the last couple of days."

Battle? What was he talking about?

"Drenneth is going to join us, Z," he added, as he motioned to the bartender for a drink. "He should be along in just a minute."

"Do we know who the fifth will be?" Zamira asked him. At my look of concern, she directed the next comment to me. "Don't worry about it, Wedd. It's customary for there to be five in the Templar party for a visit to Stonehenge."

"No one's signed up yet, but I'm sure someone will show," Sevenoir answered. "Just as well so there are no complaints about a pre-made party."

"I've got the uniform for her in my bag," Zamira added.

Listening to their exchange was starting to make me anxious that I didn't know what I was getting into here. Party? Uniform? Was this a costume blow-out Solstice celebration or something? Some kind of pagan ritual? Still, it was fun and exciting to be included with the group of young Templar agents, so I decided to stay cool so they wouldn't think I was a dork.

Around us, the revelers chatted loudly, laughed, and drank their libations. Upstairs I could hear the disco music in full swing on the dance floor. This evening was shaping up to be the most fun I'd had since I got to London. After the week I'd had so far, I needed to blow off a little steam.

We walked together to the Ealdwic Park, keeping an eye peeled for trouble. Pedestrian traffic was frowned upon in the park after dark, so we were pushing our luck with the local constabulary to be out here.

Because I was new to traveling by anima well, Zamira took my hand as we ported out to Stonehenge. Drenneth went first, disappearing in a shimmer of light before me.

When it came time for our turn, Zamira squeezed my hand and *pulled* me with her. It felt like being submerged in a tub full of seltzer water, a warm damp sizzling and a flash of golden light, and then I could see the landscape change around me.

It turned into a series of industrial walls, cordoning us off from the greater night landscape. I could see the inky sky peppered with stars above us—we were clearly outside, but the area around the well was blocked off in some fashion. On the north end in front of us was a wooden and chain-link exit, but the gates were closed. I could see lighting on the landscape beyond the gate. I wondered if that was Stonehenge itself, all lit up.

Sevenoir shimmered into the well behind me, and I stepped forward to give him a little room. Or at least I thought it was Sevenoir.

Gone were the bunny ears and the leather jacket and blue jeans. Instead, he was encased head-to-toe in a white leather uniform of sorts, with deep red accents on the shoulders and arms. There were two gold stripes on his right sleeve and a white four-armed cross over his heart on the dark red background. The uniform had a white hood with a red stripe edged in gold, and he was wearing a white mask, like a disguised reveler from Carnivàle. He had white leather gloves covering both hands, and his weapons were now prominently displayed—an assault rifle on his back and an elemental focus on his hip.

I looked over at Zamira, who was still holding my hand and saw she was in a similar get-up, although hers had more gold on the uniform overall.

Drenneth was standing to our left and was wearing a full suit of stylized armor, not unlike that of the mysterious man I'd seen at the review panel. Drenneth's armor was gray and dark red, with shining gold highlights on the shoulder guards, chest covering, and leg protection covering the tops of his thighs. He had a red hood, and a face guard with eye slits with the four-armed cross emblazoned on top. His sword hung at his waist. He pushed his mask up while we waited.

Zamira pushed up her own mask and opened her backpack. She pulled out a white and dark red uniform and handed it to me, before setting the backpack at the side of the well. "Since you haven't got one of your own yet, I'll let you use one of mine."

I stared at her, my mouth agape. "What is happening here? How did you suddenly change into these costumes?"

"Practice, and they're not costumes, they're uniforms," Zamira said with a wry grin. "Sorry for the trick. This is the Secret War, Wedd. It's a scrimmage of sorts—us against the Dragon and Illuminati here at Stonehenge tonight. It starts in just a few minutes. Get dressed."

My face went red. Trick indeed. What had I gotten myself into? I was a little mad at Zamira for her sneakiness, but I was also excited to see what the Secret War was all about. It couldn't be too dangerous if they all were here to do it.

I set my backpack on the ground near the wall of the enclosure and quickly pulled the uniform on over my jeans and T-shirt. Zamira's boots were too big for me, so I left my own hiking boots on, pulling the uniform pants down best as I could to make do. I stuffed her boots into my backpack and pulled out my blood and chaos foci.

"Drenneth's going to be our 'tank,'" Zamira continued, "which means he's going to try to hold their attention and take damage, leaving the rest of us free to deal damage to the other teams."

"Here's hoping we get a fifth team member or it will be over quick enough," Sevenoir grumbled.

A scoreboard suddenly lit up over the gate at the north end of the enclosure, with a clock timer and three icons—the Illuminati blue triangle, the Dragon green circle, and the four-armed red cross of the Templars. The scores, at the moment, were all zero.

"Here's the strategy, Wedd," Zamira said. "We're going to all run out there in a minute and start the match. We have to hold the center of the henge, like King of the Hill. Whatever you do, try to stay inside the inner circle the whole time. It's how we make points, and it's how we'll win the match. You can dodge behind the stones temporarily if you need to get out of the crossfire, but stay close to Drenneth. He'll help protect you. Sevenoir and I will be working to deal damage to the other teams and moving around a lot."

I heard a shout across the field, presumably coming from one of the other teams. Drenneth grumbled under his breath, while Sevenoir shouted back in return.

"We'll see who kicks whose ass this time, Lurdtz," he yelled.

"You know them?" I asked Sevenoir.

"Oh yeah, there are definitely Dragon and Illuminati we see on a regular basis here. Some of them are a good challenge. Others just have big mouths."

"How do we fight them without hurting them?" I asked.

Zamira shook her head slightly and gave me a strange look. "What do you mean?"

"I mean, is it like flag football, where you pull off a flag or something?"

"Nope," Sevenoir said definitively, and threw back his head and laughed. "You really fight the other team. You'll experience anima exhaustion. Maybe multiple times during the fifteen minutes of the match, if that's what you're worried about."

My face filled with alarm. I had suffered anima exhaustion back at Innsmouth Academy, and it was a devastating experience. The idea of doing it for *sport* seemed outrageous. I edged away from them both toward the anima well. Maybe it wasn't too late to leave this place if I could figure out how the well worked.

"If you back out now, we'll be short two team members, which almost certainly means we'll lose. The rest of the groups all have five members on their teams," Zamira said. I scowled at her. I didn't like being pushed into this *at all*.

Sevenoir pushed up his mask and faced me. "Look, Wedd, the point of this is to hone our fighting skills and to learn not to be afraid of 'death.' As Bees, we don't die anymore, and while anima exhaustion is unpleasant, it's a whole lot better than the alternative. To be really effective agents out in the field, we have to run *toward* danger. The Secret War gives us a chance to pit our skills against other agents to know where we stand and to see other fighting techniques and approaches. Plus, at the end of the day, it's just good fun."

Before I could respond, I heard the swoosh of the well behind me as my teammates cheered. Finally, a fifth person was here to join our team.

He was dressed in a uniform as well, but it was different than the others. He was wearing a white hood, but the white mask covering his face protruded in front into a beak, like a plague doctor mask. He had a black and gray harness with a supply pack, a white and red jacket and pants, red gloves, and black boots trimmed with gold. He popped up his mask and turned to the group.

"Hey, HolloPoint," Drenneth called. "Great! That makes five for the team, and we have a healer."

HolloPoint gave Drenneth a high five and said hello to Zamira and Sevenoir. They introduced me, and I gave a small wave.

151

A woman's voice came over a public announcement system. "It's 12:08 a.m. United Kingdom Time. The game is starting in 60 seconds."

"It's time." Drenneth nodded to the group and pulled his mask down. The rest of us followed suit.

"It's almost Solstice," Sevenoir said, rubbing his hands together with poorly disguised glee.

"Who is that speaking?" I asked.

"That's an adjudicator from the Council of Venice," Zamira explained. "They're here as neutral observers to make sure the rules are followed and things don't get out of hand. They make certain the teams are on equal footing."

Alrighty, then. I wasn't sure what to think about this. I was nervous and excited, but uneasy about what was ahead. My new friends seemed happy and enthused about the coming match.

"The game is starting in 30 seconds."

Argh. I was running out of time.

HolloPoint was wearing fist weapons and began sharpening them with a loud twang. I could feel anima radiating from the metal claws. I realized I'd better figure out what spells I was going to use.

Since this was a match against multiple players, I figured I'd choose my chaos and blood spells for broad hitting attacks. I could bring my dread sigil attack, and perhaps a runic hex. It would help heal me slightly while doing damage to the combatants I hit with it. But I'd use chaos spells for my base. Turmoil would be my primary attack, with schism as a follow-up. Entropy would increase the damage I did. And of course, I could unleash pandemonium to stop multiple attackers at once by throwing them all to the ground.

I could see the appeal of thinking through how best to attack and protect oneself from an unknown type of enemy. My experience up until now had been mainly against the known enemies at Innsmouth Academy. This was a whole different ball game.

But at last, I was ready to go, and not a minute too soon.

"The game is starting in 10 seconds." The announcer's voice cut through my thoughts, and I took in a deep, fortifying breath.

"Remember, Wedd," Zamira said, "stick with Drenneth. He'll help protect you until you get your bearings."

"The game is starting."

The gates swung open and our team ran through them onto the field. I tried not to gawk as we jogged across the grassy expanse toward the massive sarsen stones of Stonehenge. Of course, I'd seen pictures of the famous monument but had never been this close. The larger stones comprised an outer ring, and they loomed over us as we approached them. A broad fountain of gold anima energy streamed out from the middle of the monument. I could see an illuminated blue triangle roughly 120 degrees to the right of where we entered and a similar green circle 120 degrees to the left. That must be where the other teams entered.

Drenneth charged forward, headed to the center inside the first circle of stones. I followed him closely, trying to keep up, as he dodged around a smaller set of bluestones set inside the greater circle. These varied in height, but were only about as tall as a person, compared to the 30-foot-tall sarsen stones.

Zamira drew her pistols and peered around one of them at the tangle of bodies in the middle, while Sevenoir strafed to an open area on the right, firing regular bursts with his assault rifle. Drenneth entered the melee swinging his sword around him in a broad circle, hitting the green and blue uniformed combatants like a truck. I did my best to follow Drenneth, careful to stay out of his swing, kicking with my legs to create turmoil.

I felt a sharp pain in my back and realized I'd been hit by a shot from a sniper. HolloPoint sharpened his fist weapon releasing anima, and I felt a cool soothing as he healed my wound.

OK, this was definitely different.

I turned to see who'd shot at me and saw a gas-mask-wearing blue-suit Illuminati just as another bullet hit me in the chest. Ouch! Thankfully it was stopped by the armor of my uniform, but that hurt!

Argh. I was a sitting duck out here in the middle, and I was going to give a little back to that guy. I ran toward the sniper, leaving the center of the circle, trying to reach him with my chaos spells to return fire.

"Remember! Stay in the center," Zamira yelled at me. "Don't get lured away."

I broke off the chase, and he turned again toward me and shot me at range, this time hitting my leg. I stumbled and yelled as pain seared my nervous system. I was standing between the outer circle and inner circles with no place to hide. One of his Illuminati teammates turned and hit me with a hammer knocking me up in the air and flat on my back. I lay there, struggling for breath, pain searing my nerves. Beside me, I could see a fighter in a green uniform in the same spot. She rolled to her feet and struck me with a blood spell, maleficium, I think. The damage was too high. I reached anima exhaustion and collapsed on the field.

With a whoosh, I found myself ported—reassembled? resurrected?—to the anima well where we started the match. I stood there in the golden glow of the tingling anima energy, trying to make sense of what I was feeling. I could tell that I'd been hurt, but it was gone now, and the pain was like a distant memory.

The gates to the area were shut, and I stood there, shaking out my hands and my legs, grimacing with the memory of the damage that I couldn't feel any more. Endorphins flowed through me. My body's relief at being out of pain was profound, like I'd just had a shot of fast-acting painkillers.

It was much harder to adapt to anima exhaustion mentally than physically, it seemed. I remembered vividly what it felt like being shot, cursed, and hit with a hammer, and that was making it very hard to want to go experience it again. I looked around for an exit.

Next to me, HolloPoint resurrected in the well with a whoosh, distracting me.

"Bastards ganged up on me," he said with disgust. "They locked me down so I couldn't heal."

In front of us, the gates to the field opened again, and I reluctantly followed HolloPoint back out to the fight. We crossed the area rapidly, and I could see Zamira once again hiding behind one of the rocks of the inner circle, diving out to fire her pistols, and then returning to safety. Sevenoir was firing his assault rifle at the Dragon team member who was dressed in armor like Drenneth's.

The Dragon, who appeared to be a woman, and Drenneth were exchanging sword blows, parrying and blocking one another in the center of the circle. Another Dragon in armor, this one male, was edging toward Drenneth, trying to double down on the damage, while the blood magic user, the one who hit me with maleficium, struck him from behind.

I had to help him!

I ran straight for the center of the circle where they were all fighting and cast pandemonium, throwing the Dragon team members to the ground. Behind me, HolloPoint sharpened his first weapons, and I could hear Drenneth's breathing ease as the heals flowed to him.

"The Dragon is dominating the center!" The female announcer voice called out.

What? How could that be? I did a quick count and sure enough. Only Drenneth, HolloPoint, and I were in the center, whereas the Dragon had four team members there. The Dragon healer, dressed in an ornate black and gold bodysuit embroidered with exotic dragon-like imagery, also wore fist weapons. His arms steadily worked, sharpening his weapons, to generate the anima healing to sustain his team.

"Thanks, Hadad!" The female Dragon tank yelled, as she scrambled to her feet and took another swing at Drenneth.

The Illuminati sniper who had cornered me previously was now focused on HolloPoint, who dodged behind the sarsen stones of the inner heel of the henge to avoid the sniper's shots.

With his target no longer available, the sniper turned once again on me and opened fire. I backed away, only to realize that another Illuminati team member had cast an elemental manifestation of electricity and little bolts of lightning were sizzling up and down my body, messing with my muscle coordination. I moved out of range as quickly as I could and turned back to the center to see where I should go next.

I was too slow, however, and I'd moved outside of HolloPoint's healing range. Before I knew it, the sniper had a bead on me, and I once again collapsed from anima exhaustion.

And, back to the anima well for me.

I was hopping mad, and my body was tingling. This was frustrating! I could hardly get my bearings in the fight before I was down again. These Illuminati snipers were a problem, and I couldn't get near enough to them with chaos magic to do any damage in return.

With a whoosh, Sevenoir popped up next to me in the well. He dusted off his uniform and stepped out of the well, waiting at the ready for the gates to drop to let him back in.

"I am no good at this," I wailed at him.

"Stop standing in the open areas, for Pete's sake." He growled at me, apparently annoyed by his own anima exhaustion. "Use the stones to break line-of-sight with them. If they can't see you, they can't hit you. The Illuminati aren't in this to win as a team. They play a solo game trying to get a high kill count, so they sit outside of the center and take pot shots from range. You've got to stay moving to keep them from targeting you."

I looked up at the scoreboard. The Dragon had 30 points, and we had 15. The Illuminati were still at zero.

Huh. Looked like Sevenoir was right.

"And focus your fire on the healers. If they go down, so does everyone else on the team."

Punctuating Sevenoir's comment with a whoosh, HolloPoint appeared in the well next to us.

"The bastards keep immobilizing me so I can't heal," he groused. The gates to the area opened, and we ran back in once again.

"The Dragon is dominating the center!" The announcer repeated. Damn it! We were losing the match.

I ran back toward the inner area of the henge, keeping my eyes peeled for healers. I spotted the Dragon healer—Hadad, they'd called him—standing between two stones for cover. Making sure I stayed moving, I glanced around for the Illuminati equivalent and realized that I didn't see anyone on that team who appeared to be healing.

I ran from cover to cover, toward Hadad. I didn't have the best spells to use on a single target, but at a minimum, I could bring him down with pandemonium. I might not do much damage, but I could at least keep him busy.

Sevenoir and Zamira were now inside the circle as well, with HolloPoint between them. Drenneth kept swinging his sword at the two Dragon tanks. I saw Zamira finish off the Dragon blood user with a pistol shot, while Sevenoir kept a close eye out for Illuminati snipers. All five of us, I realized, were in the center.

"The Templars are dominating the center!" The announcer intoned.

Elation rushed through my body. We were earning match points!

I harried the Dragon healer with my chaos spells. He healed the damage I was causing easily, while also keeping his teammates in armor alive as they engaged with Drenneth.

Hmm. This wasn't working very well. I watched as one of the Illuminati snipers got HolloPoint in his sites, and down went our healer again.

I spied the red cross-hairs on my own chest and sighed with irritation. I couldn't get away fast enough once they had a bead on me. The shot exploded there in a fine, red mist, and I crumbled to the field a third time.

Whoosh! I was back in the anima well. I looked up at the scoreboard. There were six minutes left in the match, and the Dragon had 275 points now. We were inching up on them with 255. The Illuminati apparently hadn't yet set foot in the center as they were still at 0.

We needed to be able to take the center and hold it long enough to get a significant lead. What we needed, I realized, was a healer for the healer. If I could get a healing spell off when HolloPoint couldn't and vice versa, together we could keep the rest of the group alive. Sevenoir and Zamira did enough damage that with some focused firing, they could take out the various Dragon damage dealers. The Illuminati didn't seem to be going for a match score at all, so really, short of not letting them kill our team, there wasn't much to strategize on. Having two healers would go a long way to keep them from being able to do that.

"What if I healed too?"

"What?" HolloPoint turned from where he was standing at the gate to look at me.

I grabbed my blood focus and thought about the spells I would need. This was definitely a change from damage, but if I could keep a blood shield on HolloPoint, it would probably work. Plus, then I wouldn't have to worry about killing other people.

"I'm going to heal too so I can help keep you alive," I said. "Because they keep locking you down…?"

I couldn't see his face behind the white mask, but he shrugged. "Right-o. Suit yourself."

I cut my finger with the end of my athame and tossed it back in my backpack, then began to cast a mend spell on HolloPoint. A golden shield of anima popped up around him, and he gave me a thumbs up. The gates fell, and we ran back to the field. I stayed low and behind the stones, moving continually as I kept him targeted.

When one of the snipers took a shot at him, I cast a sanctuary spell, stopping some of the incoming damage and quickly healing him back to full health. I was starting to feel exhilarated. HolloPoint fired off a huge healing spell that brought our entire team back to full health.

"The Templars are dominating the center!"

This was working! I was filled with elation and stopped moving long enough to get winged by a stray bullet. It stung lightly, but I paid it no mind, casting a mend spell on myself and then turned back to put a blood shield on HolloPoint.

I could see Drenneth block a hammer attack from the female Dragon tank, then turn and knock the male tank in the helmet with the end of his blade. I topped off his health with a convalesce spell. Zamira moved in a circle as she fired off a round of bullets from her pistols with such grace it looked like she was dancing. I jumped up and down at her, and clapped my hands in delight and cast a big golden blood shield around her.

Yay! This was fun!

"What in the bloody hell?" Sevenoir yelled at me across the center. "What's wrong with you? Stop doing that!"

What was he going on about? I looked down as I clapped my glowing hands and then across the glowing field at the nimbus of gold that surrounded him.

Hmm…That was an awful lot of glowing for a fight on a dark night. Looked like I needed to check in with my emotions. With all these healing spells, I was in danger of magical blood martyrdom. If I wasn't careful, I would bring on my own anima exhaustion. I cast a runic hex at a Dragon damage dealer who was hiding near a swath of rocks, and she yelled as it hit her. The inherent corruption of that spell brought my blood martyrdom down to manageable levels and took the golden sheen off of the scene for me.

Yeesh. I was definitely more practiced at dealing with too much blood magic corruption, but martyrdom was equally dangerous, it seemed, because you simply stopped caring about your own safety.

A woman in an Illuminati uniform ran forward into the center of the circle and laid down a swath of frost on the ground. She then cast fireballs and fire bolts at the group in the center.

Time stopped. *Deja vu.*

Something about her seemed so familiar to me. Was this another trick of the martyrdom?

I shook my head and threw a hex at her before I began casting mend spells again. They were small enough that they did not pose a huge problem controlling the martyrdom. HolloPoint had everyone in good shape health-wise. Drenneth was beating back the tanks, and Sevenoir and Zamira had the damage dealers locked down.

The rest of the Illuminati team rushed the center, and for a few minutes there were fully fifteen of us scrimmaging against one another, bullets flying, hammers pounding, swords slashing. It was crazy and glorious. I kept an eye on my teammates, casting a nearly constant string of healing spells, but remembering to occasionally pepper my opponents with hexes to keep the martyrdom manageable.

Then suddenly, it was over.

The announcer's voice rang out. "Game ended. The Templars are the Summer Solstice Match winning faction with 592 points. Dragon in second place with 577 points. Illuminati in third with 186 points."

There were cheers from my team and groans from the combatants in the circle.

And with that, I felt a whoosh around me and found myself back with my team at the anima well, the gates to the playing field shut. We grabbed our things and chattering happily among ourselves, ported back to Ealdwic Park and headed to The Horned God to celebrate our win.

June 21, 2012

Bang, bang, bang!

Dragging myself from sleep, I sat up in bed at the noise. Knocking. Someone was knocking at my door.

My head pounded in response. Our celebration had been lively and the drinks copious. I had stumbled back to my flat around 3 a.m. I opened an eye and looked around the room. Judging by the lack of light coming in the windows, I hadn't been sleeping long.

Bang, bang, bang!

Again with the knocking! What was with these people?

I reached for my robe and shuffled across my bedroom out to the living area.

"Yes?" I croaked at the locked door.

"Message for Blodwedd Mallory from Richard Sonnac," an all-business male voice boomed from behind the closed door.

I opened the door, leaning my head against the frame, and looked up at him with bleary eyes. "We've got to stop meeting like this."

The tall, dark-haired, uniformed Templar cracked a smile and handed me a sealed letter. I took it and watched as he pivoted on his heel and headed down the stairs of my building.

I sat there a second, blinking, and cursing the fun from the night before. I flipped on the overhead light and broke the seal on the envelope.

Ms. Blodwedd Mallory
No. 5-F May Queen Market
London, England UK

Mr. Richard Sonnac
Temple Hall
London, England UK

June 21, 2012

Dear Ms. Mallory,

Your presence is requested at Temple Hall at 7 a.m. sharp
on Thursday, June 21, 2012.

I don't think I need to tell you again that timeliness and
business attire are *apropos*. Bring the uniform.

Regards,

R. Sonnac

At this rate, Richard Sonnac needed to get these little
summonses for me pre-printed. I scooted my back down the wall
and sat on the floor. Bring the uniform? Ugh. I was apparently in
trouble again, this time for my participation in last night's battle.

I held my head in my hands. Where was my backpack and was
the uniform in it? I struggled to remember the evening.

Looking around my living area, I spotted the backpack sitting on
the floor by the couch. I grabbed it and unzipped the bag, relieved
to find the uniform within. At least I could comply with that
portion of the request.

I knew from my experience last Sunday that 7 a.m. was probably
about an hour and a half after sunrise, so I stumbled into the

kitchen and put on a kettle for tea and headed to the bathroom to shower.

Freshly showered, I felt better and went to my room to get dressed. I dug through my wardrobe for something that passed for business attire. Settling on some black trousers and my white button-down blouse, I pulled my damp hair back into a bun and put the Templar cross necklace my mother gave me around my neck. I found my black low-heeled pumps under my bed and slipped them on.

The kettle started to whistle from the kitchen, so I unplugged it and made myself some breakfast tea and grabbed some digestive crackers and yogurt from the fridge. A little tea and some food in my stomach went a long way toward helping me feel human as well.

Right. No use putting it off any longer. I grabbed my backpack and emptied out everything but the uniform, my weapons, and my wallet, and slipped it on my back. I locked my apartment door and headed down the stairs to the street.

Outside, the morning light was just starting to fill the street. I stepped out on the sidewalk as Plimmy was retrieving her morning paper.

"Oh, hello dear. You're up early," she said to me as I approached.

"Yes, unfortunately," I answered her with a wry grin. "Another early morning meeting."

"Did you have fun last night with your friends at Stonehenge?"

It took me just a moment to track back to the fact that Zamira and I had been discussing the visit to Stonehenge in front of Plimmy before I knew it was part of the Secret War.

"Um yes. It was very…different than I expected but exciting and fun."

"Oh, good. I'm glad you're meeting some more people your age," she said, kindly. "As much as I enjoy your company over tea, you need opportunities to socialize since you're new to Ealdwic."

"I think I did a little too much socializing," I agreed with a sorry laugh. "It's made this morning feel even earlier."

She chuckled knowingly with me at that. I waved goodbye and headed up May Queen Market toward the Underground station. It was too early for there to be much of a crowd listening to the Fallen King, but there were still a few paying attention to his dire predictions and rumblings.

I made my way past the now familiar landmarks, Pangaea, Bartleby & Daughters, Redcrosse Circus, until I came to Temple Court. I greeted the guards and made my way to the bottom of the stairs at the hall proper to await Richard Sonnac's leisure.

I passed the time contemplating what I was being called to account for this time. Yes, it was true I had participated in the Secret War, but I had no reason to believe that I had been prohibited from doing so. It was extracurricular, to be sure, but, based on what Konrad Engel and Zamira had said, sanctioned action by the Templars. Even the Council of Venice was in on it.

The longer I stood there waiting, the more irritated I became. I hadn't done anything wrong. We'd won, for pity's sake! I had comported myself as well as I could, given my lack of experience, and had played my part with the team. Sure, I didn't score as many individual points as the others, but I'd tried to do what needed to be done for the team.

"Blodwedd Mallory?"

I heard a female guard dressed in a pristine uniform calling for my attention from the entrance. I nodded my head in acknowledgment and followed her up the stairs into Temple Hall. She led me through the hall to the now-familiar set of doors on the right side of the room. She stopped in front and knocked.

Once again the doors opened, and I was ushered inside into the tribunal room, as I'd come to think of it. I had no idea if that was actually what it was called, but it certainly seemed to be its purpose, based on my acquaintance with it.

I walked on the thick red carpet up to the anterior of the room in front of the bench. As he'd been before, Richard Sonnac was there at a table to the left. He gestured for me to sit. The same panel was gathered behind the bench, Dame Julia, the dark-haired, middle-aged woman, and the silver-haired man. I felt a little sick to my stomach.

"Richard, please start these proceedings," Dame Julia gestured from her seat in the middle.

He coughed lightly into his hand and stood to face me and the bench, his face grave.

"Ms. Mallory, we have some critical news to share with you, which may have dire implications to your continued pursuit of initiation with the Templars."

I took a deep breath at his words, my heart dropping to my feet. *No, no, no, no, no...They were kicking me out!*

I bit my lip to keep from crying out as he continued.

"At approximately 10 p.m. last night we lost contact with your mother, Elizabeth Mallory, on her current assignment. We believe this to be disturbing news as she is utterly dependable and consistent in her communication with Temple Hall. At this point, we don't know where she is or her current condition."

I looked at him blankly, and my ears began to ring. The room started to distort slightly in a peculiar fashion.

My mother was missing? I felt a gaping abyss open up beneath me, threatening to swallow me whole.

"To complicate this matter," he continued, with a look of empathy for me on his face, "there is evidence of a mass spike in Gaia-touched individuals who are swallowing bees around the globe. These individuals need to be identified, contacted, and brought to Temple Hall to be trained, lest they be lured away to other factions...or worse. We believe this surge is directly related to the attack in Tokyo."

I choked back tears and looked at the faces of the panel members, who all wore masks of grave concern.

"I know it is your wish to become a Templar. Right now," Sonnac said, "we quite simply don't have the resources to provide you the one-on-one training to ensure your safety in the field."

Grumbling erupted behind me, and I whirled to find Brigadier Lethe in a seat at the back of the room with a scowl on his face. Richard Sonnac held up his hand for silence and continued.

"You are a young recruit. Some have maintained that you are too young." He gestured vaguely in the direction of Dame Julia.

"Too untested. Too likely to be drawn off on side, ahem, adventures."

He cleared his throat again. "And so, it has been proposed that you return to Innsmouth Academy where you can remain under the care of Annabel Usher until things settle down."

No!

I jumped to my feet and opened my mouth to protest.

At the same time, one of the heavy wooden doors swung open and slammed back against its casing. I whirled around and was astonished to see Sevenoir in his full uniform, conspicuously minus the bunny ears, marching up the carpet, escorting Plimmy on his left arm.

"Julia!" Plimmy shouted, her straw hat bouncing on her head as she scurried to keep up. "What kind of kangaroo court is this?! Why are you so determined to undermine this girl?"

"Plimmy," Dame Julia scowled. "Why are you here? This is none of your business."

"Of course it's my business." Plimmy retorted with a sniff as she swept off her hat. "Wedd is my tenant. I see her and pay attention. I talk to her. I've talked to her colleagues. She's a smart, talented candidate and I, for one, don't believe we can afford to lose her because she's thwarting your desire for control."

Dame Julia threw her hands up in the air at that and then crossed them over her chest as she fumed.

Wait, what?

My head was spinning with all the revelations, and I was having trouble tracking the details. Plimmy just said, "We can't afford to lose her." Plimmy was a Templar? And Sevenoir escorting her? What was that about? Plimmy had implied over tea at The Horned God that she didn't know who he was. Apparently, that was not the case. How did the two of them even know to be here?

I looked up at Richard Sonnac, who had a slight smile on his face. Even Brigadier Lethe was standing up now, approaching the bench. And my mother? Where was my mother? I felt like a basket case with all the emotions coursing through my body.

The courtroom was in an uproar as well. The middle-aged dark haired woman grabbed Dame Julia's gavel and slammed it down hard on the bench.

"One at a time, please!" she said in a commanding voice. "Let's have some order here."

Plimmy and Sevenoir moved to sit beside me at the left table, and Brigadier Lethe joined them, leaning his hip on the corner to take the weight off his bad knee. As I glanced to my left, I could see that the two mysterious figures were once again stationed against the wall there as well, the man in the brown suit with the white mask, and his companion in full combat armor.

I was speechless. This was a lot of ruckus for just me. Maybe whoever had suggested I be remanded back to Innsmouth Academy—Dame Julia, I was almost certain—had a point. I rubbed the scar on my right palm. I had made my fair share of trouble in the past week. Had it only been a week? It felt like a lifetime of difference from Solomon Island already.

"Richard, if you please. Review the facts for us in order, so this committee has some hope of making sense of the situation," The dark-haired woman nodded and returned the gavel to its place in front of Dame Julia, and folded her hands across the bench in front of her.

"Of course, Chancellor." Sonnac stepped forward from the table, positioning himself to face all of the attendees. "The proposal to return Ms. Mallory to Innsmouth Academy was intended to be a stop-gap measure, I believe, until we had sufficient resources to focus on her training again."

"That's a load of malarkey," Brigadier Lethe spat. "Wedd has more field experience than most of our new recruits. She has a lot to learn, of course, but she's been tested in combat several times now."

The Chancellor gave Lethe a look. "If you please, George, let Richard continue. Your support is noted."

Lethe nodded and folded his arms across his chest with satisfaction.

"There is the matter of her unauthorized participation in the Secret War scrimmage at Stonehenge last night," Sonnac continued.

The gray-haired man's eyebrows shot up at that, and he sat forward in his seat. "Did we win?"

Dame Julia looked over at her colleague and narrowed her eyes.

"That wasn't Wedd's fault," Sevenoir admitted. "Several of us dragged her along. She thought we were taking her to a druid ritual." Plimmy and the dark-haired Chancellor chuckled at that. "And yes, we won. We beat the Dragon by a solid 15 points. The Illuminati were barely on the board."

"She was probably safer at the scrimmage than she would have been at one of those pagan shindigs," Lethe muttered under his breath. "The mead at those things is like to kill you."

"So the team compensated for her inexperience?"

"Actually, no," Sevenoir explained. "We were lagging just slightly behind the Dragon until Wedd realized that if she changed her tactics and helped heal the team, we could hold the center. She did it without any of us prompting her. It was enough to push us over the finish line to a win."

The grey-haired man gave an interested "hmm" and sat back in his seat.

"I know my esteemed colleague appreciates a solid win in the Templar column for the Secret War, but there's still the matter of her missing mother," Dame Julia said sharply. "And this trend of Ms. Mallory doing what she wants, rather than what she's been instructed to do. It prevents us from keeping her safe, and we have a duty to Lisbette to ensure her daughter is cared for."

Plimmy cleared her throat and raised her voice. "Why are we not asking Wedd what she wants?"

"For pity's sake," Dame Julia said with a huff. "We know what she wants. The adults in the room are making the decisions here." She looked across the room at the mysterious figure in combat armor and nodded her head.

"Plimmy has a point, Julia. We need to hear from Wedd." said the Chancellor, as she gestured to me. "Wedd, would you like to take a moment to clarify for all of us here what precisely your thoughts are?"

What did I think? I was a little overwhelmed by all the attention here directed at my behavior and dismayed at the thought of having to go back to Innsmouth Academy and put my initiation on hold, but I wanted to do what was right for the organization as well.

"At Innsmouth Academy, it was my job to manage the familiars loose around the campus. My friend Gypcie and I harvested them daily to gather anima charges to make shards to power the wards," I began. "It was dangerous work, but Headmaster Montag and Ms. Usher trusted us to do it. It was how we contributed to the fight to hold back the darkness threatening to overwhelm Solomon Island. We even successfully fought and captured a wraith that was seeking blood-debt retribution from the headmaster."

"Yes, yes. We know all about your exploits at the Academy, Ms. Mallory," Dame Julia said dismissively. The Chancellor looked at Dame Julia with a raised eyebrow, and her mouth flattened into a line.

"My point is," I said with some energy, "that I have been in dangerous situations before and I've learned how to take care of myself. Yes, it's true that I am currently training to become competent with other weapons and I have a lot to learn before I master them, but I am smart and willing to work hard."

I bowed my head as tears began to well up in my eyes, and swallowed down the emotions choking my throat. I looked up at the panel who held my future in their hands. "I have wanted to be a Templar my whole life, and nothing has made me happier than being here this past week, working toward that goal. But at the end of the day, I am also a team player, and if it isn't in the best interest of the organization to have me here now, I will accept that outcome."

Brigadier Lethe eased off the side of the table and faced the panel. "I've given nothing but favorable reports on Wedd's progress. As she indicated, she's been focused on her training and working hard to learn the things I've taught her. Why are we holding her to a higher standard than some of her peers? Her mother, as we've noted, is one of our most talented and dependable agents."

"And she's missing," Dame Julia shrilled. "Or did you miss that part?"

"I did not," Lethe responded firmly. "And of course I'm worried. But I'm also hopeful that we will yet get good news where Lisbette is concerned. What is the rationale of holding back Wedd because her mother is missing?"

"Because at least then she will be safe! Her father..." Dame Julia stopped talking with a cough.

Plimmy got up from her seat behind the table and walked up to the bench, with sorrow and compassion on her face for the silver-haired matron who was holding herself rigidly from her position at the center of the bench.

"Julia, Julia," Plimmy said, shaking her head. "You, of all people, understand that this world is not safe. It was never safe, not for an ordinary person and certainly not for a Templar agent. And we all must occasionally endure our loved ones being in harm's way. You know that I, more than most, understand what that means."

Dame Julia looked gravely at Plimmy in acknowledgment, then glanced across the room toward the mysterious figures on the left wall. The man in the hood and armor gave her a slight nod, and she looked back at those assembled at the front of the room.

"Very well. I withdraw my petition for Ms. Mallory to be returned to the Innsmouth Academy for the short term. But that means we still have to deal with the problem of her oversight and training."

"I'll do it."

I jerked my head to the right at Sevenoir's voice and looked at him in amazement.

"You'll do it." Dame Julia said flatly, drawing my attention back to the bench. "Like you left her at the Agartha portal on Solomon Island to find her own way to London?"

Sevenoir spread his hands and sighed. "That was a mistake. I was angry at the assignment. It was not my best decision. But, I've tried to make up for it and watch over her since."

Brigadier Lethe agreed. "He's been a regular participant in her training...most days."

"And I can attest to the fact that he's kept an eye on her outside of training as well," Plimmy chimed in, turning to Sevenoir as she added, "although those ridiculous bunny ears made it hard for you to be subtle. Fortunately for you, she hasn't had any counter-espionage training yet. I saw you coming a block away most times."

I gaped at Plimmy. She smiled at me and winked. "I was an agent for many years, dear. Dame Julia was my partner. Of course, I'm retired now and merely a landlady. I find it suits me as I get older. Not all of us want to devote our whole lives to the Templar task, although I do still enjoy being invited to the Christmas festivities."

Dame Julia gave her a wry smile at that.

"Well, that settles it," the dark-haired Chancellor spoke up. "Unless there is still discussion, I move that Wedd be fully reinstated as a candidate for initiation. And I further move that she be given provisional status. We can then supply her with gear and a uniform, so she'll have her own to wear next time she joins her teammates in a Secret War scrimmage."

"Agreed," the silver-headed man at the right of Dame Julia nodded.

Dame Julia took a deep breath. "Very well then. Richard, please authorize Brigadier Lethe to provide Wedd with the necessary provisions."

"Of course, Dame Julia," he said with a smile at me. "Congratulations, Wedd. Welcome to the Templars in a provisional capacity, pending your initiation."

Happiness flooded my body at his words, and I beamed. Sevenoir patted me on the back, and Plimmy pulled me into a big hug. Even Brigadier Lethe offered me a growled, "Good on you, soldier."

"But that doesn't solve the problem of all the new Bees headed our way," Dame Julia said archly. "George, you are soon to be swamped with trainees. The rest of our agents, Sevenoir here notwithstanding, who are not already on assignment are out in the field tracking down Gaia's chosen. We expect the agents to be tied up for weeks as we figure out how to process and train the influx of new candidates. Everyone will have to pitch in. We cannot afford to let the darkness get a foothold in this war."

There was an abrupt knocking at the panel door, and a young aide entered and rushed up the red carpet to the bench. He handed Dame Julia a report and stood at attention while she reviewed its contents.

Her face darkened, and she looked up with resignation.

"And I see my comments were uncommonly prescient."

She stood up at the bench and eyed Sevenoir and me, frustration clear on her face.

"We're in the middle of what some would call a 'developing situation.' Some fellows from Oxford have been excavating below Darkside. Another Roman temple, dedicated to Mithras. There's a mess of them around here, as the both of you well know. But this one's special."

Dame Julia practically spit as she said that, her anger causing her to lose her customary formality. "Aren't they all? They've found some bloody artifact. Every time that happens, things go tits up. Everyone's scrambling to get a hold of it. Like children scrabbling in the dirt for a shiny shilling."

She looked at Plimmy with what I could swear was a kind of longing in her face. "What a circus this all is."

"None better to handle it than you, Julia," Plimmy said with a smile.

"Right then," Dame Julia responded, decisiveness clear in her face. "There's a defensive perimeter, but it won't hold up against a sustained onslaught, I'm afraid. The position is already under attack, and the tunnels have been intentionally caved in to prevent us from pulling the assets out of there."

She paused, shaking her head as if she couldn't believe her own words. "We need a detail down below, and since everyone else's off fighting for home and country, Sevenoir and Wedd, you're that detail."

Dame Julia gestured to the aide to bring us the report. "Go with Brigadier Lethe and get your provisions, Wedd. We don't have time to fit you for an agent uniform now, but you'll need a headset and a cell phone for contact. You both need to get to that Mithraeum immediately."

CHAPTER TEN

The Approach to the Innermost Cave

FOR A MAN WITH A STIFF LEG, Brigadier Lethe could move fast. The next few minutes were a blur as Sevenoir and I grabbed our things and followed him swiftly out of the room and back to the Crucible. The guards there held the doors open as he approached. Lethe traversed across the carpet to the steps to the practice floor quickly, and then leaning on the railing for support, he swung his bad leg out and hopped down the stairs two at a time.

He made his way down to a black case in the center and grabbed a cell phone, and headset sitting on top of it and handed it to me. Sevenoir helped me fit the headset around my ear and jaw and turn the cell phone to silent mode.

"That'll be it then," Lethe said, clapping me on the shoulder. "Godspeed, you two. Make me proud."

I thanked him for all his support, while Sevenoir consulted the mission report the aide had given us.

"Looks like the location of the Mithraeum is in Lostbrooke Close," he said. "That's not far from here, thankfully. We can cut across Temple Court past the Honesty Yard. The entrance is down an access stair in the sewers."

Oh goodie. More sewers.

I looked down at my plain black heels dubiously. I unbuttoned the cuffs of my white button-down dress shirt and rolled up my sleeves, then checked my backpack to be sure I had my athame and my blood and chaos foci.

"Ready?" Sevenoir asked me.

"Ready."

We headed out of the Crucible, across the hall, and down the front steps, turning left at the bottom. Sevenoir was right about it being close. The Honesty Yard was just to the west of Temple Hall, and we set a brisk pace crossing the yard to Lostbrooke Close, entering through a fancy wrought iron gate.

The Close itself was a well-lit brick tunnel with a cobblestone floor, which provided access between Via Antiqua and the Temple Court for maintenance. Even though it was well maintained, it had rubbish and boxes which gave it a patina of disuse. I had to slow my pace a little there to compensate for the heels of my pumps on the cobblestones and rued my choice of footwear.

Still, how could I have known this would be the outcome of my early morning invitation to Temple Hall? I was thankful I had decided to grab some breakfast.

We followed the tunnel as it curved south, coming to the domed entrance of a metal staircase that headed down below the street level. To our right, the tunnel continued out to Via Antiqua. Ironically, I could see the Fallen King's square on the far side from where we stood. He seemed a fitting icon for this folly.

"Down we go," Sevenoir said, and he stepped out on the curved metal staircase, his uniform boots ringing out as he proceeded down them. I followed him cautiously, walking on the balls of my feet, trying to keep my heels from catching in the grates.

We came to a platform that sat level with the Bazalgette sewers I'd traversed earlier in the week. To the right of the bottom of the stairs, the entrance to the sewers was blocked with steel bars. Directly across, a path into the brick-lined sewer tunnels beckoned.

Just left of that entrance was a rusted metal maintenance door, with an industrial-looking light fixture above it.

"This is us," Sevenoir said. A combination lock was fastened to the front of the door, and after consulting the mission report, he punched in the access code, and the door popped open.

"Do you know how a sub-vocalization headset works?" he asked me. I shook my head. I barely knew how a cell phone worked.

"Have you ever heard anyone reading to themselves at the library under their breath?"

That I was familiar with. Mainly because I was known to do it. Gypcie had loved to tease me about it.

"It works like this. When you think of a word, your brain starts to shape the muscles of your mouth and throat to speak them, even if you don't say them aloud. The headset Lethe gave you is specially designed to pick those signals up. This enables us to communicate in near silence, which is important on a mission."

I nodded my head in agreement.

"Try it," he said.

OK, I mouthed. In my ear, my words came back as if I'd said them aloud. "OK."

I saw his lips move in response, but nothing came out of his mouth. "Good, good." Sevenoir's voice came in clear as a bell through my earpiece. This headset was seriously cool.

Then I heard another voice in my head. I cringed as I realized who it belonged to.

"You've arrived just in time," Dame Julia said. "There are enemies incoming. Find the main worship hall of the Mithraeum as quickly as you can."

Sevenoir pushed the door open and stepped quietly inside the maintenance access. I followed him, stepping again on the balls of my feet to keep the heels of my pumps from striking the floor.

Behind the door was the entrance way to another Mithraeum, which of course I already knew, but was somewhat shocked to step through a modern threshold into a stone temple ruin. The floor was paved with aged, dusty flagstones, and the walls were ornately carved and covered with a faded white finish. Torches lined the walls in front of us and illuminated a staircase headed down. We moved down the first flight to a small landing covered with crates and supplies. This apparently had been an active dig recently. A standing commercial light fixture buzzed on the left, lending a bright glare to the scene.

We rounded the corner to a large room, with three dim hallways, running east to west. To the left was a small space visible through a curved archway that was well lit. I could see a bank of servers sitting against the north wall through the arch.

Sevenoir set off at a quiet jog up the middle hallway. I shuffled along behind him, listening carefully for signs of the intruders Dame Julia had warned us about. All I could hear, however, other than the occasional light footstep from one of us, was the electrical drone of the lighting down here.

About halfway down the hall, we came to a large circular iron grate on the floor. Sevenoir cut left around it, and I followed him north down another hallway. We hurried through the hall until we came upon another arched entryway leading to a smaller set of stairs. We moved up the stairs and into a vestibule that opened up into the broader room that comprised what I assumed was the main worship hall of the Mithraeum.

At the center of the nave was a raised dais in the shape of an inverted "T" in front of a rounded alcove set into the back of the wall, with columns to either side. That looked like the main altar. Someone had placed sandbags in a semi-circle in front of it. We could crouch behind the fortification to avoid enemy fire.

Dame Julia's voice rang again in my headset.

"I don't know how long you have to get set up, but it won't be long enough. There are arms caches there in the room. There should be turrets and mines inside them. Set up whatever defenses you can, but carefully."

I looked at Sevenoir with wide eyes. He nodded at my concern. I hadn't been trained to set up mines or turrets.

He motioned me over to a nearby crate, removing its lid carefully.

Inside, packed in straw were round circular disks. They had a button on top. Sevenoir mimed pressing the button down.

"These are proximity mines," his voice came in clearly through the headset as his lips moved. "Set them down at the points of entry and press the button down to arm them, then back away slowly. And whatever you do, don't go near them again once they're armed."

It looked like there were six mines and three entrances to the main worship hall, so I took the task of setting up the mines, while Sevenoir found the turrets and assembled them to the right and left of the dais.

I decided that setting the mines in a staggered fashion just inside and outside of each threshold into the room was my best option to effectively stop the interlopers. Carefully, I placed the outer mine first in the central entrance, setting it enough to the side that hopefully, a careless foe wouldn't see it until it was too late. I pushed the button on the top of the mine to set it and, taking Sevenoir's advice, backed away slowly to avoid triggering it.

I repeated this step just inside the central entrance and then again at the openings on the north and south walls. When I was done, I surveyed Sevenoir's progress with the turrets. Deadly looking guns mounted on a stand with a long strand of bullets trailing from them sat on each side of the dais. I stepped up, and one of the guns swung around to target me.

"Stop!" Sevenoir's voice boomed in my ear, and I stopped in my tracks. "Match friendly target."

"Matched," a computerized voice acknowledged, shattering the relative silence of the room. Sevenoir and I both grimaced at the noise. Still, it was better than getting shot by our own defenses.

Dame Julia's voice came across the headset. "Our motion sensors down there were triggered. Someone is coming. Find your places. We'll send a team to support you as soon as we can. With everything going on, we're woefully short on personnel. Hopefully, this will be a wake-up call for the Force Marshal."

I scooted up the stairs and ran around behind the sandbags at the altar, sitting down with my back to them to hide. Sevenoir followed me, although he crouched facing forward, to keep an eye on the entrances.

"Are you ready?" he asked in my ear.

"Let me get my athame."

I shrugged my pack off my back and set it down behind the sandbags. I dug out my athame and pricked my finger, saying a quick prayer for assistance to Gaia. I wondered briefly if She granted aid when the enemy was Her chosen from another faction.

I looked up at the altar and saw a metallic golden gleam from a sword handle. My right palm tingled as I looked at it. This must be the artifact Dame Julia had mentioned! Someone had surrounded it with candles that weren't very ancient looking, not that I was an expert. Perhaps the archaeologists digging down here had used them for extra light.

"Why did they leave this down here?" I asked Sevenoir.

He shook his head and shrugged. "The mission report said they had some trouble moving it," his voice said in my ear. "Which is why we're here now to defend it."

"What is it?"

"It's an ancient sword called the *Crocea Mors*. Which means 'yellow death,' presumably because the hilt of the sword is embellished with gold. According to the mission report, Julius Caesar supposedly lost it to a British prince named Nennius. It was believed to have been buried with Nennius, according to Monmouth's history, but its presence here in the Roman Mithraeum suggests that was inaccurate, if not an outright fabrication."

Any chance I had of replying evaporated with the sound of running feet approaching from the hallway. I flipped around and scrambled to peek over the sandbags as the first explosion rang through the stone room and dust trickled down from the ceiling.

An unknown assailant in a blue uniform lay in a crumpled heap courtesy of the proximity mine in the south entrance. I winced at his cry of pain. I was glad he was down, but I didn't enjoy hurting other people, regardless of their faction. Another Illuminati assailant had made it successfully into the room, but Sevenoir neutralized him with a well-placed burst from his assault rifle.

Three Dragon assailants in green uniforms breached the threshold to the west. The outer mine exploded, but they made it through on their feet. The westernmost turret fired a barrage of bullets. I squeezed my pointer finger on my left hand to get the blood flowing from the place I'd pricked it with my athame, and cast a dread sigil at the three of them. They buckled visibly under the onslaught, but two made it up onto the dais and charged Sevenoir and me where we stood behind the sandbags. The third dove for cover behind a pile of crates near the western archway, and gave his companions covering fire with his pistol.

I shrieked as a bullet buzzed by my ear and stood to hit the attacker nearest me with three quick jabs of chaos distortion. He grabbed his chest and crumbled to the ground. Beside me, Sevenoir hit the other with repeated fireballs to his chest, until he turned and ran back toward the door he'd entered, flames catching on his uniform. The turret on the west side fired once, twice and that attacker dropped to the floor in a heap. With a flash, his body disappeared as he was recalled to an anima well.

The Dragon behind the crates fired his pistol at us again, and I dropped low behind the sandbags for cover.

Horror filled me as I realized that unlike the Stonehenge bout, their faces weren't masked and I could see every emotion that crossed them as we fought in deadly earnest, the determination, the pain, even the fear.

I sat hunched behind the sandbags, paralyzed. This was awful.

"Get up, Wedd!" Sevenoir's voice rang in my ear. "They're coming in from all sides now."

The turrets started to fire continuously, and a *rat, tat, tat* boomed off the stone walls, the noise making it hard to think. I could hear mines exploding as well. I took a deep breath and stood back up, gritting my teeth against what I'd see.

"This is what it means to be an agent," Sevenoir's voice was strained in my ear. "You don't have to like it, but you do have to do it."

Resigned, I looked at the eastern archway and cast dread sigil at the groups of blue attackers as they swarmed in the room. My right ring finger tingled sharply with the action, and I saw the attackers drop to the ground. A sharp stinging pain bloomed in my left arm, and I swung my head around to find the cause. I'd gotten nicked by a stray bullet from the side. Blood trickled down my arm inside the sleeve of my shirt, and I grimaced.

LONDON UNDERGROUND

This was no good. Standing behind the sandbags was keeping me from using the bulk of my chaos spells and leaving me an easy target to anyone fighting at range. I kicked off my shoes, leaped over the barrier, and ran out into the melee of the battle in the center of the room, and started throwing barrel kicks, hitting the assailants within my reach and creating turmoil wherever I could. I cast pandemonium and threw several blue uniforms to the ground. Behind me I felt I sword slash the back of my legs, burning as it scored my skin. I turned and hit my attacker with small bursts of chaos, creating a pocket of distortion in reality. Three singularities opened under my feet.

I reached into my pants pocket and pulled out the Electromagnet Stabilizer gadget that I carried around to purge singularities, and my attacker was knocked on her back as they exploded in a cascade of light. I felt a swell of healing anima energy suffuse me as a wellness enigma, released by the purged singularity, activated. I jumped up and, with a yell, fractured reality then watched as purple and green cracks covered the floor. The Illuminati attackers still trying to stand from pandemonium screamed as the chaos energy sucked at their anima.

There were at least a dozen assailants in the room now.

"Julia, where are our backups?" Sevenoir's voice blurted over the general cacophony in the room. "It's 12 to 2 down here!"

"They're on their way," she responded over the com. "Just hold out a while longer."

I tried to get my bearings in the room and realized that the Dragon assailants were having a lot more success staying alive. I listened through the background noise of the turrets firing and the screams and grunts of combat. From behind the sandbag barricade near the archway, I heard the faint twang of fist weapons being sharpened.

"The Dragon has a healer!" I cried aloud.

Sevenoir grabbed his ear. "Subvocalize, Wedd! You just about blasted out my eardrum, not to mention you just told everyone in the room," came his voice in my ear.

Oh, shit.

"Sorry," I mouthed.

Sevenoir fired a three-round burst at a Dragon attacking from the west, then cast a spell to overload the floor with electricity. Bright bolts ran across the floor, zapping the assailants and throwing them back to the ground. One Illuminati elemental fighter cast a fire manifestation behind the sandbags, and Sevenoir rolled over the top of the bags, across the raised front area of the dais, beating the flames out of the pant legs of his uniform. I could hear his groan of pain across the room. The wooden crates of boxes went up with a whoosh and flames leaped in front of the altar where the artifact was laying.

Damn it! The artifact was the whole reason we were down here. I spun on my heel and ran for the altar area. I had to reach the sword and get it out of the inferno burning there. I ran around the west side of the dais, ducking as bullets flew over my head, chipping into the stone pillars at the sides of the altars. The air was smoky and full of dust, both from the bullets chipping away at the stone and from the steady stream of dust coming down from the ceiling because of the exploding mines. I tried to grab the blade of the sword, but couldn't get a decent grip that would allow me to pull it toward me.

My white blouse was starting to smoke with the heat, and the hair on my forearms sizzled and stung me as they burned away where I'd rolled up my sleeves. Fire again. I cringed with the memory of my previous burns, and my palm ached with the need to have the blade in my hand. This wasn't working. I needed to try from the other side where I could get a grip on the pommel.

I ran back down the dais onto the west side of the floor where I got a glimpse of the short, dark hair of the Dragon healer, hidden behind a sandbag barricade to the right of the archway that had been set up for the defense of the room. I knew a healer was hiding there!

"What are you doing?" Sevenoir's urgent voice came across the headset. "I need help here."

CHAPTER ELEVEN

The Ordeal

SEVENOIR WAS ON HIS BACK in the middle portion of the dais, his uniform pants in tatters from the flames, and he was trying to get to his feet as he was attacked by two blue and a green assailant. I spun on my foot and sprinted up on the dais, casting pandemonium as I went. The spell grabbed the assailants and threw them to the ground. I heard a snap, and one of the Illuminati agents on the left stayed down, his body slumped across the western stairs of the dais, his neck at an odd angle. A golden light flared, and his body disappeared.

My brain noted indelibly that I had just used lethal amounts of damage on a man that I didn't know and had never met except in combat. I didn't have time to think about it right now, but I was certain it would feature in my dreams for many nights to come.

I reached down my hand to Sevenoir and dragged him to his feet. His face was pained, and he limped, unable to put any weight on his left leg, which had gotten the bulk of the burns.

Behind us, the flames continued to consume the wood of the crates and had jumped to the cloth of the sandbags. Black smoke gusted from the bags as they ignited. I could see at least six attackers still able to fight, although a couple of Dragon had begun to engage a hammer-wielding Illuminati. And that didn't take into account the concealed Dragon healer.

I looked at the two turrets, which had been helping defend our position. Both were tipped to the side, out of bullets and out of commission. It was just Sevenoir and I against all of them. The two remaining attackers at our feet began to move, rolling away and picking up their weapons to advance again.

Sevenoir still needed a moment to recover, so I began throwing barrel kicks again at the two attackers nearest us. I slammed the floor with my palm fracturing reality, damaging the stone of the dais. The attacker on the right fell and cracked her head on the stone floor.

"Stay down," I muttered to her angrily under my breath. I needed to get that sword off the altar before it was irrevocably damaged.

This was a colossal mess and attackers were still swarming in the door. The Dragon and the Illuminati were apparently pulling out the stops to get their hands on the *Crocea Mors*, which would likely be a puddle of iron and gold on the altar by the time I got back to it.

Where was the backup Dame Julia had promised? I knew the Templars were short on available agents right now, but surely the "standing army" Richard Sonnac had touted had a few soldiers running around who could help!

As if my angry thought had summoned them, I heard shouts and feet running toward us. A swarm of Templar soldiers in red uniforms ran in through the central archway and began to engage the Illuminati and Dragon attackers fighting among themselves. I hit the remaining blue suited attacker standing on the dais with a punch of chaos energy to the chest, sending him flying off the stairs, and turned and sprinted to the east side of the altar. The front of the stone was blackened with soot from the flames.

I took a deep breath. This was going to hurt. I reached into the stone opening and put my right palm on the pommel of the sword. It scalded my hand as the blade's grip touched the scarred skin there.

I was filled with a sense of rightness and the pommel, though hot, fit my hand like a glove. I pulled the sword off the burning altar, the blade ringing like a bell, and brandished it over my head.

"This is Templar ground, and you are trespassing!"

Sevenoir groaned and grabbed his ear, but I ignored it, filled with righteous anger that the attackers would dare attempt to steal the sword. I needed to get rid of that healer so we could get the remaining attackers under control.

I jumped down the stairs and landed in a crouch, then stood and sprinted across the room toward the western entrance to the sandbag barricade where the Dragon healer was concealed. He stood as I approached and I brought the gold-pommeled sword to his throat.

Time stopped.

The Dragon healer looked at me, his eyes widening.

I looked back.

His olive green uniform stretched across his broad shoulders, the golden scarf around his throat embroidered with red dragons accenting the uniform and highlighting the gold in his green eyes.

I... I knew those green eyes. I had looked into them over many cups of coffee in the Faculty Lounge. I had missed them, since leaving Innsmouth Academy. I had dreamed about them. I had wondered if I'd ever see them again.

The Dragon healer in front of me was Renee Laveau, the man I had hoped would try to find me in London. My mouth opened and closed wordlessly.

"Run, Hadad!" One of the Dragon assailants called from across the room.

Hadad? Memories of the Stonehenge match swamped me. Hadad was Renee? I dropped the sword from his throat, unable to use it.

In return, he raised his pistol and pointed it at my head.

No! My heart broke into a thousand pieces, and tears welled up in my eyes as I watched him fight a battle within himself over whether to shoot me.

His brow furrowed and he got a look of pain on his face as he held the gun to my forehead and I could see his finger tighten on the trigger.

Cold chills broke out on my body. I couldn't believe it. He was going to shoot me. I stood frozen, unable to move, my heart beat echoing loudly in my ear.

Thump, thump. Thump, thump.

"Fuck!" he yelled, then flipped on the safety and slapped my sword arm away, dropping the pistol. He lunged toward me and grabbed my shoulders. From there he moved inside my guard and twisted.

Off-balance in every sense of the word, I cried out in pain as he grabbed my left arm, pulling it across his shoulder and reopening the stinging bullet scrape there. He squatted, lifting me onto his back and slammed me from hip height onto the stone floor. My right hand hit the floor and opened reflexively, dropping the blade, which clanked and skittered out of reach, sliding into the sandbags of the barrier.

I hit the ground with a thump, and the air whooshed out of my lungs. I wheezed, trying to draw in oxygen, the muscles of my back constricting. He reached down and pressed on my windpipe with his right hand, the blades of his fist weapon perilously close to my throat, and readied a punch with his left hand. Black spots filled my vision as I struggled for air, but he continued to push.

Helplessly, I thrashed, trying to push back against him so I could breathe as the seconds ticked by, but his arms were longer than mine. Finally, I stopped struggling, my eyes wide, pleading with him to let me go.

Hadad grimaced and released me. My lungs heaved, and I dragged in a huge breath of air, which burned raw down my throat. His eyes scoured the floor for the sword that I'd dropped, and he turned away from me, bending down to the pile of sandbags to grab it.

I couldn't let him get the blade! I lifted my leg and with all my strength, kicked at the side of his right kneecap, grunting loudly. He shouted in pain as his knee buckled, and he pitched forward, scrambling to get his balance, dropping the blade. I rolled over to my side and grabbed his right leg, trying to keep him from getting away.

He kicked backward at me, but his injured knee wouldn't cooperate, and the kick had no force. I scrambled to all fours and leaped toward the blade. Hadad lurched to his feet, but I slammed into him, knocking him forward. I righted myself and grabbed the sword from where it had landed. He rolled onto his back and grabbed his pistol, firing it at me.

The shot rang out, loud in the stone room despite the cacophony around us. I froze, blade in hand, waiting for the bloom of pain to let me know where I was hit.

It didn't come. The bullet had gone wide and missed me.

He rolled to his feet, favoring his right knee, watching me closely as I stood, hunched over, the golden pommel of the blade in my right hand, panting. As I stared back, I realized he also had a golden-pommeled sword in his hand.

"It's the job, Wedd. I have to finish the mission."

Outrage filled me, and my vision narrowed to red. What trickery was this? Were the Dragon attempting to plant a decoy in the confusion of the fight? My palm tingled and itched at the sword in my grip, and I calmed down a little. I was sure I had the *Crocea Mors*. He could take the fake, the chimera back to his masters.

Hadad sprang toward the western archway, limping away as fast as he could on his bad knee. Woozy, I stumbled backward, tripping. My legs buckled beneath me and I fell back hard again to the stone floor.

Around me, the chaos of the fight continued. I lay there on the floor, my ears ringing and my lungs laboring for breath a second time in as many minutes. I looked up at the stone of the ceiling, trying to process what had just happened.

"Get up, Wedd," Sevenoir's voice buzzed urgently in my ear. "Get up. The fight's not over."

Dazed and emotionally raw, I climbed to my feet, dragging the sword up with me. My head was swimming as I looked around the room.

Red uniforms had closed in with the remaining blue and green in the room, and I moved back to the right of the dais where Sevenoir had propped himself against crates stacked in a pile so he could remain upright. His legs were a mess. I could see raw red burns through the tatters of his uniform pants. Despite the pain he must have been in, he was still firing on the remaining Illuminati and Dragon agents when he could get a clear shot as they struggled with the red-uniformed Templar soldiers.

I cast a few half-hearted blood sigils at the attackers and climbed back up on the dais with the sword in my hand to survey the room.

Two attackers, one Illuminati and one Dragon, made a last-ditch attempt to rush me to get the sword. The Illuminati struck first, swinging at me with the sharp prongs of his fist weapon. They connected with my hip, drawing blood with a cold burn.

The pain of the new wound infuriated me, and I grunted at him. I clenched the fist of my left hand, casting a blood rupture spell which caused his heart to stutter and stop. He fell back, grabbing his chest, and rolled off the stairs to the Mithraeum floor, disappearing in a flash of light.

I pointed the blade at the Dragon who was scuttling up the stairs toward me on the right with a shotgun held at his waist and feinted an angry jab at him. Finding himself alone on the dais with me and the sword, he backed away, raising his hands and the shotgun in a gesture of surrender. The scar on my middle finger tingled fiercely as if urging me to continue attacking with the sword.

Luckily my blood corruption was low, so even though I was furious, my mind was utterly clear. I kept the sword trained on the Dragon, ignoring the desire to exceed my training and pursue him. One of the uniformed Templar soldiers captured him from behind by the arms and walked him off the dais, keeping me from second guessing my resolve.

Taking a deep breath to calm my roiling emotions, I looked around the room and realized that now the fight was over. There were a very few blue- and green-uniformed combatants left standing, and they were being taken into custody by the Templar soldiers. The bodies of those agents who had suffered anima exhaustion had disappeared, leaving only the aftermath of the damage in their wake. Bullet shells, dropped weapons, splatters of blood, chips of stone and dust littered the room as a red-uniformed clean-up crew entered the room and began to tidy up. I looked out the western archway, but there was no sign of Hadad.

I limped over to Sevenoir who had moved to sit on the dais stairs, his burned legs clearly causing him significant pain, the raw wounds weeping fluid onto his ruined pants. His face was drenched in sweat, and he grimaced as he adjusted himself trying to get more comfortable.

"Just my bloody luck. My legs will be ruined with scars for beach season," he said as I approached. "Give me a little nick with the sword to put me out of my misery instead?" He was trying for pithy, but a certain sincerity rang in his words from the pain.

I cast a mend spell on him to take the edge off his agony, golden light rushing to heal the raw and blistered skin there. He thanked me, panting, as the healing spell brought him some relief. I had a clear recollection myself of how badly burns hurt, and he had endured the pain while continuing to fight.

Admiration for his skills welled up within me. Sevenoir had guided me throughout the fight as well, even while dealing with the combat and his own injuries.

"Thank you for helping me with the fight," I croaked out, my throat still raw.

"I promised," he said, wiping his forehead. "And I keep my promises." He lifted the headset from his jaw and ear and leaned over to me and said in a low voice. "But we need to talk soon about that Dragon you let get away."

I nodded and cast my eyes to the floor.

Dame Julia's voice crackled through my headset. "Job well done, soldier. I'm actually impressed. How did you manage to pick up the sword? The archeology team has been complaining for weeks that it couldn't be moved."

I looked down at the blade, the golden pommel pressed against the coin-scarred marking in my right hand. I looked up at Sevenoir's face, and my eyes widened in the alarm at not knowing how to answer her.

"I'm not sure," I mouthed and shrugged my shoulders for emphasis.

Sevenoir put his headset firmly back in place against his jaw. "We'll make sure all the details are in our report, Dame Julia."

"Very well, then. For now, bring the artifact out of there and take it to Mr. Gladstone in the library," she continued. "Sevenoir, get yourself patched up. This will be a promotion for you. Come see me, and well done."

CHAPTER TWELVE

The Reward

W E REMAINED down in the Mithraeum long enough for a healer with the clean-up crew to triage and heal the burn wounds on Sevenoir's legs and for someone to chase up a new pair of pants for him to wear. After a little searching, I found my black pumps and slipped them back on reluctantly.

I held onto the sword. I didn't want to put it down, and no one seemed intent on asking me to. Dame Julia had told me to deliver it to Mr. Gladstone—the Templar Chief Librarian according to Sevenoir—and deliver it to him I would. I was actually delighted to have a reason to go there and meet him. Not only was I looking forward to seeing the library and its infamous magical tomes and artifacts, but I still needed access to a good Latin dictionary. Handing over a historical sword seemed like a good way to get started off on the right foot with the guy in charge of all the books.

When Sevenoir was ready, we made our way out the same way we'd come in, although climbing the metal stairs in the Bazalgette was no fun. My legs were tired, and my feet ached from tromping around underground barefoot, then stuffing them back into the pumps. Once again I stepped on the balls of my feet to keep from breaking off a heel in the metal grates of the stair treads.

By the time we got back to Temple Hall itself, Dame Julia was back at her usual station in front of two giant, ornately carved wooden doors on the far wall of the hall. Sevenoir explained that in addition to being the Special Assignment Supervisor, Dame Julia was also the Outer Warden of the inner Temple itself, the holiest of holies. I asked him if he'd ever been inside the Temple. He smiled enigmatically at me and didn't answer the question, although he did point out that the Templar structure — the Temple, the hall, and the outer court — was positioned to point to the southeast and Solomon's Temple in Jerusalem.

"That's all the mysteries you'll get from me today," Sevenoir added as he finished with the explanation of the architecture. "The rest will need to wait until you are a full Templar."

I pouted, but by then, we had crossed the hall to Dame Julia. She greeted Sevenoir, then turned to me.

"I see you're back as well. I'm not sure I asked you specifically to return, but," Dame Julia made eye contact again with Sevenoir as she gestured to us both, "it's good to see you two in one piece."

She put her hands back on her hips. "Sevenoir, this is a step up in rank for you for your excellent work in protecting the sword and Ms. Mallory here, as well as holding your ground until reinforcements could arrive, and all while you were injured in the battle. We'll see to your advancement shortly. Thank you for your good work."

Sevenoir nodded, and I muttered a half-hearted thanks under my breath, thinking to myself, "What am I, chopped liver?"

Dame Julia narrowed her eyes and scowled, visibly counting to ten, and Sevenoir looked at me in horrified amazement, stifling a laugh.

Whoops. I may have actually thought that out loud. Damn it. That sub-vocalizing headset had me all confused as to what was inside my head and what wasn't.

She scowled at Sevenoir, who was struggling to keep a straight face, and drew in a deep breath, before continuing. "Look, I've been a soldier all my life, Ms. Mallory, and I'm not sure I can give you the appreciation you're looking for and, maybe, deserve. You remind me of myself at your age, going on wild adventures with Miss Plimmswood, saving the world and turning conventions on their head."

I looked up at her, surprised and pleased, giving her a bright smile. Maybe there was hope for me yet.

Her eyes widened with alarm, and she shook her head at me sternly in response. "Don't take this as a sign that we're becoming friendly. I do not fraternize with anyone, least of all those below my rank. I believe in rules, traditions, and decorum. Still, you are showing promise. We will talk again, I'm sure. Until then, go take that sword to Gladstone as I asked."

Dame Julia shooed me away with her hand while she indicated to Sevenoir that he should stay so they could talk about plans for all the new recruits anticipated to start hitting Ealdwic in the next week.

Ugh. I was still being treated like a child, being sent from the room whenever the conversation got interesting.

I scowled in frustration as I shuffled back across the hall. I was at a loss as to what to do. I thought I'd done a good job down at the Mithraeum and held my own in the fight. However, Dame Julia had boiled that all down to "showing promise."

Clearly, I was not yet welcome at the Templar bosom. I looked down at the priceless sword still in my hand, I figured that like a good soldier I had better do as I'd been told if I had any hopes of winning Dame Julia's acceptance for real.

CHAPTER THIRTEEN

The Road Back

I WALKED DOWN THE STEPS and west across the courtyard to the Library, which sat on the left side of the road in front of Temple Hall. Temple Library had a suitably grand entrance in keeping with its collection's prominence in the occult world. A set of stone stairs led into the building, which was lit up like candles on a birthday cake.

Inside the main foyer with the four-armed cross etched into the marble floor was a grand staircase that branched gracefully to the right and left. There were Templar guards sprinkled throughout, impressive in their red and black uniforms. I had read that the library was at the very heart of the building, surrounded on all sides by meeting spaces and lounges and that it was a frequent spot for people to gather to chat or study. I trudged up the staircase to find out, beginning to feel somewhat awkward about wandering around with an unsheathed ancient sword in my hand. However, it didn't garner much notice. Apparently, historical artifacts were commonplace in the heart of Templardom.

On the second floor, I stepped off the landing through the threshold into one of the lounges. The room was boldly decorated in deep red, from the carpet to the walls, the color broken up only by the sparkling white crystal chandeliers hanging from the wooden paneled ceiling and the golden sconces which lined the walls. Even the overstuffed leather seats and couches were red, and I ruminated sourly to myself that this would be a great place to stage a bloody massacre. No one would ever know it had happened.

I turned right to move toward the inside of the building, and at last, the glory of the Templar library itself was revealed. It was a circular, two-story space, the walls lined with bookshelves, a giant translucent dome of leaded glass overhead filling the space with ambient light. There must have been thousands of texts here. Delicate wrought-iron staircases wound around to the second-floor catwalk, the shelves of volumes there broken up periodically by large classical oil paintings of scenes from antiquity. The center of the room was filled with wooden reading tables, lit with low golden lamps.

It was a book lover's paradise, and I took a deep breath in to enjoy the evoked scents of chocolate and coffee that wafted from the antique pages. I could hardly wait to spend time here looking at the collection in more detail.

Almost directly across the room from where I entered, I could see a bearded man in a black tunic talking to two short-haired women in very short dresses. I wondered if this was who I was looking for.

He looked up from the conversation and waved me over.

"You must be Wedd," he said as I approached. "Dame Julia sent a courier, although I could hardly miss you. Not everyone runs around with a sword, at least in here." He smiled and gestured around the room. "I'm Iain Tibet Gladstone. Welcome to my library. Or, at least, a tiny part of it."

I cocked my head at him. "Where is the rest?"

"Oh, underground, of course," he answered.

Well, of course it was. I fought the urge to face-palm. I'd been underground quite enough for the past few days.

"Let's have a look at that sword, shall we?" Leaving his companions standing at the wall, Gladstone directed me to a big desk in the center of the room. I placed the sword on the wooden top carefully, feeling a twinge of regret as it left my hand. To cover the feeling, I rubbed my hands together briskly.

"Ah, the famed sword of Caesar, the 'yellow death' as it was called, or *Crocea Mors* in the historical vernacular."

"Why 'yellow death'?" I asked.

"Well that's a good question, and I'm not sure we know the answer for certain," he said, scratching his beard. "Depending on who is telling the story, it was also called 'red death' or 'grey death.' It was Geoffrey of Monmouth in his *History of the Kings of Britain*, however, who called it 'crocea' after the 'crocus sativus,' the flower which was cultivated for saffron. The golden yellow of that spice is perhaps a good match for the pommel of this sword, is it not?"

He pulled a glass jeweler's eye ring out of his pocket and bent down to look closely at the gladius, which was in fantastic shape for a weapon that was nearly 2,000 years old. Gladstone mumbled and oohed under his breath as he examined the sword.

Finally, he stood up straight and clapped his hands with glee. "My favorite kind of artifact! A magic sword, with a checkered past, not unlike my own. There are a few, you know, which are reportedly lost here in the British Isles. Some of them quite well known. This one is perhaps not as infamous as some, but all the more interesting because it is apparently not the conjuration of a lake undine or a would-be historian."

He paused and cleared his throat. "Oh. You're no doubt related to old Tom of Warwick. Sorry. No offense intended."

Huh? I stared at him in bafflement. Old Tom of Warwick? What was he talking about? A lightbulb went off in my head. Sir Thomas Malory. *Le Morte d'Arthur.* Magic swords. Excalibur. Right.

"The question in my mind," Gladstone said, changing topics, his right eye overly large and startling behind the jeweler's ring as he peered at me, "is, how did you pick it up? The archaeologists who were excavating the Mithraeum were convinced that the sword was fused in some manner to the altar there."

"I... I don't know. I just put my right hand on the pommel and picked it up." I said "The area near the altar was on fire and I was afraid the artifact would be damaged. I didn't realize it wasn't supposed to... move."

"You did the right thing," Gladstone assured me. He stretched a bit, the beaded pendant he was wearing around his neck bouncing off his breast. "It needed to move. Protecting that Mithraeum, as you know, was becoming a bit of the bother with the Dragon and Illuminati hot on the trail."

Gladstone leaned in conspiratorially, "Did you know that this particular sword is alleged to kill everything the wielder strikes with it instantaneously? In a battle between the Romans and the troops of Canterbury and what is now London, Nennius, an ancient British prince, captured it from Caesar in personal combat when it got stuck in his shield. Nennius wasted no time and freed the sword to use it to massacre the rest of the Romans who got within reach. Unfortunately for the prince, Caesar had clobbered him in the skull with the sword before it got stuck in the shield. Ultimately, that did him in."

Gladstone clucked his tongue ruefully. "Infection, two weeks later. Well, I suppose to a magic gladius, a death is a death..."

I gave him an awkward smile, suddenly glad that I hadn't actually hit anything with the sword myself. There was no need to tempt fate. With my luck, I was surprised I hadn't tripped over it or something. Or accidentally stabbed Renee with it, I thought, with a gulp. I rubbed my hands together again, nervously, running the fingers of my left hand over the scar on my right.

"Nennius was supposedly buried with the sword near the North Gate of the old city, which is..." breaking off from his story, Gladstone eyed my palm as I rubbed it.

"Say, what's that you've got there? That's quite a scar."

I turned my palm over so he could inspect it, the precise brand of Caesar's profile and name imprinted there from my run-in with the superheated coin. The scar now looked years old, even though it had only been there a few days.

"Hmm..." Gladstone looked at me speculatively. "And you say you just picked the sword up by the pommel."

I showed him the scars of the sun and the moon on the ends of my fingers as well.

"Oh! To have the sun emblazoned on your finger. The sun! There a topic close to my heart. And close to yours too, since it is branded onto your heart finger!" he crowed with delight. "What this all means shall be a fascinating set of events to watch unfold, Wedd."

At my look of concern, he gestured to reassure me. "The unconquered sun, defining your heart's purpose and your ability to distinguish right from wrong. It's only natural, of course, to be alarmed. Light and darkness: life and death. The sun has fascinated and frightened humanity from the day we crawled out of the black oceans."

I was further alarmed by his glib explanation and pulled a face.

He chuckled and gestured to the south wall of the second floor. "And there are a hundred books on this topic right up here for you to study to consider the implications."

I followed his gesture with my head and looked in awe at the sheer number of volumes that awaited me. Still, this was worrisome information. "What do you think the moon on my ring finger means?"

"It could mean any number of things. Affinity with blood. Eternity. The feminine balancing force…to the masculine force of the sun." Gladstone tapped a finger against his lips. "We shall see what it means in the future."

"You mean…you don't know now?" I asked anxiously. "It's not in one of these books?"

"Bah," Gladstone said with an irritated swipe of his hand at the room. "One thing you learn quickly in a place like this is that there's no singular truth. There are no facts. History is…is mutable, history morphs, in form and shape, context and content. All us historians can do—arcane or not—is pick through the wreckage and attempt to piece together the broken bits in the hope that it'll teach us something."

He gestured to a Templar guard standing at the wall, who joined us at the desk, and gave him instructions as to where to place the gladius in temporary storage pending further investigation. Rather than invite the question of whether anyone else could move it, I picked the gladius up off the table and placed it in the guard's gloved hands, who gave me a brief nod and retreated to follow Gladstone's instructions.

"I'm looking forward to getting a little more time to look at that in my workshop," he said watching the guard leave with a jolly chuckle. "Well, I best get back to the Stewart twins. They get bored so easily, and then they get vicious."

He gave me a wry smile and turned to rejoin his female companions standing over near the wall. He took two steps toward them before he turned back to me.

"Come join me here in the library to study any time you like, Wedd," Gladstone said, "but in the case of the real import of your scars, my dear, I suspect you'll best learn the implications by experiencing them."

CHAPTER FOURTEEN

The Resurrection

June 22, 2012

I WAS EXHAUSTED by the time I was able to return to my flat and overwhelmed with all the things that had happened in the last 24 hours, even though it was only mid-afternoon. The streets were swarming with people—all the new recruits come to Ealdwic, I suspected—and I kept my head down as I trudged home.

Gladstone's vague ruminations on the meaning of the scars on my hands left me feeling more unhinged than ever. Back on Solomon Island, things were very cut and dried. It had seemed to me a month ago that by leaving the island, I could leave the things of the island behind.

My hip twinged suddenly where it had been scored with the Illuminati fist weapon as I walked down Antiqua Way past the entrance to the Lostbrooke Close tunnel. It was fully healed thanks to the triage efforts by the clean-up team down in the Mithraeum, but the memory of receiving it hadn't yet faded.

That seemed like a good metaphor for my pondering as I headed home. I was learning that there was no casting off of experiences. I might be effectively immortal now but, for good or otherwise, I carried the scars of my adventures—mental, emotional, and sometimes physical—with me.

I dodged a crowd gathered in front of the Ealdwic Station and headed up May Queen Market, through the blue door and up the flights of stairs to my third-floor flat, tromping my feet in lassitude.

The rusted old key squawked in the lock as I turned it and opened my front door. I latched it behind me, walked over to my futon, and plopped down in a heap, kicking off my black pumps. My feet sang with relief, and I pulled my right foot up into my lap to rub my toes.

I was dirty and tired from the day. Pulling off my business attire, I jumped in the shower to clean up then threw on some comfortable clothes.

So much had happened that I'd barely had a chance to contemplate the implications of the Secret War and celebrate our victory before I found myself dragged before the panel, then embroiled in the mission to protect the gladius. I felt like I needed to think it all through to catalog the information, but I didn't even know where to start.

Dear Gaia. My mother was missing.

I felt the sharp burn of adrenaline as this information clicked home, and I stifled a shriek of horror and shame that I was just now tracking to this information I'd gotten hours ago. I started to hyperventilate a little as I imagined dozens of terrible scenarios that she could be in.

But my fear was too big to stay focused on, and I had many years of practice coping with my mother being out of reach on dangerous missions. She was smart and capable, and she had been doing this for a long time. The more I thought about it, the more confident I was that she would report in soon.

As I calmed down a little, my mind wandered over the other things that had happened. I was excited about the panel's decision to once again consider me a candidate for initiation, but disturbed

199

by the experience of fighting agents from other factions in real action. Stonehenge was one thing, but to set up mines and turrets with the intent of wounding and maiming them sat very poorly in my gut. I thought about the combat and wondered what had become of the assailants who had experienced anima exhaustion. Were they sitting in a pub now, in New York or Seoul, nursing their loss of the artifact over a beer? I let my eyes lose focus as I imagined them commiserating with their other faction members.

Without asking my permission, my brain immediately served up the image of dark hair and green eyes firing the pistol at me and limping out the archway of the Mithraeum with the other sword.

The muscles of my chest clenched tight. Renee.

I covered my face with my hands.

What was I going to do about Renee? Hadad. Whatever his damn name really was. My heart broke anew as I tried to reconcile the man I'd gotten to know and begun to care for at Innsmouth Academy holding a gun on me. Throwing me down and holding my throat to keep me from breathing. Trying to steal the blade from the Templars.

I shook my head. I still couldn't believe it. My heart didn't care that he was a Dragon, while my brain launched into a thousand recriminations about how naive I'd been. I had believed the difference in our factions wouldn't matter when I became a Templar.

I couldn't have been more wrong.

I felt sick from all the emotional upheaval, and I swallowed bile in the back of my throat as I wandered into my kitchenette to get a glass of water and some aspirin. Turning on the faucet, I filled a glass and gulped it down.

Oh, shit.

I put the empty glass down on the counter, my heart sinking. The Dragon wasn't the only enemy of the Templars. Someday, I might have to face off against my best friend, Gypcie.

Leaning over the sink, I covered my face with my hands and wept. I couldn't bear it. This had all been a terrible mistake. I should have never come to London after all.

I stumbled back to the futon, where I laid down and cried until I drifted off to sleep.

Knock, knock.

I looked up groggily. I felt nauseated, woken from my exhausted nap. Who the hell was at my door?

"Who is it?" I growled from where I was laying.

"Wedd, open the door. What are you doing in there?" Sevenoir's voice drifted into my flat.

"Go away." I groaned.

"Come on, Wedd," Zamira said. "Let us in."

"I'm tired. Please leave me alone." I rolled over on the futon and put my arms over my head to try to block their voices.

"Dear?"

Now Plimmy?

I grumbled and rolled off the futon and stumbled to the door. I unlatched and threw it open. The three of them stood in my doorway looking vaguely chagrined.

Zamira cleared her throat and braved a start. "We're here to check on you, yeah? It's been a lot for you in the last couple of days. We thought you could use a friend or two." She held up two bottles of St. Swithin's as a peace offering. Behind her, Plimmy wiggled a bottle of Scotch.

"I haven't got enough glasses," I mumbled lamely.

Sevenoir held up four teacups, which he held by the dainty handles. "We've got you covered," he said gruffly. "Let us in. Trust me, you need to debrief about everything that's happened, and there's no better way to do that than with a glass of, er, tea. We'll order in a pizza and have a good cry. This area has a great delivery service, and I'm hungry."

I choked back a laugh and opened the door wider for them to enter. Plimmy and I sat down on the futon while Sev and Z made themselves as comfortable as they could on the floor. Plimmy cracked the bottle and poured out generous libations of Scotch in the teacups, which Sev handed around. Z wandered into the kitchen looking for a church key in my drawers to open the beer. She returned triumphant with two open bottles and plopped them down on the coffee table. We clinked our teacups, and everyone had a deep sip. Sev pulled out his cell phone and ordered a pizza.

"OK, dear. Start from the beginning and tell us what's been happening," Plimmy said as she set her teacup down on the coffee table.

I looked at the three of them, sitting there for the sole purpose of supporting me, their familiar faces in expressions of sincere interest, and something in me that was broken mended. I had been wrong. Moving to London hadn't been a mistake. In the past week, I had started a new life and made new friends, friends I could count on.

Between the three of them, they listened while I talked about everything that had happened to me in the last week, about my hopes for the future, and my fears for my mother, my sorrows about Hadad and Gypcie.

"I can't believe you let him get away," Sev said, shaking his head. "Julia will have your hide for that if she ever finds out."

"I didn't let him 'get away,'" I protested. "He ran away as I was trying to get enough air to breathe. What does it matter anyway? We got the sword."

"I certainly hope so," he said. "Based on what you said about the chimera, I'm not so sure. We'll have to be creative in our mission report."

"Give it a rest," Z held her hand up. "I thought our plan here was to cheer Wedd up, not drag her through a hostile debriefing."

Sev shook his head, ruefully. "You're right, Z. Wedd, you fought well, all things considered. It was crazy down there."

"What are you going to do about your young man, Wedd?" Plimmy asked, empathy for me evident in her eyes.

I choked back tears. "I don't know what to do. I don't even know what to think about it right now." I wanted to be angry with Hadad for hurting me, but this past week had shown me that as an agent for a faction, you didn't get to choose your fights.

Plimmy made a comforting noise, and pulled me into a hug, patting my back. "You'll work it out, dear. The politics of the secret world make for some strange bedfellows, there's no doubt. There's nothing that says you can't have relationships within the other factions, but you have to remember where your loyalties lie when it comes down to a fight."

"Yeah, I see Dragon and Illuminati in The Horned God pretty regularly," Z agreed. "I'm friendly with some. Doesn't mean I won't put my boot on their heads when I need to."

Sevenoir nodded. "I have friends of my own who turn up regularly to the matches wearing the wrong colors. We have good fun fighting to see who's the best."

Plimmy watched us all with a sad smile. "I'm glad I'm not a Bee," she sighed. "The choices you three have to make are so much more difficult because they're so long-term. I'm not saying it wouldn't be nice to stay young. Julia and I are getting older — and that brings its own sorrows, to be sure."

"Surely she'll retire someday," Z said.

"That stubborn old bird will never retire," Plimmy muttered under her breath in response, then added, "Well, that's a topic for another time. We are here to lighten your load, Wedd, not to dwell on things that can't be helped or changed."

There was a brisk knock on the door, and Sev got up to answer it, saying, "That will be the pizza." When the transaction was completed, he turned back to us, placing the box on the low coffee table. We all dug in, reveling in the taste of the hot, cheesy slices. I was famished, and the pizza was a comforting reminder of home. Plus, I was glad for a little food to help absorb the alcohol that was warming my belly.

While we enjoyed our meal and drinks, Z regaled us with Council of Venice conspiracy theories from Konrad Engel and shared her tales about the various grudge matches of the Secret War. Plimmy told stories about her days as an agent partnered with Dame Julia that had us in stitches as the drinks flowed.

Even Sev got into the act, reciting from memory some of the lesser known works of Thomas Payne. That was some funny stuff if you'd had enough tea.

"The harder the conflict...wait! Hic!" he said, punctuating a story from Z while spilling Scotch and his bunny ears onto the floor. "The harder the conflict...the more glorious the triumph."

I bent over at the waist laughing inexplicably, my face red, at the sight of the ears next to the puddle on the floor.

"Awww, party foul," Z said with a pout, holding up the nearly empty bottle. "Quit wasting the liquor, Sev."

"S'not liquor, it's Scotch," he said while Plimmy simultaneously said, "Tea!" and the two of them cracked up.

"Ah, brilliant. And here I thought you were a bit of fluff, Sev." Zamira said with a smirk.

"Nah. I'm a hopen book," he added. "Ashk me anything..."

"Did we tip the pizza guy?"

Sev scowled at Z. "Of coursh. That's a ridiculoush thing to ask." We all laughed at his look of affront.

"I got one," I said, wiping the tears of laughter from my eyes as I sat up.

"What?"

"Why do you wear those damn bunny ears?"

He reached across the floor to try to grab the ears and toppled over. With a huff, he grabbed them, jammed them on his head, and pushed himself back up to a sitting position.

"I have...you might shay," he said, wobbling side to side, making the bunny ears bounce. "A schlight problem with authority. The earsh fix it. Drivesh Julia mad."

I laughed harder at that.

Plimmy poured the last of the Scotch in my teacup and stood. "The rest is for you, dear. Come on you lot. We're pissed, and it's dark. Time to stumble home and let Wedd get some sleep."

She patted my cheek and gave me a hug. "Sleep tight. We'll see you on the morrow."

They said their goodbyes and shuffled out the door. I latched it behind them, went into my bedroom and crawled under the covers. I was asleep as soon as my head hit the pillow.

Rap, rap, rap.

The sound of light knocking flitted into my dream, rousing me. Nope. I was ignoring it. Sevenoir could go hang. I wasn't getting up again.

Bang, bang, bang.

The knocking got louder. I pried my eyes open and lifted my head. It pounded with a bass thud in time with the continued pounding on my door.

"Are you kidding me?" I cursed under my breath as I kicked the covers back violently. "What do you people have against sleep in this country?"

I stumbled into the front room, still wearing my clothes from the day before. Was it the day before? There was no light coming in my windows, and the streets were quiet.

What kind of inquisition was this now? Not only did the English lack appreciation for a decent night's sleep, I decided, but the Templar organization as a whole was in collusion against me getting one.

I opened the door and stuck my hand out, startling the knocker.

"Give me the damn letter," I growled.

The tall, dark-haired Templar guard who had drawn the short straw for this particular visit grinned at me. "No letter. You're to come with me."

"What?" I said crossly, pointing to my red eyes and rumpled shirt. "Hungover... Nope, actually, still drunk here. I'm in no condition to go anywhere."

"Those are my orders, miss."

I put my hand on top of my head and pressed down to keep it from exploding.

"What time is it?"

"About a quarter after 11."

"P.M.?" I squeaked, then winced as the headache drove a spike through my brain. No wonder I was so tired. I hadn't been asleep for more than an hour, two tops. "Do I get to know where or why, at least?"

"Temple Hall. Why is above my pay grade."

I scowled at him, my hands on my hips. "I'm taking a shower first."

He nodded with equanimity. "I'll wait outside the door. Hurry."

I showered quickly, pressing a cool washrag to my eyes to try to relieve their puffiness, then threw my wet hair back into its neat bun and pulled on a pair of jeans and a clean shirt. I looked at my shoes and decided it was definitely going to be sneakers. If I needed to dress for success, someone needed to give me more than 20 minutes warning. I grabbed my backpack and a hoodie then stepped out into the landing of my apartment building and locked my door, before following the guard down the steps.

We reached Temple Hall just shortly before midnight on Saturday morning, June 23, a little more than a week after I'd arrived in London. Funny, so much had happened in the past couple of days, it felt like more time had passed.

The guard escorted me up the front stairs, where we were met by Richard Sonnac. He bowed to Sonnac and turned to me with a wink, mouthing "good luck," before he headed back down the stairs.

Sonnac motioned me to follow him into the hall proper. I complied, interested to note that he did not head toward the tall doors I was all too familiar with on the southwestern side.

Instead, he strode all the way across the hall to an alcove on the east corner. Two sets of doors were visible there, one set directly to the east with two guards in front, a bald black man and a white woman with a blonde bob. On the left was the other set on the north side of the hall, but there were no guards there.

"Grand Temple will be convened shortly," Sonnac said, "Remember, your word is your bond. Ready your heart, mind, and soul for what is to come." Then, he turned and left me gaping at the eastern doors.

This was disconcerting. I wracked my aching brain to figure out what I was in trouble for now.

The blonde guard knocked on the door, and it was opened by a female attendant in a Templar uniform, but one far more ceremonial and ancient looking than I was used to seeing. She was wearing a chapeau with a large white feather and carrying a staff.

The attendant motioned me inside to a small wooden paneled room—much smaller, but no less ornate than was typical to this building—dimly lit with candles in two wall sconces. I could see a second door on the wall across from the entrance. The room was roughly rectangular with a chair and a small couch, and an ornate wooden screen along the back.

"Divest yourself of all your worldly possessions," she stated, holding a bag out in front of herself. When I didn't move, she added, dryly. "This is not a symbolic request."

At last, the coin dropped, and a thrill ran through my body. This was my initiation! A broad grin broke across my face, and I hurried to comply with her request. I removed my backpack, the Templar pendant my mother had given me, and the rest of my jewelry and placed it in the bag the attendant held. When I was done, she handed me a set of clothing and told me to remove my clothes and dress in the garb to prepare myself, pointing to the screen along the north wall, apparently set up for privacy.

"Don't forget to take off your shoes and socks," she added.

I stepped out from behind the screen, barefoot and wearing the garb—a plain white robe—that I had been given. I handed the attendant the rest of my clothes to put in the bag. She set down the bag of my possessions on the small couch and drew a black cloth from behind her back.

Motioning me to be still, she placed the cloth, which turned out to be more of a sack, over my head so I could no longer see in the dimly lit room. The folds of the sack covered my shoulders, and it felt soft where it touched my face.

I could hear her rustling around beside me, and I jolted a little as I felt something heavy placed around my neck as well. I reached up and felt coarse hemp twisted into a noose at my throat.

What was that for? I swallowed nervously.

The attendant put her hand on my shoulder and squared me in front of what I assumed was the other door. I had lost my sense of direction with my sight and had to rely only on the sounds I could hear in the room.

"There is a door in front of you. Knock three times if you would gain entrance," she advised me.

I lifted my hand and knocked sharply, three times, on the heavy hardwood of the door. It made a loud *rap, rap, rap* in the small room, even from under the dark hood.

There was a long pause as we waited. I fretted. Would there be a response?

Finally, there were three loud answering raps on the far side of the door, and I could feel a slight gust of air and change of pressure as the door opened.

"Who comes here?" a deep stern voice intoned from the now open space in front of me, startling me slightly. I thought I recognized the voice as Richard Sonnac's but couldn't tell for sure. The sack on my head prevented me from confirming. I itched to pull it off to see what was happening.

"Blodwedd Mallory," the attendant said formally in a clear voice from my right side. "A poor blind candidate who has long been desirous of having and receiving a part of the rights and benefits of this Grand Temple, dedicated to the Light and Faith, and held forth to the holy order of King Solomon, as all true followers have done who have gone this way before her."

The voice that sounded like Sonnac said, "Blodwedd Mallory: Is it of your own free will and accord that you make this request?"

"It is," I said as steadily as I could manage.

"Steward, is the candidate duly and truly prepared?"

"She is," the attendant answered promptly.

"Is she worthy and well qualified?"

"She is."

"Is she properly avouched for?"

"She is."

"By what further rights does she expect to obtain this benefit?"

"By being chosen of Gaia, free and of lawful age, and under the tongue of good report."

The deep stern voice responded, "Then, all these questions being answered in the affirmative, Blodwedd Mallory, you will wait with patience while I inform the Grand Master of your request and return to you her response."

And with that, the door shut, and I waited.

And waited.

And waited.

Patience had never been my strong suit, but I tried to cultivate it here. Behind the door, I could hear low murmurs and the occasional footfall. However, the solid hardwood of the door and paneling on the walls of the small room, not to mention the dark sack over my head, obscured me learning anything useful, so I resigned myself again to be patient.

Eventually, the door opened, and I could feel the presence of the speaker once again, just shortly before I heard his voice.

"Blodwedd Mallory, it is the order of the Grand Master that you enter this Temple."

Eagerly I took a step forward to enter the door. A sharp pain pierced my chest above my heart, and I stopped abruptly.

Ow! That hurt!

I waited anxiously, uncertain of what to do. I could feel the blade in my skin and a trickle of blood running down my chest inside of the garb. The sound of my breathing was loud inside the hood.

What was happening? Why was I being stabbed? Did I want to go through with this or yank off the hood and run? My thoughts spun through my head.

I reached a decision. I *did* want to go through with this. I was ready to become a Templar. I fought for calm and resolve, quelling my nerves, which were telling my body to flee, and decided to put my trust in whatever would come next.

After a moment's pause, the stern voice continued, "and I receive you on the point of a sword, piercing your breast. This is a torture to your flesh. So may it ever be to your mind and conscience if ever you should attempt to reveal the secrets of the Temple unlawfully."

And with that, I felt a pull on the back of my neck and the noose tighten around my throat, as I was led blindly into the inner Temple.

CHAPTER FIFTEEN

The Return

June 24, 2012

66 CONGRATULATIONS on your novitiate, Wedd. I'm very proud of your progress."

It was Monday morning, and the initiation ritual was complete, its secrets laid bare to me. My oaths were taken, and the obligations to those oaths spelled out. I was back in Richard Sonnac's office, talking to him across his desk still filled with papers.

I smiled and thanked him for his support.

Inside, however, I contemplated how little of the hero worship for him that I'd had on my arrival to Ealdwic still remained. Oh, I was thrilled to have my initiation under my belt and be a Novice in the Order, but the events of the past week had opened my eyes as to the reality of what it meant to be a Templar. I moved over in front of the fireplace, gazing at the giant oil painting of St. George slaying the dragon. Things didn't seem quite as black and white to me anymore.

"I called you here to discuss your next assignment," Sonnac said, standing up from his desk and crossing the room to where I stood. He clasped his hands behind his back. "As you know, Solomon Island has been overwhelmed these past months, dealing with the aftermath of the incursion of sea draugr and the reanimation of its citizenry as zombies."

"Yes. The events of last October have had a terrible impact on the island," I agreed, soberly.

Sonnac looked at me for a long minute, as if trying to anticipate my reaction, then paced away across the carpet. "We've received word that the Sheriff's Office in Kingsmouth could use assistance. We feel that you are uniquely positioned to be of help there. Sevenoir would be there to support you, of course."

I considered what he was saying. It would be good to help out on Solomon Island for a while. I knew what I was getting into there, and I had been worried about Ms. Usher and Carter since I left. Not that I wasn't concerned about Headmaster Montag, too, but they had been foremost in my thoughts.

It made sense that I was being offered this assignment. I knew that all the factions regularly assigned agents there to help out, hence how I had met Renee. I wondered if Gypcie might also be assigned back to the island when she finished her initiation.

"We must find the root of whatever doom has come to Solomon Island," Sonnac said, his voice rising with emphasis, drawing my attention back to the conversation. "But let me stress that this is *not* a rescue operation. Our goal is the salvation of all mankind, not survivors on a case-by-case basis. I understand that may stick in your throat, but... well... halos are fading all over town, now that there is so much more at stake."

My eyes narrowed. He was right. That stuck in my throat badly. I believed it was possible to do both at once.

I knew that Gaia was creating Bees in unprecedented numbers—Ealdwic was swarming with them at the moment. I also suspected that my so-called dreams of the Tokyo subway were nothing of the sort, and that was the root of where the problem lay—some massive global catastrophe was underway. Gaia herself was under attack by dark forces of an unknown origin. The sooner I got more experience under my belt as an agent, the sooner I could help the Templars get to the bottom of it.

And, a rebellious voice whispered in my head, I was pretty sure I could help *both* my friends and humankind.

"When would I leave?" I asked.

"The assignment is relatively simple but urgent."

I put my hands on my hips and turned to him. "So, pretty much immediately."

"That's correct. Leave as soon as you can. Your travel arrangements have already been made with the Station Master at the Ealdwic Underground. You'll travel through Agartha," Sonnac smiled wryly, "but you've made that trip before. Good hunting and I'll be in touch."

Unofficial Legends of the Secret World Website, Mailing List, and More

First of all, thanks for reading *London Underground!*

If you enjoyed this novel and want to read more of Wedd's adventures, stay tuned for the next installment of the *Unofficial Legends of the Secret World* in mid-2019. If you'd like to stay in the loop to learn about more book releases and other cool stuff as it develops, visit the webpage at http://www.blodweddmallory.com. Don't forget to subscribe to the ULotSW mailing list. I promise never to share your email address and to only send you emails on the stuff you want. You can unsubscribe at any time.

You can also check in with Wedd by liking the Unofficial Legends of the Secret World - Blodwedd Mallory Facebook page at https://www.facebook.com/BlodweddMallory.

Reviews and word-of-mouth are critical to the commercial success of any self-published novel and would-be novelist. I welcome your support should you choose to leave a short review on Amazon and/or Goodreads to help spread the word about this series of forthcoming books set in *The Secret World* and *Secret World Legends* universe.

And, if you've never played *Secret World Legends*, get on over to http://www.secretworldlegends.com and sign up to play this terrific Funcom game for free! There are hundreds of missions available to you in game and more than 100 hours of story to discover, investigate, and explore. Create your faction agent, whether you prefer Templar, Illuminati, or Dragon. Remember, dark days are coming. Join the battle against the forces of darkness today!

About the Author

Blodwedd Mallory is the Secret World alter ego of Amber McKee, a Utah-based writer, editor, and Jill-of-all-trades.

Over the course of her career, she's been a newspaper reporter, movie reviewer, bartender, tarot reader, magazine editor, advocacy trainer, instructional designer, service delivery manager, and more. Now, she realizes what she really probably should have been all along was a video game developer. So, she assuages that pain by creating urban fantasy fiction books based on her in-game experiences of an urban fantasy/horror video game. Go figure.

She lives with her hubby and two rescue pups in a formerly haunted house.

Made in the USA
San Bernardino, CA
15 January 2020

63236148R00124